BOB—

MAY YOU ENJOY

THESE STORIES FROM

THE "SOUTH",

David A. Peterman

"To Vicki"

CAPE HORN

AND

OTHER STORIES
FROM THE END OF THE WORLD

CAPE HORN

AND

OTHER STORIES
FROM THE END OF THE WORLD

by

FRANCISCO COLOANE

Translated & with an Introduction by

DAVID A. PETREMAN

LATIN AMERICAN LITERARY REVIEW PRESS
SERIES: DISCOVERIES
PITTSBURGH, PENNSYLVANIA

YVETTE E. MILLER, EDITOR

1991

The Latin American Literary Review Press publishes Latin American creative writing under the series title *Discoveries*, and critical works under the series title *Explorations*.

Translation © 1991 Latin American Literary Review Press

Library of Congress Cataloging-in-Publication Data

Coloane, Francisco, 1910-
    [Short stories. English. Selections]
    Cape Horn and other stories from the end of the world / by
Francisco Coloane ; translated & with an introduction by David A.
Petreman.
        p. cm. -- (Discoveries)
    Selected and translated from several Spanish collections.
    ISBN 0-935480-50-1
    1. Tierra del Fuego (Argentina and Chile)--Fiction. 2. Patagonia
(Argentina and Chile)--Fiction. I. Petreman. David A. II. Title.
III. Title: Cape Horn. IV. Series.
    PQ8097.C55A26   1991
    863--dc20
                                        90-19924
                                            CIP

Cover by Andrés Jullián

Cape Horn and Other Stories From the End of the World may be ordered directly from the publisher:

    Latin American Literary Review Press
    2300 Palmer Street, Pittsburgh, PA 15218
    Tel (412) 351-1477 Fax (412) 351-6831

Acknowledgments

This project is supported in part by grants from the National Endowment for the Arts in Washington, D.C., a federal agency, the Commonwealth of Pennsylvania Council on the Arts, the College of Liberal Arts of Wright State University, and the William C. Archie Fund for Faculty Excellence of Wake Forest University.

The stories translated in this anthology were selected from the following Spanish collections:

Cabo de Hornos, Editorial Andrés Bello
Golfo de Penas, Editorial Cultura
Tierra del Fuego, Editorial Zig-Zag

Some of the stories in this volume have appeared in the following journals:

The American Voice ("Gulf of Sorrows")
Stories ("The Kanasaka Iceberg")
City Lights ("Cape Horn")

TABLE OF CONTENTS

Introduction

"If Francisco Coloane didn't exist, I would have to invent him."

—Pablo Neruda

When one thinks of Latin America, places such as Ultima Esperanza (Last Hope), Golfo de Penas (Gulf of Sorrows), Puerto Hambre (Port Hunger), Isla Desolación (Desolation Island) and Bahía Inútil (Useless Bay) are not locations that normally come to mind. They seem to be fictional names or places devoid of any sign of life. In reality, life flourishes in them with more force than many other regions of the world. People tend to reject, or forget, that there is anything beyond the forty-second parallel South in Chile. It is a strange world, an unreal reality that combines the most concrete elements of our existence with a magic and fantasy to which we are unaccustomed. It is a region in which man communes with Nature, while trying to survive within, or in spite of it, in which man has been able to resist the pressures of modern civilization's degrading aspects. Nature itself has fought against the exploitation that has been suffered elsewhere, maintaining many of its primitive characteristics. Southern Chile is a universe that has survived perhaps because it has been forgotten. While at one time this region was visited by more ships than any other in the world, it is now one of the most sparsely populated areas of the planet.

There is still a rich, profound life in this lost, forgotten land, one in which mankind looks for, and often finds—even without looking— his primitive roots. The desire to seek them is in Patagonia and Tierra del Fuego something inherent to man's nature. Everything around him, from the perennial western winds to the eerie cry of the guanaco, is important. Animals, especially, play a vital role, for they share everything with man. Chile's South is a region made up of labyrinths of islands and channels, floating and submerged icebergs, a wild and solitary Patagonian pampa, and plants and birds seen nowhere else. It is where the Andes mountain chain lowers its shoulders and breaks up into thousands of little pieces at the end of the world. The real—sometimes too real—daily events here are often magical, fantastic, beyond our own realities, simply because they occur in such a strange land, inhabited by lone and rare beings with unusual names.

Captains' logs and geography books inform us statistically about this place, but its very heart is brought to us in the literature of the

Magellanic region's principal spokesman, Francisco Coloane. He has dedicated his literary work to the artistic recuperation of this land, where he lived and worked for many years. A life-long friend of Pablo Neruda, Coloane is a frustrated poet who constantly recites Neruda's verses, sometimes changing his voice to the low, morose tone that was characteristic of the Nobel poet laureate. His conversation poetically engages one in the brilliance and darkness, the storms and the calms of his experiences. While he most often turns to Neruda for poetry, Coloane dominates the short story, giving new life to the genre that in Latin America finds itself in an equal position with the novel, as evidenced by the mastery of Jorge Luis Borges and Julio Cortázar, among others. As a man of action in his youth, Coloane lived what he writes. He portrays for us human beings fighting the most essential battles against Nature, solitude, animals and other men; he presents a man who understands that friendship and camaraderie can translate into life itself, whether that relationship be with man or beast.

In his story, "Cape Horn", the most sinister side of mankind's greed leads three men into dark caverns, both physical and mental; yet in the same story he develops a creation scene that moves one to again feel the majesty of life. In "Cururo", Subiabre saves the life of a sheep dog puppy who then becomes integral to his life as a supportive, hard working comrade within a mutually dependent relationship. "Submerged Iceberg" is a psychological study of a man's unwillingness —or inability—to communicate with others. The unexpected appears in "Gulf of Sorrows": five men in a tiny boat, rowing for their lives on the open sea in the midst of a severe storm, pull alongside a ship and request aid. A short time later, after the boat's skipper has consulted with the ship's captain, the rowers mysteriously head out again into the storm. The inexplicable remains intact, even as we learn more about the extreme south. In "The Bottle of Caña", two men encounter one another on the snow-covered pampa of Tierra del Fuego, and leave behind an empty bottle as the only clue to their existence. But what has happened out there within their shared moments of solitude?

Our centuries old image of Latin America as a jungle, of venomous animals and Amazon Indians disappears before the austral world of low temperatures, polar winds, an abrupt geology and dangerous seas.

Coloane's style is simple and direct, in the vein of realism. Even though he is a precursor of Latin America's most well-known literary tendency, magical realism, whose leading exponent is Gabriel García Márquez (*One Hundred Years Solitude*), and also utilizes many modern literary techniques, such as the manipulation of temporal planes and "elliptical art" or understatement, he has done so in a subtle fashion, never losing the realistic presentation of his material. It is his clear-cut imagery and realistic descriptions of these "forgotten" lands that stand out. His literature has proven to be ever popular and contemporary, shining through all of the trends in recent Latin American literature due to the experimentalism that was a product of the great "boom" of the novel during the 1960's and early 1970's. Since the appearance of his first story in 1928 to the recent re-issue of his collections, *El témpano de Kanasaka* (*The Kanasaka Iceberg*, 1986), and *Cabo de Hornos* (*Cape Horn*, 16th edition, 1990), his literature continues to excite and intrigue his readers as he has remained one of Chile's most beloved and widely read authors.

David A. Petreman
Barcelona/Dayton

Cape Horn

The western coastline of Tierra del Fuego breaks apart into numerous islands, between which wind mysterious channels that disappear there at the end of the world in "The Devil's Tomb". Sailors from all latitudes assure you that there, one mile from that tragic promontory that backs up the constant duel of the world's two largest oceans, at Cape Horn, the devil is sounding with two-ton chains, which he drags, grinding the shackles in the depths of the sea on horrible, stormy nights, when the water and dark shadows seem to rise and fall from the sky to those abysses.

Until a few years ago, the only ones to venture into those regions were the most audacious hunters of sea otters and seals, people of distinct races, tough men whose hearts were nothing more than another clenched fist.

Some of these men have remained stuck on those islands all their lives. Others, strangers, intimidated by the whip of hunger that seems to drive them from east to west, arrive from time to time to those inhospitable lands, where very quickly the wind and the snow cut them to the soul, leaving them only wounds as hard as icicles.

At the end of the channels exists a place of gloomy renown: the Ushuaia prison. From the bloody prison escapes some have also been scattered around the islands, sometimes among the Indians, men who have won their freedom fleeing, and who cannot show their faces wherever there might be a light of justice.

Nothing should surprise a man of those lands: that a little boat should go out to sea with four sailors and return with three; that a cutter should disappear with its whole crew, etc. Nothing should surprise him when pelts and gold are divided evenly among crew members...

At the end of those channels, near Cape Horn, is Sunstar Island.

The only two inhabitants of the island, Jackie and Peter, are seated in the doorway of their hut in an interminable December twilight. The hut is a two-room construction made of coarse tree trunks, upon whose roof the greenish-yellow lichen and moss grow upwards, like a stiff smile of that rough nature, toward the sky, which, loaded with misfortune, lets its snows fall during most of the year.

The hunters say that they are brothers, but no one knows for sure; they have never said it, since they never open their mouths except for violent purposes or to gulp down food.

Jackie has the vague, impersonal face of a new-born; he is of average height, with a sparkling glare in his sunken eyes, in reddened, swollen and lashless eyelids; he seems at times to be a large fetus, or a red seal.

Peter is more interesting with his fox-like features, like a tired and hypocritical feline. At first sight he has a gentle attitude, but on that sun-baked head of oakum, there are some cloudy tufts of hair, darker than the rest, which warn, without knowing why, of something sordid and aggressive hidden within that apparent gentleness.

They say that they have some sterling pounds hidden and that they are accumulating more in order to return to their own lands...To what lands? Where have they come from...?

No one knows the origin of many men from those places, no one knows where they will end up; indeed, they seem to have emerged from the earth itself, from those strange and lost waters at the edge of the world.

They speak a mixture of Spanish and a guttural English. Their dealings with the Indians and with solitude have caused them to lose the ability to form long thoughts or sentences. Their speech is broken and is difficult to understand for the slightly more civilized men who come down from Magallanes to search for the coveted pelts.

After eating some fish they sit in the doorway to rest in the middle of a waning afternoon with the strangest reflections in the southern twilight.

In front, the waters of the channel are calm and deep; in the depths of the coves, surrounded by oaks, they are darker in color and disturbing black vapors seem to move over the smooth surface.

The silence is complete, static, cold.

From his seal-like jaws Jackie emits a yawn, leans his head on his hand and looks at a faraway snow-capped mountain just to rest his eyes upon something, more than for some remote instinct toward beauty.

Suddenly he makes a disturbing movement and turns his ear toward a noise that he perceives coming from the nearby beach. At first it is a splashing sound like an otter makes coming out of the ocean and clambering up on the rocks; then it becomes a soft, tender movement of oars in the water.

As is the hunter's habit, he goes into the hut for his Winchester and waits in the doorway. Peter also gets up to wait.

After a short while, the splashing noise ceases, and soon a movement is heard in the thicket among the oaks, which in part surround the hut. They no longer have any doubts; someone is advancing through the short, dense oaks.

Among the men there, weapons are not used; Jackie reluctantly leaves his rifle behind the door.

No one uses weapons because every cartridge is worth a seal's or otter's pelt; and when someone wants to avoid the bothersome division of the skins, partners are eliminated by abandoning them on a solitary rock in the middle of the sea or better, a quick push from the rail of the easily capsized cutter while sailing along on some calm night.

From the green of the foliage appeared something dark, and a man, leaning forward, with torn, soaked clothes, moved toward the small clearing like a beaten animal emerging from a pool.

The brothers looked at each other; the man stopped a few steps from them; tall, lean and noble, in spite of the fact that he was completely destitute; his thick moustache and beard were extremely black. He lifted up his head, and with a strange pleading look, as if his whole being had been lashed against the ground, he said, "Some food! I have escaped from Ushuaia!"

His voice came out strangely, as if during all these risky days he had not used it and now it had no timbre.

Peter, the one with the dark streaks in his mop of hair, shook his head and lifted his hand, pointing in the direction from which the man had come. Stumbling on his words, he said, "Go on! Move it! Get away from here!"

The man did not plead, he knew it would do no good; he was resigned to leaving when he caught sight of a pile of baby seal pelts stacked up along the walls of the hut.

The pelts most coveted by the hunters are of the double-skinned seals; but the European manufacturers have imitated this fine skin very well with the hides of single-skinned baby seals which are killed within eight days of their birth, and skinned within twenty-four hours after their death. Those skins are known as "popis" and the buyers from

Magallanes pay at the rate of forty to fifty cents for each one.*

The abundance of single-skinned seals in the Antarctic regions is enormous. The difficulty lies in the inaccessibility of the places where the females give birth and the time of the hunt, which must be, as is known, within eight days after birth.

"You hunt 'popis'!" said the fugitive with a look on his face that wasn't quite a smile, and he continued, "I know a cavern, an enormous rookery where there are more 'popis' than you could hunt."

Peter's face widened, and on his lips a smile appeared, like the dark swamp that on some silvery night is lit up like a fountain.

"But first—something to eat! I'm dying of hunger!" continued the fugitive.

"First tell us: where is this rookery?" one of them exclaimed.

"Have you heard of the 'Aviary'?"

"Yes! What a surprise, we already know that in its interior there is a rookery and also that no one has ever been able to get to that fiendish island, because the cave's mouth is right in the sea, full of rocks and reefs."

"That's right!" said the fugitive smugly. "No one has gone in there, but where there are birds, there are seals, and where there are seals, fish. Before heading out to sea, in the bend of the center of the island, right where the herds of seal swim and play, there is a hidden entrance."

"Come on, stay here," smiled Peter with his evil face.

The man ate some dry fish, some leftover toast and then settled down to sleep on some pelts behind the messy, mildewed kitchen.

The gringos stretched out on their rough oak plank bunks attached to the wall, which was caulked with oakum and pieces of rotting hides to offer protection against the wind and snow.

Silence reigned again. The southern night outside was quiet, frozen.

In that land as everywhere, everything was a matter of money. At dawn, right around 2:30 a.m., the three men were already aboard the small cutter with its rowboat astern, working together to set sail, as if they had known each other all their lives.

* Story takes place in 1941

The semi-polar sun began obliquely to illuminate the landscape, like a pale, faraway reflector, when the explosions of the cutter's kerosene motor pierced the region's peace and the boat moved slowly along, heading south down the channel.

After navigating for three hours they reached the mouth of the channel. Beyond, one could see the great ocean waves, which lessened their fury upon approaching the narrowness of the opening. This transformed them into a choppy and torrential sea, extremely dangerous when the tides rose or fell.

The cutter began a tenuous balance by the tack on port side and, turning, sought the bend in the island, where, after looking for the bottom, Jackie tossed the small anchor into the sea.

"The Aviary" is a long island in the form of a reclining monster or seal, whose head, bent by the strong southwest winds of the Cape, seems to cower defiantly and to vomit pieces of rock where the ocean eternally hurls itself.

"There it is!" said the fugitive, pointing out, from the prow of the cutter, a difficult-to-see crevice that penetrated the island, and which was lost again in the thick foliage. And contemplating the grayish wall of the island, he felt a breath escape from the depths of its being.

That was his "Aviary"; eight years without seeing it. The cavern that only he knew. Among those same winding rocks he had hidden once, when in Ushuaia the cursed Coast Guard lights found his contraband brandy...; there were shots and the need to shoot well. Who knows how many! Everything was left behind.

The tall rock was cut in a smooth line leaning toward the sea. The shadow of its projecting top stole away a clear area in the waters.

It would have resembled a part of a strange, dead world if in its tiny crevices, like steps formed by some natural whim, there were not thousands of birds constantly crowded together; like inhabitants of a curious skyscraper, sea crows, patoliles, white caiquenes, thrushes, albatrosses, seagulls and Cape doves congregated on its balconies.

An admirable order was maintained in that "Aviary", which had given its name to the island. In the lower part, the penguins with their snowy chests and stupid seriousness crowded together; just above them the crows and patoliles, with their simple inquisitive stares, were scandalized by everything. At the top, the seagulls and albatrosses screeched in the background, flying off and returning as if on determined expeditions.

Every now and then, a good peck in the middle of a quarrel would send a crow off the ledge, a flap of wings sustaining his fall; another would arrive in direct flight, ready to open a space for himself and a tumult of wings, beaks and squawks would rise up.

"Where there are seagulls, there are seals, and where there are seals, fish," the fugitive had said. The current which narrows in that area and the deep, sheltered inlet of "The Aviary" made up the main route for the incessant traffic of the ocean inhabitants.

The eternal struggle appeared from the depths of the sea when a seal, with a sudden bolt, broke the surface with its round nape, biting a sea bass that twisted like a shining, white arm.

It was a sculptural spectacle of the sea: the seal's skin, black and shiny, its neck stretched in a vigorous form, dog-and-man-like jaws, with its moustaches drooping wet, like pieces of crystal, clenching the tail of a fish that was twisting and slapping the anxious jaws of the beast.

Beyond, in small groups, with thin, dolphin-like bodies, fine double-skinned seals swam, leaping in pairs.

The three hunters, embarked in the small boat, approached the hidden crevice through a curtain of lichen and creepers.

Spreading the green curtain, they entered a dark mouth. It was the hidden entrance to the cave. The rock sweat humidity and the water from a small spring fell to the sea in big, inflated drops.

Illuminated by a lantern, they advanced pushing themselves with the small oars against the smooth, slimy walls.

They had gone in some thirty meters when they witnessed, little by little, the appearance of a vague light and that tomb-like peace was disturbed by a muffled, faraway sound, like rumblings from colossal drums. It was the wild sea that crashed upon the inaccessible entrance of the cavern that lay back out toward the Cape.

Little by little the half-light diminished, it became smoother. They guessed the walls to be cut straight down and toward the cave's roof only a dense and overwhelming blackness was seen.

The fugitive took the boat's pole, advancing it along with a thousand precautions. The oar, gently flapping, serving as a propeller, produced scarcely a sound whose echo was swallowed by the emptiness.

The three men crouched, instinctively looking forward, to a place that seemed inhabited by fear.

Suddenly, in warm, nauseating waves, a strange odor of rotten fish blood rushed upon the three men. The odor worsened; the warm waves became heavy, suffocating swells, and they heard a gentle, muffled sound.

Suddenly, the cave's gallery widened and at the far edge of an enormous pool they spied heaps of large, dark, round bodies, moving slowly, heavily.

"There's the rookery!" said the fugitive, and his hoarse voice continued, "You have to watch out for the old males, those big, bearded ones who are the only ones who stay with the mother while she's giving birth. Get the rifle ready and when we get close, fire some shots so that the females move away and we can climb down on the flat stones of the little beach."

The bodies stirred with the shots and at a small clearing on the beach the men tied up the boat; each one got out carrying in his hand a wide stick in the shape of a club.

A huge male, with horrible, stiff whiskers, moved the wrinkles in his lips; his eyes moved with strange reflexes and he rose up on his flippers with a ferocious attitude...a single shot resounded from Jackie, who carried the rifle, and the seal collapsed, emitting a muffled, deep bellow.

In the depths of a cavern, in the bosom of an island, surrounded by shadows, and a heavy odor and heat that weakened the senses, the men suffered a momentary tremor and their toughness weakened somewhat, when they heard that bellow from the dying seal...

Sure, they were hardened...but out at sea, where the waves and the wind strike head-on and attack ferociously; while these deep black spaces, this heaviness of caves made for monsters...

"These guys have had it!" said the gringo, when he saw the beast collapse from the bullet.

Birthing was at its peak. Some females in a difficult moment lay on their sides and from their wombs, open and bloody, came forth confused little animals, moving like thick, enormous worms with rudiments of flippers. Others emitted strange, intermittent moans, almost human, during the last pains of birth. In their movement, they sometimes crushed each other and, mothers to the end, in their desperation, they pushed and bit in order to save their tender little ones from being crushed. The biggest of these climbed on to their mothers' backs like little odd toy bears, or they clambered down, tumbling for the first time in their lives.

A rare palpitation of life, slow and acute, emanated from that distressing, formless mass of round, dark brown bodies.

Moans in low, muffled tones. Collisions of soft masses. The unfolding of flippers, heavy breathing. Viscous clicking of wombs in contraction. Something sinister and vital, just as the conjoining in the softened wombs of nature should be.

If that was not a rookery, it was an island in a painful trance. An island giving birth! The groaning of nature in the act of creation, in that pocket of foul-smelling air and dark waters!...The fertile womb of the island, incubating its favorite children of the sea!...The sea, that devastating, fierce male who bathes its shining rocks from the outside!...The progenitor who returns the birthing pains of the island with white caresses of foam stuck on the steep rocks. Region from a distant world!...Seals, hunters, strange islands! An awesome, haunting, beloved land; the man who has trembled in fear of her mysteries will be tied up forever to her memories! She and her men are like the iceberg. When life has spent the blue, frozen foundations, it gives a sudden turn and the hard white mass appears again, navigating among forgotten things!...

But it is useless for life to hide itself in the depths of its womb: man, with his instincts, enters in there to rip it out.

The three hunters began their everlasting, universal task: to kill..., to kill, to destroy life even when it has just begun.

With their deadly clubs raised high, they jumped over the bodies that were giving birth and delivered well-aimed blows to the tiny heads of the newborn. The tender cubs did not utter a cry, they fell inert, giving up the life they had only possessed an instant.

Killing and killing!...The more quickly done, the better! As if possessed by a strange insanity, the men aimed their clubs and stacked up the little bodies.

Sweaty and tired, they stopped for a moment to take a breath. A big, old male sea lion frightened them sometimes, and they had to use the rifle. The females did not defend themselves, and their eyes, with an inexpressible radiance, fixedly contemplated the task of their offspring's assassins.

When they had calculated the capacity of the boat, they began to throw the dead seal pups into its hold, until the water line advised them to be prudent.

Then the boat, full of dark, shiny baby seals, was heading out between the rocky entrails, and the men, with their cargo, came out into the light like strange fishermen who had gone into the abyss to spread their nets, for there those seal pups seemed to be fish.

They had two successful killing sessions that day, from the cavern to the cutter. And with the advancing shadows of night they reached their hut and began skinning the seals, since the skins spoil from one day to the next.

The next morning, all of the available boards of the hut were covered with the staked out seal pup skins.

"It's as if we had finished a whole season!" said one of the gringos, jubilant.

For five days they continued bringing the cutter loaded with furs. The hunting job was coming to a close. The eighth day after birth had passed.

In the evenings, during the brief rest that the skinning and staking left, the gringos had become more obliging with their valuable guest. His expression, always frozen in an attitude of expectancy, changed to a smile that began to develop under his extremely black moustache.

In the austral morning, cold and luminous, the cutter with its noisy tiring motor slid along once again and found refuge, with its echo muted, within the channel boundaries.

"Today is the last day and we'll try to do three boatloads of seal pups," said Jackie, undoing a reef in the sail to help the motor, with the fine breeze that joined the propeller.

The fugitive ventured a hopeful smile and he said, slowly, while looking at the sky, "After this, I'm heading north. You know. I'll just take a few skins and give them to the captain of the first cutter that can take me. I'd stay here, but I'm no longer any use; the hunting season is over and one is never too far from Ushuaia."

Something very cold was understood in the glance exchanged between the brothers. The two gringos had always questioned each other, for a long time now, in such circumstances in life when they looked at each other that way. Both of them were swine, but it cost them to really be that way...they had always been able to toss the black ball of their thoughts from one to the other.

Dividing shadows, as in previous days, they penetrated the cavern and tied up the boat at the clearing that the female seals left in the last days of birthing.

The instant wound in which life is born to its course smelled, as always, like death and life.

With his teeth showing as if in a gritty smile, the fugitive headed into the cavern, clubbing fragile little heads left and right.

He had gone in rather far, blending in among the shadows, obsessed with his desire to kill, moving astride the backs of seals like a strange demon who explored the thick dark spaces with the movement of his club, when the brothers suddenly looked at each other. It was only one supreme instant! Their looks clashed; there was even fear in their eyes. They hadn't spoken a word, but from that moment their evil thoughts were in agreement. They understood each other...and with one single impulse they jumped aboard the boat and quickly undertook their escape.

The fugitive, tired, suddenly stopped the killing—and, slowly, he turned his head back. The boat was already disappearing down the passageway out.

He had no time for anything. He was astonished, as if the entire earth had disappeared, leaving only him, floating and swallowed up in the void, without a floor, without a roof...

When we have loaded up our boat with our baggage, with the most beautiful illusions and dreams, and we become dumbfounded on the beach of deceit, seeing the boat leave, far away, carrying everything away from us, leaving us the empty feeling that doesn't amount to anything...then we become weak; but we look back, we see that there are paths of return, we recover, and although we move along hunched over because of our heavy cross, with our souls bent, we will still lift up our shoulders, throw the cross into some dusty riverbank and we will become again what we were before.

But when there are no roads of return, the soul is on the cutting edge, wavering there, forever falling. The dividing line can be a thread of lacerating light or an abyss.

The fugitive headed toward the edge of the water. He sat on the sand and projected a kind of gaze over the brown backs of the beasts, on the shadowy walls, on the tranquil and sinister waters of the black cavern.

Outside, the rowboat was heading into the channel, smiling with light and birds...

*   *   *

A suffocating heat...an odor that comes in waves...in masses of white oakum like cotton. And it gets up into the nostrils..., into the mouth, stopping them up.

A huge, black seal..., a seal, yes, with his stiff whiskers in the loathsome soft flesh of foul-smelling lips, with a heavy stench, which comes to crush his chest with its enormous, flabby, sticky, heavy flippers, like the beams of death.

But it's not a seal! It is Luciano the Italian, who, drunk, comes to hurl his massive body on top of him. Luciano doesn't move his thick Tuscan-smelling lips, but his eyes ask about the sealskins.

The skins over which they had fought and after which he had left him stretched out on the sand with a stab wound in his belly.

Blood!...Relief! Now he swims slowly in the sea; familiar seals plunge in next to him in the clear, green waters; then the waters go dark...but, they are not waters...it is thick, cloudy blood, and by his side he sees two large, red seals...no; they are monsters, half men, half seals...but no; they are Jackie and Peter, showing their clenched teeth and they are smiling...

My God, what is that? A she-seal is opening up her innards over his face. Her pup comes out of her belly like a black slug...and it smothers him... Ah...it went away!...What a relief; but the innards withdraw, they absorb him, they are huge and drag him inside... squeezing him horribly...

The seal is going to birth him but then cannot. The viscera push him, draw him in, make a knot of him...and everything is black, it is black blood, thick slime.

Quiet!...Slowly a sound rises up from afar. The noise becomes a harmonious canticle of thousands of children's voices. And on the now-celestial walls of the cavern groups of children begin to appear...no, they're birds...; no, they're seal pups with their flippers turned into wings...and they sing...and fly...

And he, what does he do?...He has stabbed the seal that swims by his side, and this seal is Luciano and he has buried him in the sand...but, my God, he is good, how has he done that? And why does he attack the baby seals who come to his side to sing to him with angelic voices? He continues killing them with the handles of his knife...and he cannot detach himself from his cruelty...and the baby seals continue falling one by one...and little by little their celestial songs die out...

Everything is peace, sweetness, silence...and now he has flippers, he is light-weight and he wants to flow into a long thread that moves toward the light...he rises nimbly, flying toward a brightness that opens up among the rocky clouds...and he ascends...he ascends toward a place of light and peace.

*   *   *

A few years later, in a Punta Arenas newspaper a laconic news item appeared that didn't surprise the people who were accustomed to reading about the mysterious tragedies that from time to time occur in those oceans:

"The commander of a coast guard cutter who undertakes expeditions to the channels of the extreme south, has communicated to the maritime authority that he has found a cutter, apparently long since abandoned, in the region near the island known as 'The Aviary', located near Cape Horn."

An old seal hunter who heard the news next to the counter in the bar of Paulino, the Asturian, commented between sips of "grapa":

"This cutter must have belonged to the gringos Jackie and Peter...those gringos were so ambitious! They probably tore themselves to pieces wanting to enter the cave's mouth at 'The Aviary'. The mouth is right out in the ocean, full of breakers and they say that inside there are big rookeries."

The two gringos entered; but it is certain that they never came out, nor will they.

The Kanasaka Iceberg

We were the first to know about the seal cutter that we found anchored behind some rocks in Desolation Bay, that opening in the southernmost route in the world, the Beagle Channel, where the massive waves rolling in from Cape Horn come crashing down.

"It's the strangest case I've ever heard in my long life as a hunter," said Pascualini, the old seal hunter, from the rail of his boat. He continued: "I haven't seen it, but the crew members of a schooner we ran across yesterday at dawn in Occasion Channel were terrified by the appearance of a strange iceberg that surprised them in the middle of the storm while they were crossing Brecknock Strait. But more than the storm itself, it was the pursuit of that enormous mass of ice, guided by an apparition, a ghost or whatever it was, since I don't believe in hoaxes, that made the schooner take refuge in the Channel."

Brecknock Strait, as formidable as the difficult bonding of its consonants, is very short; but its waves are so big, they tower like craters that are going to explode next to the dark masses of rock that rise up to a great height and then fall, crashing in such a way, that all of the navigators suffer nightmares when they cross over.

"And this is nothing," continued old Pascualini, as he exchanged some hides for brandy with the skipper of our cutter, "Mateo, the Austrian, who keeps giving me competition with his dilapidated 'Bratza', told me he saw the phantom iceberg behind Devil's Island, that damned black rock that marks the entrance of the northwest and southwest branches of the Beagle Channel. They were beginning to tack in the Beagle, when from behind the rock the terrifying vision appeared, rubbing against that old heap of the 'Bratza'."

We said good-bye to old Pascualini and our "Orion" headed toward Brecknock Strait.

All of the names in that region recall something tragic and harsh: Dead John's Stone, Devil's Island, Desolation Bay, Dead Man, and so on, and they are only minimized by the moderation of the names given by Fitz-Roy and the sailors of the French sailing ship "Romanche", who were the first to draw maps of these regions shaken by the strong winds at the conjunction of the Pacific and Atlantic oceans.

Our "Orion" was a four-ton cutter captained by its owner, Manuel Fernández, a Spanish mariner like so many others who have come and remained among the large rocks, Indians and seals of the Magellan Coasts and Tierra del Fuego; he and a young apprentice mariner of

Italian parents were the crew; they didn't need anyone else: with a few loops of rope he lashed the boy to the mast so that the waves didn't carry him away and so that he could freely handle the operation of the foresail for forward tacking, and he managed the rudder, the mainsail, the crotch, and reefed in the sails, all at once, if necessary.

On a stormy night, upon crossing Cape Froward toward Magdalene Channel, I saw him, ferocious; his eyes flashed in hatred toward the sea; short, and stocky, with his face of earthly debris, where it seemed that the drops of water had torn away chunks of flesh, I saw him move toward the prow to untie the cabin boy, unconscious because a heavy sea had knocked his head against the mast.

I volunteered to replace him: "Let's go!" he said, dubiously, and he tied me to the mast with a rope.

Waves came like soft and agile elephants, and they fell with great hands of water which slapped my face and at times heavy liquid tongues engulfed me, soaked me.

At the moment of tacking, when the wind hit us in the prow, he untied the foresail and pursued the wind that was laying us out to one side. That was a supreme moment. If my strength had not withstood the lashing of the canvas which was relentlessly beating me, the tacking would have been lost and we would have run the danger of being driven ashore and, with our movement paralyzed, one blast of wind would have shipwrecked us.

After suffering for two hours, Captain Fernández untied me, without telling me if I had done well or poorly. From that night on, I often relieved the ship's boy during navigation.

I was making a trip whose destiny was Yendegaia, to become a foreman on a sheep ranch. The cutter was carrying an official load of merchandise; but hidden in the depths of its small hold was another, unofficial, cargo: contraband brandy and condensed milk for the Argentine prison at Ushuaia, where the first is prohibited and the second has a high tax.

There were two other passengers: a woman who was going to sell love in the penal colony and an obscure individual named Jiménez, who disguised his lowly profession as a pimp with some film cannisters and an old movie projector, with which he said he was going to entertain the poor prisoners and earn a few bucks.

This guy was hysterical: when we broke loose from the dock in Punta Arenas he proclaimed boastfully to be a real sailor and to have gone through great storms. Upon facing the first squalls, at about Cape San Isidro, he began shouting like a madman, crying out to heaven to have mercy on his destiny; in the first serious storm we had, he was a prisoner of his own panic and, as seasick as he was in the hold of the cutter, he had the strength to come on deck screaming crazily. Some cursing and a good kick in the rear end by the skipper Fernández sent him back to his cabin, putting an end to his detestable screaming. The prostitute, more valiant, cried with resignation, pressing her dark face into a filthy pillow.

But the sun appeared and Jiménez was another man; with his repugnant face and flat nose he emerged from the depths of the hold like a rat, having forgotten the captain's kicks and he spoke again, happy and stupid.

By the third day of the trip, those of us who were traveling on those four planks upon the sea had already defined our categories. The severe mettle and courage of skipper Fernández; the eager gesture of that adolescent who swallowed his tears and wanted to be a man of the sea; my inexperience which interfered when I tried to help; and the prostitute dragged along by that worthless screamer. A whole human scale, as happens with the majority of passengers on those boats that cross the waters of the extreme south.

Gentle, slow pitching indicated to us the proximity of Brecknock Pass and then we embarked upon the massive open sea. Our cutter began to skillfully ride the crests of the waves and to descend, creaking, to the depths of those ravines of water. The southwest wind pushed us quickly along; Brecknock wasn't as bad as other times and in less than an hour we already had in front of us the impressive mass of rock that forms a small but fearful cape; after that the large waves began to diminish and we penetrated the northwest mouth of the Beagle Channel. In the distance, bordering on the solitude of the open sea, every now and then we could make out the white crests of the waves of the cape which broke upon some isolated rocks.

Our navigation had no major setbacks; the small auxiliary engine of the "Orion" and the wind that pushed us on the starboard side had us moving at six miles an hour.

We were in the middle of December and in that season the nights in this latitude are almost non-existent; the days bite their own tail, since the afternoon twilight only just begins to spread its painted shadows when the milky light of dawn is already beginning to brush them away.

We sighted Devil's Island about three in the morning. The day was clearly beginning, but the elevated rocky walls trimmed the clear route of the channel in black, with the exception of a few stretches in which the glaciers streaked those shadows with their white steps descending from the mountains.

The cataclysm which in the beginning of the world split the Beagle Channel into two branches, the northwest and southwest, left as a strange point of that angle, Devil's Island, where swirls from the currents of three channels make crossings very dangerous, so much so that navigators, upon referring to the island, have come to use that frightening name.

And now it had one more surprise: prowling the area was the sinister white mass of the iceberg which carried on board an apparition that terrorized the navigators of the route.

But we crossed, avoiding the complicated current, without glimpsing the strange iceberg.

"They're just stories!" exclaimed the skipper Fernández, while we avoided collisions with small icebergs which, like a curious caravan of swans, small inclining elephants and Venetian gondolas, continued by our side.

Nothing weird happened to us and we calmly continued on toward Kanasaka and Yendegaia, where I was to assume my rural labors.

Before crossing toward Yendegaia we were to pass through the tranquil and beautiful Kanasaka Bay.

All the coastlines of the Beagle are rough and cut sharply all the way to the depths of the sea; it was said that the sea had risen to the highest peaks of the Andes range or that the Andean cordillera had sunk there in the sea.

After miles and miles between the hostility of coasts of rocky walls, Kanasaka, with its beaches of white sand, is an oasis of gentleness within that rough nature; beyond the beach lie green rushes that cover an extensive valley and then oak forests rise up until they become stunted by the dryness of the peaks. An uncommon flora for that zone has taken refuge there, the sea zigzags its way inland and forms small, mysterious lagoons where fish leap to kiss the sunlight, and behind all this, at the tree line, is the house of Martínez, the only white man who, alone and exiled by his own will, or for whatever reason, lives surrounded by Yahgan Indians. In the midst of that savage land, my good friend Martínez discovered a refuge of peace and beauty and—oh, what an incurable romantic—many nights I found him out riding at the pace of his steed, next to the sea, accompanied only by the moon, which was so close that he seemed to carry it on the haunches of his horse.

"We're going to have a headwind and the Channel is going to bloom with the east wind!", said Fernández, interrupting my fond memories. And, sure enough, the surface of the Beagle Channel began to blossom with white gardens; the easterly squalls speckled the sea with black and white, and suddenly the cutter had to hoist its sails and run from shore to shore.

The old Spanish mariner looked at the sky and frowned. The slow nightfall had begun and the sea continued to increase its fury. The cabin boy was strapped to the mast in order to work the foresail for tacking purposes. The skipper diminished the mainsail by reefing it in and everything was trussed up to face the ensuing storm.

The most dangerous thing about storms in the Beagle Channel are the swirling gusts of wind; the capricious coves and mountains form them and hurl them to the middle of the channel, lifting up real columns of water. During the daytime it is easy to ride them out. A black shadow coming over the waves announces them and permits the boat to head prow forward, but the night falls and its more intense shadows swallow those other shadows and then no one knows when those treacherous, sudden huge waves are coming. Those waves that can capsize a boat with one blow.

Even all of skipper Fernández' instinct for sniffing out the nighttime squalls was not enough, and, from time to time, one would sneak through and surprise us like some kind of vengeance of the sea against that old mariner.

The skipper locked up the hysterical screamer and the prostitute in the cabin, secured the hatches, and asked me if I wanted to be locked in as well.

The arms of death have rocked me a number of times on the sea and I did not accept the invitation, since the situation of being in a mousetrap, battered around by the waves and not knowing when it is going to sink is very agonizing. I have learned to know the sea and I know that an approaching shipwreck is less distressing when one is on deck during the storm. Besides, waiting for death is not nearly as bothersome on a small boat as it is on a ship of great tonnage. On the small one, you are only a few centimeters from the water; the very waves, soaking us, already give us the salty taste of the few moments our agony will last; we are at the boundary itself, wavering; a short step and we find ourselves on the other side.

This was our situation in the middle of the Beagle Channel around midnight. Despite having reefed in the sail, the wind had us running over the waves, from shore to shore, and skipper Fernández shouted at the boy at the moment of tacking just when the blackness of the hostile walls of rock placed an even more startling note over our prow.

"You can relieve the boy while he goes down to recuperate with a shot of brandy!" skipper Fernández shouted at me; his words were wrenched away by the wind.

I was strapped tightly with my back to the mast. The skipper's shout announced to me the moment of tacking, and, seizing the foresail, I tried my best to realize the maneuver of catching the wind.

The hurricane worsened; at times I experienced a kind of starvation, my strength diminished and only the satisfaction of serving in such serious moments obliged me to remain firm before the dashing of the sea.

With each passing moment I thought I saw death's arrival among the characteristic three waves which are always preceded by another three smaller ones; the squalls dangerously listed the cutter, making the whole freeboard sink; the mast bent like bamboo and the canvas rustled with the wind that was tearing apart tne rigging. It could be said that we were becoming part of the storm itself, we were going arm in arm with the waves, sunk into the elements and death would have merely been one more thing, for which we were already prepared.

We navigated with the sheet caught up, tilted extraordinarily over the sea, when I suddenly saw the cutter swerve rapidly; the sprit creaked, the pull on the sheet was tremendous and, there in the darkness, all of a sudden, emerged a great whitish mass.

Fernández, the skipper, shouted something to me that I did not understand and I instinctively put my hand on my forehead in a manner of defense; I expected death to emerge suddenly from the sea, but not in such a strange form.

The whitish mass approached: it had the square shape of a statue's pedestal and on top—oh, what a terrible vision—a cadaver, an apparition, a live man, I couldn't tell, since it was something inconceivable, was lifting one of its arms, pointing out the distance swallowed up by the night.

When it got closer, a human figure clearly stood out, on its feet, sunk to the knees in ice and dressed in flamboyant rags. His right hand, raised and rigid, seemed to say: "Get out of here!" and to indicate a route off in the distance.

Upon glimpsing its face, that attitude disappeared and gave way to another, still stranger, impression: the horribly corroded set of teeth, frozen in the biggest laugh, in a static, sinister laugh, to which the howling wind sometimes gave life, with a shuddering howl of pain and death, as if sprung from the string of a gigantic violin.

The iceberg, with its strange navigator, passed by, and near the stern turned around, driven by the wind and showed for the last time the terrifying vision of its macabre crew member who was lost in the shadows with his sarcastic, howling, guttural laughter.

In the night, the symphony of the wind and sea has every human tone, from laughter to weeping; all the music of orchestras, and what's more, soft murmurs, faraway, lacerating lamentations, voices that the waves chatter; those two impressive elements, the water and the wind, seem to tone down to imitate the barking of little dogs, the meows of cats, inharmonious words of children, women and men, which remind us of the souls of the shipwrecked. Voices and noises that only men who have spent many nights awake on the sea recognize and know how to listen for; but that night, this symphony made us feel something more, something like that inexpressible anguish that overpowers the spirit when mystery approaches...it was the iceberg's strange apparition!

At dawn, we cast anchor in the peaceful waters of the protected Bay of Kanasaka.

"I wouldn't have believed it if I hadn't seen that horrible smile of those who freeze to death and that hand stretched out that brushed the main sail upon passing by; if I hadn't swerved on time, it would have broken us into pieces!", exclaimed skipper Fernández.

When we told what had happened to Martínez, the white settler, next to the fire in his hut, one of the Indians who was helping dry our clothes suddenly opened his eyes wide and, speaking to the others of his race, uttered faltering sentences in Yahgan, and among them he repeated in a frightened tone: "Felix! Anan! Felix!"

The oldest Indian calmly spoke and told us: the previous autumn, Felix, a young Indian, tracking a fine-furred animal, crossed the "Italia" glacier; nothing else was heard from him and no one dared to look for him in that immense frozen wasteland.

And so all of that was easily explained: the youth, in his ambition to hunt the animal, went out on the glacier and low temperatures halted his pursuit, freezing him; the winter snows came and covered his body, until summer made the ice resound, breaking it into pieces, and the Yahgan Indian, attached to the iceberg, headed out to rove the seas like some strange phantom.

Everything was easily explained that way; but the hieratic, sinister figure of the cadaver of the Kanasaka Yahgan lingered in my mind like a symbol, pursuing by sea the profaners of those solitudes, the "civilized" white men who have come to disturb the peace of his race and to degenerate it with their alcohol and other disasters. And as if telling them with his extended hand—"Get out!"

Flamenco

I

Just as among men a genius appears from time to time, so among animals, sometimes an extraordinary example emerges, whose existence brings us closer to nature's mysteries, if only to make them more inscrutable for us.

He who has seen killing, from men to sheep, and knows the last scream of terror, the bellow, the last neigh and who even believes to have heard the exhalation of a pinned butterfly, knows how equal these last voices of life are in all beings.

Death not only makes all men equal, but equalizes men with beasts and even with worms.

If we were to take this into the account of our lives, our conduct with animals would be very different.

What campesino has not known some solitary ox who isolates himself in order to ruminate the grasses in the woods, a horse that follows a little girl or a dog who sees death?

There are also lands suitable for the mystery, which influence the conformation of strange beings and animals that do not appear in other places. The eastern foothill region of the island of Tierra del Fuego seems to be one of them.

On its coasts washed by the surge of the Atlantic, curious fish and marine monsters have been seen; on its plains gallop flocks of guanacos who differ from common ones; the fox is very different from the Patagonian one; owls and even that small rodent, the "cururo", sometimes seem to be peculiar to the distant island.

Even men suffer from the strange attraction of those lands and never get accustomed to living in other parts. I have seen many who curse upon departing, and then return a few years later, declaring that they haven't been able to live in other regions. Who knows if this narration is not the product of the nostalgia that one day may corral me too much and make me return to her to again gallop over her vast meadowlands as in the time of my youth.

II

The case of "Flamenco" began one morning in which the drove of horses was being branded. That is, it began for me then, since I didn't actually see the wild life of this beautiful sorrel horse on the Carmen

Sylva range. It must have been very interesting, because the story of his captivity certainly was, and not because I followed the animal like an entomologist does his insects, but because the chain of events made it stand out for me this way.

That morning I was left alone in the corral of the troop of horses while everyone had gone to eat lunch.

Calmly smoking my "Caporal", I was contemplating the hundred little colts and small mares stabbed by that ferocious Jackie. Their haunches were shiny; their thin extremities, ending in small, fine hoofs, looked like the tiny arms of dead children; their chests broken open by the knife thrusts, the tender little heads with fixed, glassy eyes and their manes mixed with blood and sand presented a rather bothersome sight.

"These gringos are cruel," I thought. "Instead of giving those animals away or selling them to the sheep herders and laborers of their own ranch, they prefer to kill them in order to thin out their land and to not propagate the race and breed."

A brilliant sun fell directly on the corral and from the blood, coagulated by the dust, a stimulating vapor rose up, an odor that made the end of one's nose tense.

The atmosphere produced a peace laden somewhat with anguish and an indifference to life.

"It must be because I haven't eaten lunch—because I'm hungry!" I told myself, and I began to leave; but suddenly, a strident neighing lacerated the midday calm.

I turned my head, and behind me, between the rails of the enclosure, a sorrel horse was, like me, contemplating the spectacle of the massacred colts and young mares.

The extraordinary beauty of the animal surprised me. It was a sorrel, between three and four years old, tall, svelte, with a straight back, a belly tight with muscles, thin legs wrapped up in a vigorous nervure and a small head. But what most captured my attention in this extraordinary example was the hide and eyes; the first, shiny and as velvety as that of the fur seal, of a bright red and changing color like flames when the tense muscles made some movement; and the eyes were two balls of viscous light, latent, that went from a steely brilliance when he reared up, to a serene and profound opacity.

He stood out as the best horse of the herd which, separated by the taming, rested at the back of the corral. Further back, the herds of mares moved in the pasture with their small ones castrated and selected to survive.

What was the cause of the curious manner of neighing and staring of this solitary steed?

Did he remember, perhaps, when three years earlier it was his turn to take part in the slashing of knives and his miraculous escape from the certain stabbing by the campañista, bespattered with the warm blood of his brothers and sisters, that young blood with as lively a color as his hide? Did he, perhaps, take that beauty from it, like the agility that Indians acquire when their parents anoint their knees with the blood of baby guanacos?

I stayed there enthusiastically contemplating him, until the kitchen boy came to call me to lunch.

In the afternoon we continued the task of separating and branding, but this time I had another attraction besides roping colts in the corral: the sorrel.

Jackie, sleeves turned up and knife in hand, had scarcely begun to look for the small ones that he would kill when the sorrel, with his head erect, approached to look between the rails.

The victim, once identified as inferior according to the criterion of the killer, was approached by him and was stabbed right in the chest with a fierce blow; with a skillful movement he turned the steel blade inside until it reached the heart, and the animal collapsed.

Then, before the stream of blood that spurted forth, the sorrel's eyes lit up, he arched his neck and stamped, making the ground rumble with his hoofs; afterward, neighing, he entered in with the herd of horses and scattered them.

He repeated this movement all afternoon. One time I pointed it out to Jackie.

"I left this one for my own troop; I noticed him three years ago, in the last branding session!" the campañista responded, selfishly interpreting my interest in the sorrel. "So don't have your eye on him now!" he finished, as a warning.

The two thousand wild mares returned to the hilly country to live their untamed lives, while some two hundred wild horses remained at the ranch to be broken and turned over to the service of the sheep herders, post workers, etcetera.

One morning all of us, from the Administrator down to the last apprentice, met in the corral in order to choose, by order of hierarchy, our future work horses.

This ceremony is very important, because it demonstrates the knowledge and the good eye of those who select, since the animals are young and wild and can turn out just as bad as good for a lifetime.

Everyone, of course, turned their gaze upon the sorrel, but Jackie, who had more authority in the corral than even the Administrator, warned:

"This is 'Flamenco', I named him three years ago when I spared his life to leave him for my own troop; he's very flashy and long-boned; who knows if he'll serve for rough work or not!"

Afterwards, everyone continued their jobs, and the campañistas, theirs: the breaking of the herd of colts.

One morning when I was to have run the range I stayed in the corrals longer than usual to see a horsebreaking.

"Today I'm going to put the leather to the sorrel you had your eye on!" Jackie told me.

And actually, the beautiful horse was tied to the railing.

I stayed then, waiting for an emotional country spectacle, since the first mounting of this steed was to be something extraordinary.

The "pialador" threw the lasso at its hoofs, made it move, and then, with a strong, traitorous pull, they rolled him over on the ground, pulled the lassos tight, and began to put on a saddle with the customary precaution.

The animal moved restlessly for a while, then let them calmly put on the leather cinch and reins.

They loosened the ropes, gave him a lash, and while he jumped up, Jackie got up onto the saddle like a cat.

The animal stayed with its four feet open and firm on the ground and lowered its head as if resolving what it was going to do.

We were all tense with emotion. The assistants opened the gate and another with the back-up horse pulled up alongside.

Man and beast were rigid, not moving a muscle, the one waiting for the formidable buck and the other for whatever surprise in this first adventure.

"Now-w-w-w-w!" Jackie shouted, and while he hung on like an eagle with his spurs, he fiercely whipped the animal's haunches.

But that beautiful brute, instead of giving the tremendous leap that we all expected of him and starting the fierce fight that his strong contexture foretold, went out through the gate with an open, harmonious gallop, just as smoothly as can be.

We were stupefied.

In a while, after taking a few turns on the track, Jackie returned.

"As soon as he learns to run, this is going to be the best race horse on the ranch!" Jackie exclaimed jubilantly, and continued, "This is the first time in my life that this has happened with an animal of such character."

"Do you want me to try him out?" an assistant exclaimed.

The youth, dark-complected and robust, got ready to mount him. He mounted up in one jump, confident; but no sooner had he steadied in the stirrups when something surprising occurred: the animal hunched over, seemed to touch the ground like a cat; then it lifted up its front legs and with a terrible jump shot out through the gate.

Like elastic he took off toward the open spaces, twisted in the air like a fish, his hide shined like leaping flames, he dropped his head and fell down, shaking himself with an intolerable shuddering.

The horsebreaker suffered three great jumps like these; on the fourth he was thrown to the ground like a rag; when they went to pick him up, he had a broken leg.

Jackie was a mestizo, the son of an Englishman and an Ona Indian, raised on the back of a horse and considered the best bronco - buster in Tierra del Fuego; when he found himself with a wild horse, all these things sprang forth, and his blood boiled.

"Leave him to me!" he shouted. "I'm going to teach him!"

Again we had a few seconds of expectation.

The great breaker got up silently, like before, and, just like the last time the sorrel began a gentle gallop.

"I wonder if Jackie has bewitched him," one man said.

"This is a one master horse, no one will be able to mount him!" the campañista exclaimed as he returned and dismounted.

And so it was. No one other than Jackie could get on "Flamenco"; everyone crossed themselves while commenting on this strange event.

III

After a month and a half we received from our bronco busters' legs the brand-new wild horses still semi-broken, since the definitive taming was to be done by our own skill and experience.

Jackie remained with his extraordinary sorrel. Time passed by and no one commented anymore about it.

No one commented until one afternoon in which the campañista, who had gone out to the open country with his "one-master" horse, didn't return to the ranch.

Knowing the experience of this great country man, we didn't worry.

But the night passed, and we became very concerned when on the next day they found "Flamenco" in the corral, saddled, with the lasso dragging, that is, part of it, since it was cut off at the end, with his belly and flanks split open and bloody from spur kicks.

"It's been cut with a knife!" one man said, checking the end of the lariat and he added: "Jackie must have cut it; he could still be alive."

Two of the campañista's helpers immediately took off to look for him.

In mid-afternoon, one returned, with long, slow strides, bringing a wounded Jackie in on the front part of his saddle.

When they took him off, that long-suffering man, tightening his mouth in pain, exclaimed: "I don't know how many broken ribs I have, but I'm sure of a dislocated shoulder and a broken shin."

"Your bones will heal up again," a companion consoled him.

The mestizo smiled from his bunk, his white beaver-like teeth showing through his faded blonde moustache.

About his bones healing up again for him was true; his forty years of breaking horses had not left him a single unbroken bone, but the splinters knitted themselves together, the joints went back into place and the enormous vitality of that man worked the miracle of his return to breaking colts as if nothing had happened.

Except that with every broken bone Jackie became smaller, his body more bent and his gait more and more full of strange movements that made him resemble a monkey.

Every time he got thrown he paid for his triumph over the animals and over nature; he got up from the ground more stunted, like those Fueguian oaks that resist the hurricanes from the west by crouching so low that they end up acquiring strange shapes, extended level with the ground, twisted and frayed, like old, gnarled hands, begging for mercy for that piece of the world lashed by storms.

"Careful! Don't go near that animal who has the devil himself inside his body!" Jackie told us when he was better, and he added, "It seems like he was waiting for the opportunity to break me to pieces, since he appeared as gentle as a lamb and had never bucked underneath my legs.

"In spite of all that," the campañista continued, "I never had much confidence, because sometimes I found him looking at me with eyes full of rage, like those of animals that you have beaten a lot."

"One time he looked at me in such a way that it bothered me; I raised my whip and struck him. 'What's the matter with you?' I asked him, and he remained so tranquil, looking askance at me."

"That day we were going along as nice as could be through the large grassy plain of Section 17, when suddenly, when I least expected it, he bucked fiercely and really gave me a jolt in the saddle.

"Why would I lie to you! I swear that I 'jerked'; if not, he would have thrown me!" the campañista said, smiling, alluding with that term to the action of grabbing the leather straps wrapped around the horse, so as not to fall and something which the campesinos consider shameful.

"He didn't give me any chance to steady myself," he continued; "he took off for a slope, prancing and leaping like a whirlwind. I have rarely seen such a fierce thing; he doubled over, turned himself into a knot, and dragged himself like a cat, neighing with his mouth wide open and me, womp! womp! lash after lash, sinking my spurs into his flanks, my sandals bathed in blood.

"We fought like that for I don't know how long; he didn't let me do anything.

"Suddenly I was about to turn the whip around to grab it by the tip and beat him between the ears and knock him over, when, for the first time ever in my years as a campesino, I let go of my lasso and it began to get tangled up with the horse.

"This is it, I thought, in the middle of my exhaustion and anger!

"In one of his buckings, his foot got caught in a turn of the lasso, which got hold of one of my legs and spread them open so far that it almost split me apart, and I was helpless, he was superior to my strength. I didn't realize what moment it was when I rolled on the ground caught up in my lasso.

"That animal ran, dragging me, like he had never run in his life, heading toward the river. When we got to the edge, I was already all broken and half stunned.

"'You want to drown me, you bastard!', I thought, and I managed to pull out my knife and as if in a dream I blindly, wildly cut the rope, luckily in the necessary part.

"And you're not going to believe it!" the campañista exclaimed, getting halfway up. "That beast came up to me snorting, like fire and full of blood; he looked like the devil. I have never seen an animal like that; I swear to you that I was afraid! He came closer, I had almost fainted, he sniffed me, panting, with his burning breath, and, do you know what he did to me?

"He pissed on me, he dirtied me, kicked me a couple of times in the ribs and left, believing I was dead!

"But don't do anything to him; just let him loose in the country, because when I get up I want to have the pleasure of settling accounts with him," the campañista finished.

IV

As in other occasions, Jackie's bones healed up and completely revived now, he headed out again to work with his horses.

"Don't get on that sorrel anymore," the Administrator himself, Mr. Clifford, said to him one day.

But Jackie mounted him, gave him his series of blows, "grabbed" him again with his spurs, and "Flamenco" remained gentle and calm as if he didn't feel any pain.

Ranch work is full of incidents; new events came to make us forget that one.

Only Jackie must have remembered it, since he had become even more stunted and his gait was no longer that of a monkey, but rather like a skeleton inside a badly sewn bag.

But time passed and even Jackie himself forgot it.

"He must have been crazy that day," he said to me one afternoon in which we were riding, he on his sorrel.

"Animals, like people, become idiotic and crazy!"

The campañista was a primitive man; the Indian and white man within him constantly fought with their instincts. With an infantile tone he told me: "Look, me myself, I'm a good man, but how many times have I, for no reason, sent a companion off to the other world!"

"This is called 'good'," I thought, and I smiled upon remembering the dark accounts that the horsebreaker had with his conscience.

"Perhaps he had eaten some bad grass that day," he continued, justifying the horse, which he surely hated and loved, "and the poor animal went crazy! Just like in the plains there are those grasses that make entire flocks of sheep drunk and stretched out, there must also be grasses that make horses sick. And once drunk, what is it that you can't do?"

"Don't forget that he doesn't let anyone but you mount him," I said to him.

"Hey, that's why I love him!" he responded.

I looked for a while at the beautiful animal that galloped next to my horse and I remembered that scene in the corral, his big, strange eyes, the way that he looked at the killing of the colts and I thought: I wonder if the person of that cruel campañista has not been forever recorded on those retinas, when the beautiful sorrel was saved from being stabbed among his brothers?

Who knows anything about anything?

My thinking that there was a hatred on the part of the animal against the man and that he was planning a real vengeance for the "executioner", I kept very much to myself. It would never come out. My companions were somewhat simple and they would not understand me; they would have roared with laughter at my observations. "He's making it up! He's nuts! He's eaten bad grass, too!" they would have said.

And since on the island "bad grass" really does abound and people go crazy because of the solitude, abstinence or alcohol, I chose to keep quiet.

And wasn't I perhaps going half crazy?

No! I wasn't crazy! The epilogue of this strange story of a horse fighting against a man demonstrated that I was truly in my right mind.

V

"Jackie hasn't returned!" the Second Administrator said under the eaves of the stall.

"And he's riding the sorrel again!" an assistant answered.

"But it's a lamb now," another said.

"It was like that that other time and it almost killed him!" the Second declared.

The Fueguian afternoon was declining, the sunset extended its light across the plains, enhancing the gentle hills and lighting up the tall pastures on the faraway plains.

The campañista had left early with a message for a mountain outpost and should have returned by mid-afternoon.

He didn't return in the afternoon nor at night.

The next morning it was up to me to go scour the countryside looking for him.

The outpost was in some volcanic mountainous region about ten leagues from the ranch. The overseer informed me that, sure enough, Jackie had brought him the order to round up the sheep in two days and that after lunch, he had departed on the return trip.

I began, then, to fruitlessly retrace my steps, always looking from right to left, since I couldn't follow tracks on that ground covered with a hard, stunted grass.

Shortly after galloping, I turned the reins toward the mountain range and decided to circle widely through some hills, with the object of making a thorough search.

In this part of Tierra del Fuego the last chain of hills from the Cordillera ends, and the mesetas that descend to the shores of the Atlantic begin, and then level off, successively, into plains, lowlands and dunes.

The topography is strange; some small lakes among holes in the mountains, eyes of water in the bottom of precipices, gaps between hills, pools among walls of rock, all give it an overwhelming aspect, like the beginnings of the world. Not a single bird is to be seen, and horses that are forced by their riders to cross there point their ears and walk restlessly.

From the top of the hills I looked down to the lower reaches with no result.

"The campañista could have passed by here," I thought, "in order to observe some unknown pass or to discover some good pasture land."

I was about ready to end my search when I spotted, on the top of a kind of meseta, a horse nibbling on some stunted underbrush. It was "Flamenco".

I quickly ascended and approached him. He didn't flee; he didn't even move. He was saddled, without reins, but with a muzzle and halter.

I took him by the halter and tied him to my lasso; at once I carefully contemplated him: he had traces of blood on his flanks and his hide revealed that he had sweat.

I dismounted, went in front of him and stood there looking into his eyes.

At times, one, without wanting to, looks at animals, at nature itself, as if asking them something and they, it would seem, return the look to us inexpressively; but a current is established, something happens in our minds, a light goes on, and we discover what we were looking for, even though it may not be anything more than the peace from our own uneasiness.

My look seemed to bother "Flamenco". In a contact of pupils I asked him, "Where's Jackie?"

And his beautiful eyes, other times lively, blinked without responding; they were calm, and like two balls of glass, opaque and expressionless, they floated, avoiding my gaze.

I mounted up and covered the surrounding area with him by the halter, without finding a single trace.

Nature did not respond either. Not a premonition, nor any tracks, nor any idea to lay hold of.

Suddenly I realized the presence and gravitation of three things: the Horse, Nature and Silence; the three of them formed that impenetrable solitude; the three united and associated, like accomplices form a triangle of a crime.

Ah! But our steps never move at random.

I headed up the hill to find the end of that meseta; but after riding a while I realized that the land curved and I dismounted to continue on foot, since it could be the sign of the edge of some precipice that could break off with the slightest weight on its surface.

Then that summit curved in a way that indicated its end. I lay down and began to drag myself headlong. Guessing that I was near the edge, I hugged the land even more and crept along like a lizard, until....

I still tremble upon recalling it: I was at the very edge of an abyss! I closed my eyes, distressed, and I clutched the earth by sinking in my fingernails! Something in my head generated the feeling of the grazing of a cold blade, as if a guillotine had been at the point of detaching my head from my body and hurling it into that void.

That was a huge gap, an extinct crater, a cliff, whatever!

The attraction of vertigo must be like that of suicide. I gritted my teeth as if expecting an intense pain and opened my eyes again. This time I could see better: I was precisely on the edge of a cliff, as if I were looking inside a gigantic barrel, whose sides, after a very brief layer of debris, sloped downward, curving toward the inside, black and shiny like a blackboard, until the bottom, which was also smooth and bright; the bottom of that fantastic mortar was what I had not seen when I first looked and I had confused it with a black, bottomless pit.

And Jackie?

Only in the end, when I had revived my very marrow, distended my nerves and my head no longer felt that torturous blade of vertigo, could I make out down below, just on the vertical of my vision, a sort of coffee-colored rag, like the ratty skin of a big dog. It was the campañista.

I crawled backwards, and when I sat up and my senses readjusted I realized another reality: how did Jackie fall at that cliff?

The campañista was not a curious man, and if he had come to the edge of the gap, his nerves would have resisted more than mine, since he was stronger.

And the horse, in his battle with him, how could he have thrown him to the bottom without having fallen too?

Unless he had stopped abruptly at the edge of the abyss after a fast run; but this supposition would be rejected before the recognized strength of the English-Ona's legs!

He could have gone crazy and thrown himself into the abyss! He could have done it without going crazy, too, like other men of that land who have ended their lives by killing themselves in strange ways.

I looked at the horse, then into the distance, and again I felt the presence of solitude and silence. Nothing. The three accomplices of that mystery were again united.

VI

It was almost nighttime when in the horse corral I told what had happened to the Second Administrator, an austere, silent Scotsman.

We had "Flamenco" in front of us, whose eyes turned from time to time to look at us.

When I finished the narration, in which I mentioned the observations I made from the first time I saw the sorrel, with his strange look, contemplating the killing of the colts in the corral, and when I had manifested my opinion to the Scotsman that that animal had behaved almost like a human being with the fixed idea of vengeance, I was afraid that he wouldn't understand me and would consider me crazy or a crackpot.

He stared at me, intensely, looking right through me in the semi-darkness that became accentuated with night's arrival. He didn't say a word, nor did his face show any expression. His hand went to his belt, he took out a long-barreled Colt, approached the sorrel, pointed at his head, shot him, and "Flamenco" fell dead in the corral.

The Second Administrator had understood me.

The Australian

I

"The new foreman should arrive today!" said Arentsen, stretching out his long legs in front of the fire, where thick balls of glowing peat cast a soft enchanting light in the room that was invaded by the last shadows of the snowy day.

"What kind of 'animal' do you suppose this one is?" asked MacKay, slyly chewing his words and his pipe, from which spread strong puffs of "octoroon".

"The letter from the Company," began explaining the bookkeeper, an Englishman from the Falkland Islands, with stiff hair and a freckled face, "says that his name is John Larkin, who has been contracted by the representatives in Valparaíso, that he is coming from Canada, is an Australian and that he has a great knowledge of cattle, acquired on the ranches of his country, New Zealand and the American West."

"Good grief!" MacKay exclaimed. "We'll really have to learn, especially me, who came from my mountains in Scotland to bury myself on these pampas of Tierra del Fuego."

A prolonged silence followed the Scotsman's words; the snow outside was falling heavily; at times a huge snowflake fluttered at the windows like an ash-colored bird and stuck to them, lying there like a strange, heavy tear, which stressed our lethargy and the melancholy emptiness of our unoccupied minds.

We were four typical men from the Fueguian ranches: MacKay, the Second Administrator from the Vaquería Ranch; Arentsen, a Chilean son of Norwegians who was the general foreman; Stanley, the Falklander, and I, who tells this story, Chilean and at that time overseer of the "Las Curureras" section of 25,000 animals, to where the man we were waiting for had been destined. This section of the ranch was twenty leagues from the Administration's houses and was situated in the mountainous part of the immense island, from where I had descended to wait for the new foreman.

We four companions rested in that calm, homey atmosphere that the employees' houses on the Magellanic ranches acquire during the winter. We had taken off our leather clothing and boots and had put on, instead, flannel clothes, with vertical stripes, with which the tough MacKay looked more like a prisoner smoking his pipe of sorrow than a "gentleman" at rest.

Nevertheless, those clothes made us forget for a while our ranch life, the daily battling with men and beasts and from time to time they transformed us so much that we even uttered courtesies which made the morose Second wrinkle his eyebrows and the delicate Arentsen smile with a kind of sadness.

Men alone in solitude, sometimes we came to hate our country attire; we tossed it far away and, with a childishness that only those who live in those desolate lands can understand, we would put on the best clothes that we had brought from the city, many years ago, and would sit for entire hours in front of the fire, looking and talking as if we were in a bar or cafe right in the city, until, bored with the farce, we would go to sleep long past midnight.

"When it snows on the glass over on this side, the weather will change for sure," said Arentsen, gazing at a thick glob of snow that blurred the window.

The impenetrable silence of the snowfall was suddenly pierced by the faraway drone of an automobile running at full speed. At times the noise, which was similar to that of a powerful airplane, weakened, then returned strong: it was the hills and ravines that made it move to and fro in its speedy ride over the snowy trail.

Just then the roar invaded the ranch's enclosure. The dogs barked from their kennels and an automobile with a roof covered with ropes and suitcases stopped in front of our house, panting like a tired animal.

Stanley, the bookkeeper, got up to meet the new arrival. In a while both of their steps resounded in the short corridor.

MacKay, Arentsen and I waited for the stranger with a certain uneasiness; that anxiety that waiting for a man who is to live closely with you produces; since a co-worker in Tierra del Fuego is more than family, more than a close friend. Many times one shares his own bread with the anguish of hunger, one frays the same knot, you move your hand toward the same knife and the weakness of one can cause the death of the other.

In almost everything it is necessary to form a pair, from morning to night, where envy, cowardice, egotism, the small yet great defects cannot be hidden and it is difficult to have to put up with them.

The door opened and next to Stanley appeared a very tall and thin guy with dark complexion and green eyes, dressed in a gray raincoat and riding boots who, bending with a certain courtesy, said good afternoon to us.

"Mr. MacKay!" said the Falklander, introducing the newcomer.

The Second Administrator came forward, but at the moment of shaking hands, the two men looked at each other, amazed.

"You are...," stammered the Australian.

"Yes, I am...," stammered the Scotsman. Their hands hesitated and they avoided the handshake. From the same height their eyes exchanged penetrating looks and something like a reflection, like an imperceptible, frozen vapor passed over their serious faces of sure features, like spades pass over dry earth.

The Scotsman bit the handle of his pipe; the Australian was the first to recover his composure, and said: "Excuse us, we already met each other. It is a small world!"

Tierra del Fuego is a place where strange things often occur. Where one meets from Hungarians to Japanese; but this encounter really surprised us. Australia, Scotland, and Tierra del Fuego are not really suitable points at which to meet.

We moved into the dining room and ate almost silently; an awkward atmosphere surrounded us. Only Stanley asked about the trip, the new man answered with short sentences as if he didn't want to talk, either.

No sooner had we gotten up from the table than the Second Administrator said good night and went to his room.

"Our beds are in the guest room," I indicated to Larkin. "You can rest whenever you want; tomorrow after we greet the Administrator, we'll leave immediately for 'Las Cururreras'."

No one said any more; we drank a swallow of whiskey in honor of the new arrival and went to our respective beds.

Stanley, too curious, tried to hold us back to tell us something; but Arentsen cut him off:

"Shut your trap. When will you learn to be quiet? Here no one is surprised about anything or anyone; just keep your eyes wide open and your hands ready."

"Everything will clear itself up and besides, what do we care?" Arentsen told me as he passed by.

II

We arrived at the pinnacles of Camp 24, winding through the low shrubs. The outline of the snowy hills stood out sustaining at times among its crowns small frozen lakes, like mirrors suspended in the middle of the mountains, from which some frightened flamingos would take flight.

"My Section lies right in the Carmen Sylva mountains," I told Larkin, who was trotting at my side; "it's bad for working from a horse, but very good and tranquil for living. The plains of the ranch, the meadows and dunes of the Atlantic are monotonous in comparison to the variety of surprises that these ranges hide, where you'll find deep holes, eyes of water, strange, ancient glacier beds and even rock structures that make you ponder this nature's cataclysms."

My English was very poor; sometimes it made my companion smile, while he, in turn, answered me in an also rather precarious Spanish.

"You will certainly stay in the Section until shearing time," I continued, "a period when we need people who understand work on the ranch."

"I hope to never go down again to the main ranch," he replied.

The confident tone with which he said it surprised me. We continued a long stretch without speaking.

"Let's gallop a while," I said, and I slapped the horse that carried our suitcases. We began a lengthy gallop. My companion had very good riding gear; an Australian saddle with big pads and ample flaps. And at the haunches, instead of a lasso, he carried a beautiful whip of braided kangaroo hide.

When one gallops next to a recent acquaintance, there is a certain discomfort produced, above all upon conversing.

Both of us wanted to get to know each other and the rising and falling movements didn't permit it; even though we spoke from time to time, when we did so it was maddening: the galloping of the horses made our words jump like the bark of dogs, but curiously, we understood each other in spite of it.

And so, getting along well with each other, we carried on with our lives, later, in the Section called "Las Curureras".

III

Larkin was a man of some thirty-five years, tall, wiry and thin; his long face indicated a mixture of English and native Australian; agile and strong, it was amazing how this guy, without a strong physical appearance, used to bend like bamboo, take calves or a heifer by the jawbone and with one jerk would throw them to the ground, where he held them with his knee in their flanks until the branding iron arrived.

He rode Australian-style, without cushions, and with stirrups so long that his feet seemed to reach the grass.

We spent all the spring workdays together: round-up and branding of beef cattle; round-up and branding of wild horses; the care of birthing sheep, and so on. This hard-working man was easily better than me.

On the ranches in Tierra del Fuego, one is not only a foreman because of the title, but also, with very few exceptions, one holds this job because he has more ability in every phase.

Larkin came to be the second overseer of the Section, and despite this natural competence in his work, he never challenged my authority.

Without exerting himself he did the work of two men wherever he went. While we laid out an animal, he stretched out two.

I tried to equal him, but I couldn't. One afternoon in which I rolled over, holding on to the lips of a heifer that I couldn't knock down, he ran quickly to my aid and afterwards, out of breath, inhaling the smoke of his half-lit "Capstan", he said to me:

"Sorry, Che (Che was the first Tierra del Fuego expression that he picked up), you still have soft bones!"

"The gringo turned out well for you!" one of the sheepmen said to me one day.

"What do you mean 'gringo'!" the horse boy replied, demonstrating a certain knowledge. "Don't you see how his face is like ours? He just has longer legs, that's all. A gringo would never work for you like that. He had to be Australian, because they say that they are more or less the same as we Americans."

With modesty, simply, as if he didn't want to attract attention to himself, Larkin would, from time to time, show off extraordinary qualities as a rider and as a man accustomed to easing the monotony and solitude with some rustic act or ability.

With great skill he had trained his troop of dark brown sorrels by means of the Australian whip; while we were twirling the noose of our lassos in the mornings in the horse corral, he, more quickly, would make his whip crack like a lion tamer and would stop, right in its tracks, his chosen horse, which then remained quiet to be bridled. On those occasions when he wasn't obeyed, a rain of snaps on the snout and rump punished the rebel until he was brought under control.

This kangaroo-skin whip was for him what the lasso and bolas were for us; but, besides, he performed true displays of his skills. Sometimes when he was in a good mood he had me hold, at the very end of my thumb and index finger, a blade of grass or little piece of straw. He would step back several meters and with the flexible whip he began to measure the distance two or three times until, all of a sudden, with a violent lash he made the whip, which ended in three horsehairs, crack, and he cut the straw held between my fingers as if he had used a razor.

I never managed to get him to go from the Section down to the ranch.

"Let me be, Che; I'm fine here at the Section; when I leave here it will be to go to other lands," he would tell me. A tough friendship, through our work, was developing between us. That friendship made through effort, in the daily struggle with nature, animals and men; very different from that other kind, born at the counter of a bar or in city pleasures.

From the last nights of winter, in which he arrived at the ranch, to those afternoons at the beginning of summer, which were relatively warm for those latitudes, when we were returning from our riding with slow strides, we had changed a great deal. Our imperfect Spanish and English allowed us to understand each other adequately.

I told him stories, legends and customs of Chiloé, from the north of Chile, my trips through eastern Ecuador, and he, the extraordinary tales of gentlemen bandits in old Australia, the heroic battles of the country people against the "dingo" dog, the dog-wolf of that mysterious continent, and his travels through South Africa, Canada, the United States; he was always in the countryside, a hardened lover of cattle, trails and remote places.

Our talks were truthful, authentic. Who, furthermore, would invent stories or novels, if for five months we were actually living the most complex part of a novel become reality: the strange encounter between the Scotsman and the Australian?

At least my ranch companions and I were living it. There Arentsen had closed the Falklander's mouth with a "Don't meddle in something that doesn't involve you," and here in the Section I never alluded to nor thought of alluding to that strange meeting between MacKay and Larkin.

For that very reason I was quite surprised that Saturday morning when I told Larkin:

"Listen, I haven't seen anyone's face but yours and our sheepmen's for more than a month; I feel like going to the ranch today just to experience the sensation of other people in the world."

And he answered, "Me too, Che."

"What? You're going down, too?"

"Yeah, I changed my mind!"

We had our best horses brought; "Nene", a half-blooded chestnut, the best of my troop, and "Reno" for him, a dark brown sorrel whose mane was clipped in the style of the American west.

We shined our boots, chose our best riding outfits, and upon leaving our rooms I saw Larkin take down his Colt from the wall, check to see if it was loaded, and tie it on his belt.

"Why the revolver?" I asked. "Our road is the most peaceful there is. I barely carry a skinning knife in case we see some stretched-out animal."

"The only things I know are you and the countryside of this Section, and life has taught me that this is good security," he replied, touching the revolver.

"Well," I said to myself, "it has taught me not to interfere in the affairs of sensible, adult men."

It was the last trip we made together, and perhaps for that reason I remember it so poignantly.

We left with our shining, spirited horses. "Nene" was a chestnut that I only rode on special occasions; a good, strong runner, with just slight pressure from your legs he took off like a flash. "Reno" was finer and more delicate; a groove in his right ear indicated his origin from one of the purebred stallions.

Upon descending to the plains of the ranch, a gentle breeze combed the bright pasture; in some low areas where grass did not dominate with its lichen-like stiffness, the meadows were sown with little white daisies and other tiny flowers which dare to appear in those tough climates. We felt the enervating power of full springtime, the throbbing muscles of our steeds, our thick blood that wanted to burst through our fingers and a sensation of youth and strength that made us breathe deeply the fragrant air and to look with yearning at the distant sights, which gave us the urge to gallop to infinity.

"I've never tried 'Nene' against 'Reno'," I hinted; "I think the sorrel can win a short race and the chestnut a long one, since he is the son of the best stallion on the ranch."

Larkin's face filled with joy. We were really in a good mood.

"Let's bet a bottle of 'King George', and so that no one has an advantage, we'll run 500 meters!" I proposed.

"You're on!" Larkin answered.

When they have a few kilos of weight on them, it is dangerous to make a horse run all out; it takes a certain mastery and also a bit of courage, which always makes a race an emotional spectacle.

We calculated the distance to a white rock which lay at the edge of the road and we agreed to start out "English-style", without the classic native "invitation".

We were stopped still when, suddenly, in unison, we yelled "N-o-w-w-w" and took off.

The chestnut gave a powerful starting jump, taking a half-length lead over the dark brown sorrel; I leaned over the animal's neck and at the hundred-meter mark I began to whip the horse, from left to right, without missing a lick. Then the half-a-body lead increased to more than a full length.

I didn't see Larkin, I just felt the blowing of his horse behind me; at the half-way mark, this noisy breathing began to press on my spurs. A dozen meters more and, little by little, the breathing was at my side. Then we entered into a fierce battle between animals and men.

The chestnut made the earth thunder, but the dark brown sorrel stretched out like a greyhound and with each stretch his head moved past the chestnut's shoulder blade.

Larkin shouted next to his horse's ear like I had never heard him, but we were already at the stone, which I crossed by, beating my opponent by a neck.

"We ran tough!" he said to me, excited.

"A few meters more and 'Reno's' class would have prevailed!" I answered.

IV

"What side did he run on? The right! Ah, no wonder he lost; he doesn't know this 'criollo' who has pulled one over on him," Arentsen exclaimed, laughing, in the small dining room, while we drank the bottle of whiskey from the bet.

Sometimes we took to killing with alcohol the anguish of solitude and other things that happen to men who spend months and years without seeing a woman. That night we drank ourselves into oblivion. One by one we retired to our rooms, drunk, until only Larkin and MacKay were left in the dining room.

My limbs were weak, but my head, still somewhat lucid, made me remember the encounter of these two men and, since my room faced the door of the dining room, I left both doors open.

I looked at them in sort of a bewildered way and in this manner I saw them suddenly get up. Each one grabbed a glass, filled it, drank it down, and remained there holding it in his hand. They leaned on each end of the table as if they were two travelers who had stopped to rest or to talk.

And then a strange conversation began, tough but not angry. I couldn't tell what they were saying but a murmur could be heard, like a brook in the woods, its waters gently flowing over a bed of sandstone.

Sometimes one of them talked a long time and the other was silent; other times both voices mingled or they suddenly interrupted one another, leaving a half-frozen void through which a monotonous murmur began again.

From time to time my mind escaped to rest, and at times it got extremely worried thinking. Could they have become reconciled? What is it that separates these men who have come from so far away to these solitudes? Are they just now explaining it to each other?

The tone of their voices was terribly opaque; it didn't suggest anything.

On occasion I nodded off and upon waking I found the presence of the voices again and I saw them in their position as lingering travelers, leaning with their hands on whiskey glasses as on the handle of a cane. My mind grasped them and let them go, like faces lost in water.

"Come on, these guys are cranked up with whiskey," I told myself and I decided to go off to sleep.

V

When one awakens from a drunken state, it's as if you resurrect, and I believe that those who are not addicts drink sometimes to die and to be reborn, thus changing with these stages the monotonous continuity of life.

It is, really, a return from the tomb: your bones and fingernails hurt as if you had been scratching the earth, packed up in your eyelids are webs of dreams and on your lips you feel an aftertaste of eternity.

After detaching myself from all of this, my first impression was that the Scotsman and the Australian were still talking, and I even thought I heard again the suffering of those voices involved in a muffled monotonous dialogue; but in the small dining room there was only a cold, lacerating light of dawn.

"They have probably finally gone to bed, drunk," I told myself.

However, I got up quickly, with the desire to verify that supposition as soon as possible.

I went through the dining room; the bottles were next to the empty glasses. I went to MacKay's room, knocked, and no one answered. The room was empty; in the middle of it, his "house" clothes had been changed for the work ones.

Nor was Larkin to be found in the guest room. Everyone else slept deeply.

Buttoning up my leather jacket, I crossed the enclosure and headed for the ranch's horse corral.

"Reno" and the Second Administrator's horse were not in the stall. I quickly saddled my sorrel, mounted and took off. Over the animal's neck I observed the tracks: they took the public road and then headed inward on the pampa; the horses' tracks were always together. The pronounced crevices made by the hoofs in the grass indicated to me that they had begun a strong gallop, ascended a ridge and headed for a meseta.

I extended my horse to a full gallop toward there, under the impression of a troublesome certainty.

The chestnut realized my urgency and climbed the slopes of the meseta by leaps, like a guanaco.

This undertaking was useless; when I was almost at the edge of the flat terrain, I heard two shots break the tranquility of that place.

I stopped the horse; something inside me sank, and I dropped the reins, weakened.

"Why didn't I gallop from the beginning? I would have gotten here on time," I thought, with deep bitterness.

After the almost simultaneous shots, a great silence invaded the countryside again and an even more egotistical thought shook me: I wonder who fell?

Before this anxiety, I grabbed the reins, spurred, and climbed to the plain.

I will never forget the view that awaited me: Larkin, on his feet, was next to "Reno", with his arms crossed over the saddle, his head resting on them and his gaze fixed upon the faraway mountains of Carmen Sylva, shining with the golden sunlight which at that moment appeared from the east; he gave the impression that he had ridden a long road and had reached exhaustion or peace at the end of it. MacKay was lying on his back on the ground; his sharp nose protruded strangely from his face and a nickel-plated pistol shined like a chrysalis in his twitching hand; his horse, indifferent, was grazing a few meters from the body of his master. All of this was enhanced by the light of the rays of the rising sun, which crossed the meseta almost horizontally, cutting through the grass. Overwhelmed, I advanced by the strides of the horse. Larkin was so removed that he didn't hear me; from my horse I had to put a hand on his shoulder for him to realize my presence. He turned his emaciated face. A couple of more years had fallen upon it.

"We fought a duel," he told me. "He hurried his last step a little, fired first, but missed. I had better luck!"

"Let's go," I told him, "Hurry and mount up. We'll get to the Section, there you'll change your saddle to one of my personal horses and tonight you can cross the border into Chile. The sooner, the better!"

"Oh, no. I'll answer for what I've done!" he replied.

"Do it!" I shouted at him vigorously. "They don't understand duels here. You killed a man. You don't have the money to bribe the police and therefore if you stay you will have to fall into the dungeons of Ushuaia! Let's move!" I ordered, and I went over to close MacKay's mouth, hobbled his horse and at once we headed at a full gallop toward the Section.

We arrived without exchanging a word. The horses were sweaty. I had a mare from my personal troop brought for the fugitive and I mounted up on the freshest horse I found closest at hand.

While he put on some wool and leather clothes, I put together some lamb chops, bread and whiskey, and we took off again in the direction of the border mountain range, cutting through the countryside and fording rivers without paying attention to any dangers.

Luckily, an almost-full moon rose over the mountains.

Past midnight, we sighted on a hill the geometric silhouette of a boundary post on the Argentine-Chilean border; then another and others, until we finally arrived to the border.

Using one of the boundary posts as a table, I made a quick map of the roads Larkin should follow.

"Well," I told him smiling, "Now you're in Chile, in my country, and to celebrate before we say good-bye, we'll eat some chops and have a drink of whiskey!"

We dismounted in order to do that. I handed Larkin the rest of the meal and the bottle, and we got ready to part. At that moment the moon was moving along brightly; that austral moon of Tierra del Fuego, large and strange, which rotates through a very curved sky like a slow tram-car with its big basket of diamonds, so slowly that sometimes morning surprises it half-way along in its journey to other gilded mines in the west.

Once mounted, we looked at each other for an instant. I was calm; on the other hand, underneath the brim of Larkin's hat something occurred...

"Well, Che, thanks!" he said to me, extending his hand.

We shook hands briefly, and "see you later" were our last words.

Whenever sentiment gets the best of me, I swim against the current. This time I told myself an egotistical vulgar remark which I did not feel: "You lost a horse and a friend. You're all right, friend. It's better for you not to leave your ranch!" and I galloped off toward the "Las Cururreras" Section.

VI

Some months later, at the moment of leaving for a drive, a messenger from the ranch came with mail. Among the letters was one addressed to me, with big letters and a strange stamp. I opened it; it was from Larkin. He was writing to me from some place in South Africa.

After recalling—half in English and half in Spanish—the past times in Tierra del Fuego and his escape, he ended in this way:

"I am here, Che (you're going to laugh) trading camels; I buy them in the south and I sell them in the interior of Africa.

It's going well for me; if it were not so, I wouldn't be sending you these paper pounds, more or less equivalent to the value of the mare you provided me, which I sold for a very low price in Río de Oro to some guy named Antúnez, so that you could recover him some day.

Come on over, Che, we'll work together here. That cursed land isn't for you; it's not worth it to live in one place like the rocks.

Ah, look; this letter has another purpose and that is to thank you for something: that you never asked me, during my stay with you in the Section, nor during my escape, the cause of the hatred and the duel with MacKay!

In the war of '14 we met in Gallipoli; I was in an Australian cavalry regiment and he in a Scottish infantry corps; but, my good friend, the subject doesn't matter: it was a dark thing, between men, that began in Gallipoli and ended in Tierra del Fuego.

Your friend,
Larkin

Gulf of Sorrows

Our boat rested between waves like some wounded animal in search of a way out through that closed horizon of dark and shifting ridges.

"Hold on, old man!" said a sailor, grinding his teeth and tightening the muscles of his face as if a painful obstruction knotted up his insides. The boat, as if it had heard him, creaked at the edge of a forty-five-degree roll and suddenly ascended the ridge of another wave, semi-resting, now free from completely turning over as well as from finding the way out.

Storm clouds closed in all around us. The sky was just one more huge wave suspended over our heads, from whose bulge a heavy, tormenting rain let loose.

Suddenly, emerging from the dark clouds, an even darker shadow appeared on the back of a wave; another wave hid it and a third one raised it up again, presenting us with the most unusual encounter possible on the open seas: a rowboat with five men in it.

A strange happening, because only ships of great tonnage venture through that gulf. Ours, with its ten miles of machinery, had been fighting to cross the gulf from south to north for over twenty-four hours. A nutshell like that minuscule rowboat couldn't hope to cross to the San Pedro lighthouse, to the first mass of dry land to be found in the south of the fearful gulf, in less than a week.

In the midst of the sounds of the storm, the machine bells resounded like a heart pounding its metal walls as the ship lessened its speed.

The rowboat was wide, made of cypress, with thick ribs which exposed a rosy pulp from so much soaking in the sea and rain water. Four boaters rowed vigorously, then haltingly, steadying one foot on the bench and the other on the matting at the side of the boat. They stared strangely at the sea, especially on the fall of the wave, when the skirt of water slipped rapidly toward the abyss. The skipper, firmly grasping the tiller, was on his feet, and with one hand he helped the oarsman at the stern with a push of his body, which seemed to give strength to them all, because they followed the rhythm of his drive as if they were one. Every now and then a ridge rose up and hid the rowboat, and in those moments, they seemed to be rowing suspended in the sea by some strange miracle.

When it pulled alongside us, a cable lashed to a lead was thrown to them, which the oarsman at the prow tied with a running hitch to a shackle on his bench. The proximity of the boats was becoming more and more dangerous. The waves lifted and dropped the ship and the rowboat, irregularly, in such a way that at any moment the skiff could be dashed to pieces against the iron sides of the ship. A rope ladder was thrown to the rail, and when the crest of the wave lifted the rowboat up to the very davits of the bridge, the skipper grabbed the ropes, and on the fall of the wave climbed up the ladder with the agility of a cat. He set foot on deck and like lightning he ascended the gangway to the bridge.

There, the skipper and the captain shut themselves up in the cabin. We waited to see what would happen. The oarsmen held on from a safe distance in their nutshell; the ship thrust its prow between the waves and lifted it up again like a tired head tossing off the foam. The boatswain and sailors were ready with the rigging to raise the rowboat on board, as soon as the captain gave the order.

The minutes dragged on. Why such a delay to save a boat in the middle of the ocean?

Our expectations diminished when we saw the skipper leave the cabin. He made a strange gesture with his hand and descended the ladder with the same agility as before. The order to lift up the shipwrecked sailors was never heard. Our amazement, at that moment, increased.

The skipper passed by me, confronted me with a cold, forceful look. I wanted to speak, but his expression stopped me. The man was drenched; he was dressed in coarse wool pants and a thick sweater; his head and feet were bare; his face was beaten by the water just like the cypress of his boat; and in his whole being there existed a sort of defiant agility with which he almost seemed to hide himself from the relentless punishment of the storm.

Again he moved like lightning, jumped over the railing, grabbed the rope ladder and, taking advantage of a certain roll of the waves, he was suddenly again holding the tiller of his boat.

"Clear o-f-f-f-f," he shouted, and the bowman untied the cable, tossing it in the air with a very natural yet disdainful expression. The oarsmen rowed vigorously and the boat disappeared behind a mountain of water. Another mountain lifted it to its summit, and a moment later it vanished just as it had appeared, like a dark shadow swallowed up by the storm.

On the ship, the only command heard was that of the bell of the machines which increased our speed. The sailors were astonished, empty-handed, as if awaiting something. The boatswain slowly picked up the cable and the lead, embittered as if he were gathering in all of the ocean's scorn...

"Why didn't we pick them up?" I asked the captain later.

He answered: "The skipper didn't want us to pick them up as shipwrecked sailors."

"Why not?"

"He told me, 'We are seal hunters from Lemuy Island and we're going to the Magellan Channels in search of hides. We are not shipwrecked!'

"Don't you know that the Maritime Jurisdiction prohibits crossing certain limits with an undersized craft? Do you intend to cross the gulf with that piece of bark?

"It's not an undersized craft, it's a boat with five rowers and we cross the gulf with it every year at this time! All we are asking is that you pick us up and drop us off a little closer to the coast, that's all."

"If I pick you up, I must turn you over to the Harbor Master of the port holding jurisdiction.

"No. They'll register us as shipwrecked—and we will not accept that, dead or alive! We are not shipwrecked, captain."

"Then I shall not pick you up."

"Fine, captain."

And gesturing with his hand, the skipper ended their meeting.

Not able to contain myself, I uttered: "So you left them fighting against death here in the middle of this watery hell; you could have given them a chance by taking them closer to the coast. Who would enforce the regulations in the open sea?"

"That skipper was pigheaded!" the captain replied, and looking at me out of the corner of his eye, he added, "If he had begged a little, I would have picked him up."

Outside, the storm in the Gulf of Sorrows worsened.

Five Mariners and A Green Coffin

One day at the beginning of winter, a boat arrived in Punta Arenas that was so unballasted that more than half of a propeller blade was out of the water; the lead-colored hull, peeling somewhat from the bad weather or because of the job of painting on the high seas, was streaked with large stains of bright red that looked like wounds whose blood still had not been stanched.

In their prolonged runs, these vagabond ships generally pass through the Strait of Magellan without stopping, and if they do stop in the port they only do so to fix some engine problem or because of some vital breakdown.

This one asked to be admitted by the captaincy of the port; but along with the flag of petition it had raised on the foremast a flag made of large pieces of black and yellow cloth which indicated "dead man on board".

And as a matter of fact, after the maritime authority's cutter had cleared off from its side, a lifeboat was lowered from the ship's davits, and, manned by four rowers and a skipper, it headed at a full row toward the port's wharf.

The boat tied up near the sea wall, which at that hour of low tide stuck clear out of the water.

Two of the crew climbed agilely along the piles to the platform, and those down below threw them two pieces of rope which they began to carefully pull in, and rising from the interior of the lifeboat, as if they were pulling it up from the depths of the sea, was a strange, big box painted green, which, although roughly made, had the characteristic shape of a coffin.

It was carefully placed on the edge of the dock and, after leaving the lifeboat secured, the other three sailors climbed up, removed the mooring lines and lifted it up in the air. Four of them placed it on their shoulders and with the fifth one escorting them, they took off in search of the port's outlet to the town. The streets were snow-covered and the mariners had to walk carefully, stepping uncertainly, which gave a certain sway to their shoulders and to the coffin, whose green color made one think of a portion of the sea carried on those sailors' shoulders.

At the entrance to the dock they asked a guard for the road to the cemetery, and toward it they directed their measured steps. It was around noon and in the deserted white streets they encountered only a passer-by or two who were hurrying to get to lunch, but not so much so as to not remove their hats out of respect before the encounter with death, and after turning their heads several times, they stopped to watch the strange funeral of the four mariners with the green coffin on their shoulders.

Upon turning a corner they ran into a short, coarse individual who uncovered his big, thick head with a flat nose and who, with an unusual gesture, began walking next to the coffin, with his eyes cast downward and an obvious look of remorse on his face, as if it dealt with a relative. It was Mike, the pastry cook's idiot son, who had the morbid custom of accompanying every funeral that came across his path, with the most pathetic sorrow possible...but he must have perceived something strange about this one, for after walking just a short way he put on his hat again and left the entourage to resume his wanderings of a crazy one on the loose.

On arriving to the outskirts, a blizzard began to whip the pall-bearers, who had to protect their faces by changing shoulders more often in order to hide behind the side of the box less beaten by the strong wind. One man always stayed behind resting, so as to become a fresh replacement.

During one of these changes a somewhat old and graying crew member got his turn to put the coffin down, and he stopped to rest fully, while he used his handkerchief to wipe his face, which was just as wet from the sweat beading on his forehead as from the blizzard. He was Foster, the one who was the most of a friend to Martin, the boat's lamplighter, who they were now going to bury; they shared the same cabin on the "Gastelu" and who knows why he was sweating so much...perhaps the coffin weighed more upon his shoulders than on those of the dead lamplighter's other companions...

But, suddenly, his eyes caught sight of a sign that stood out over the doorway of a house which said, in blue and red letters, "Hamburg Bar". He glanced fearfully at his companions who moved on unaware of his delay, laying to the blizzard with persistent steps; looking at the sign again he quickly entered the bar.

At the counter he asked the bartender for a double gin which he swallowed in one gulp, then wiped the back of his hand across his lips which joyfully sucked on his moustache. And he felt more relieved, not because the coffin had weighed more for him than for the other men, but because it had to do with Martin the lamplighter, his cabin-mate, whose eyes, upon rolling with the last look of his life, had dumped a weight into his own greed-filled soul; a weight that he had tried in vain to lighten.

It was he himself who proposed to bury him on land and not at sea, for fear of an old sailors' superstition which says that those who are buried at sea always return to their homes or often visit the places where they lived, many times avenging themselves of those who have done them harm. And when it has to do with a crime or something similar, the legend exalted the vengeance in such a way that the soul of the victim came to embody that of the perpetrator, until he became sick or died...superstitions! Nonsense! But so certain at times, like the San Telmo lights that light up on the tops and crosstrees of the masts just before a ship is going to sink in the middle of a storm!

Even before their ship had passed by Froward Cape, the last continental rock of South America, he, Foster, had hurried, with hammer and saw, to make the rough pine coffin that he had to paint green because there was no other paint on board other than the black tar, which was impossible to use because of the length of time it takes for it to dry. He had hurried, and insisted to the first mate so that they wouldn't toss Martin's body to the sea, so that on the other hand he could rest in peace in the earth, and perhaps it would let him rest, too..., because as long as he was above the ground or wandering in the depths of the sea, the weight that the lamplighter's last look dumped upon his soul would not be lifted by all the glasses of gin he could drink in his lifetime.

He couldn't continue with his thoughts: there was a sudden turbulent invasion in the Hamburg Bar by his four companions who, upon realizing that he was no longer following them, stopped for awhile to wait for him; but one of them, like all thirsty sailors, had also seen, out of the corner of his eye, the red and blue Hamburg Bar sign on the side of the house, and they had no doubt whatsoever that their missing friend had slipped his head in there to stingily have a few swigs. They set the coffin down in a depression in the semi-urban terrain, between the sidewalk and the street, so that their disrespectful abandonment might be less obvious, and the four of them headed after the scoundrel who had come to drink by himself.

Foster welcomed them, not without surprise; but putting on a front, he immediately asked for a round of drinks for everyone and, a rare thing because of his reputation as a miser, then he asked for another, and went to pay for them.

"Did you inherit from Martin, is that why you are so generous?" a red-haired man with a face full of knife scars said, laughing.

"You old rascal, we caught you—I bet you're drinking up the money Martin had in the hiding place that only you and he knew about!"

Foster wiped his forehead again with his handkerchief and tried to smile while he raised his glass to his lips, inviting the others with this gesture.

"And you were going to suck it up all alone, eh, old man?" said another.

"Don't be like that. I have always drunk alone, but with my own money!"

"Then bring us a whole bottle of gin," the red-haired man exclaimed. "Old Foster is buying!"

The tavern keeper uncorked a clay bottle and put it on the counter...the mariners came closer and read the label—"its pale yellow color proves its age"—and began to pour it.

Outside, the blizzard was turning into a heavy snowfall and only the snow's lifeless wings came to accompany Martin, like a gift from all immensity upon his abandoned coffin.

*   *   *

"If you have green with green,
        and red with its own
        then no one gets lost
        on his way home..."

Everyone sang the chorus with which Martin the lamplighter remembered the position of the lights when ships meet each other at full sail in the night; a chorus that every lamplighter or helmsman repeated often so as not to err in the route that they should take in such circumstances.

Lights had also been lit in the interior of the bar, because night had fallen outside, without the mariners having noticed its arrival. Sea people, fishermen, drank noisily, and the strong smoke of their pipes and Tuscan cigars filled the bar with a heavy atmosphere.

From time to time someone put a nickel coin in the slot of the music box bolted to the wall and the chords of some old march, polka or waltz broke into the air with a great stridence of drums and cymbals.

One of the mariners looked through the window toward the night and stopped a while to melancholically contemplate how the snowflakes played on the glass, like a flock of butterflies who fought to pass through the crystal toward the light, then slid down in big tears that sketched the blurred glass by evaporation. The music, the awkward dance of the winged feet of snow on the glass with their agitated rhythm...who knows? Perhaps they brought an obsession to the sailor's mind, and he got up to speak to one of the bartenders. Afterwards he remained pensive, leaning on the counter and looking toward his four friends; old Foster was nodding off and the other three drank slowly, annihilated by the alcohol. He emitted a concealed whistle that was heard only by the red-head with the slashed face, who instantly approached the counter.

"Let's go have a good time, eh?" he proposed.

"All right!" the red-head answered, making his tongue crackle, but then, suddenly in doubt, he added "What about Martin?"

"Let them bury him...if they can!" he replied, making a disparaging gesture toward those who remained at the table.

They left silently and the night swallowed them up. Only after a long while did those inside become aware of their absence; but the binge had been so sudden, that they paid little attention to the time or the circumstances in which they found themselves.

"Let's...bury Martin," one of them stammered.

"When the others return!" proclaimed the other.

Foster continued dozing heavily and he would awaken from time to time only to stretch out his hand and unsteadily bring his glass to his withered lips, which revived for a few moments because of the burning contact with the alcohol.

"Poor Martin," the one moaned.

"Poor guy," repeated the other, in litany.

"Do you remember when he bought all of us drinks in Tocopilla?"

"Yes, I remember; he paid for all of us with his generosity."

"He played better than this cursed music, with his harmonica..."

For a few moments, the unforgettable image of the Gastelu's lamplighter, the ship's best companion, passed through the minds of the drunken men: the vision of when he cheered them up with his mouth organ, or of those occasions when, without a penny in his pocket, in a bar in whatever port, he would dance with one of his companions, playing the harmonica and accompanying himself with a real battery of spoons placed between his fingers, which he drummed to the beat of the dance on his head, forehead and back, in a strange, grotesque dance. After the dance, which made the customers laugh, Martin bowed and shortly thereafter he was invited to all of the tables; but he could not drink at them without his beloved companions...

"Do you remember the shipwreck of the 'María Cristina'?"

"When he took off his lifejacket and handed it to Foster?"

"So that he could save him, because he was older than he was..."

"And he almost died, swimming from the high seas without a life preserver..."

"And now the old bum is sleeping and doesn't even bury the man who saved his life..."

"Neither do we..."

"Nor those traitors who took off and still haven't returned..."

"Nor anyone else...(hiccup...hiccup)...this is a wicked world ...you barely turn around and nobody remembers you..." moaned the drunkest one, his face filled with big tears, and between hiccups and his crying, he added, "Poor Martin! 'If you have green with green, and red with its own, then no one gets lost, on his way home'..."

A ship's siren began to intermittently and grievously penetrate the late hours of the night; it could be heard inside the bar, piercing the noise and the music. It was a howl that came from the immensity that had something like a human voice, a ululant voice, touching. It was the 'Gastelu's' whistle calling for its five crew members who had disembarked on a mission of mercy...

"Hey,...sailors...a ship has been calling its crew for half an hour!" the bar owner exclaimed, shaking the two men who were still sleeping on the table at which all five had been sitting during the afternoon.

It was difficult to wake them up. Luckily he was able to do so at the same time the ship's siren renewed its grievous and prolonged laments, again calling its crew members to set sail before the tide resisted their leaving the Strait.

Still rubbing their eyes, the two mariners recognized the 'Gastelu's' voice in the intermittent whistles.

"That's it, our ship!"

"It's insisting!" the other exclaimed.

"And our companions?" one of them asked, somewhat clear from his sleeping.

"They took off...a few hours ago...looking for fun elsewhere!" the owner replied.

"Foster, too?"

"Who is Foster?"

"The other two probably went to see women; but Foster, the old guy, should be with us!"

"Ah...the old man, yeah; I saw him stay with you, but he disappeared a while ago...maybe the older you get, the more of a womanizer!"

At that moment the 'Gastelu's' horn began to clamor again with its intermittent whistles for its men who had been swallowed up by the city, and the last two customers of the "Hamburg Bar" quickly put on their hats and left.

Outside they ran into the black night; but the frozen tentacles that came out of the darkness fanned their faces and cleared up their drunkenness a little bit.

"And Martin?" one said, suddenly remembering the coffin that they had abandoned along the sidewalk.

"We didn't bury him!" the other exclaimed, like an echo in that drunken litany.

"Quiet then...and we'll make an agreement with the others in the lifeboat."

"Someone will bury him tomorrow when they find him!" the other replied, and they disappeared on their way to the docks like two shadows darker than the night itself.

But the next day no one found any coffin in the port...because the snow had fallen all night long, forming a layer about a meter deep and covering everything with its pure whiteness, and it continued snowing, slowly, but so abundantly that no one was going to go around looking for coffins on the stone pavement of the streets that day. Not on that day nor on the others that were solidifying the thick crust of ice...

It was as if Martin the lamplighter had again returned to the sea after dying, like the souls of those shipwrecked who follow the wake of their former ships or the trail of those who tormented them in life or in the very hour of death.

About mid-morning of that day, Don Erico, the owner of the "Hamburg Bar", began to clean up his establishment, and imagine his surprise upon finding, behind one of the barrels in a room adjacent to the bathroom of the bar and which served as a wine cellar, an old graying mariner still sleeping off his hangover.

"And you?" he said to him, waking him up with the tip of his foot.

"Me? I'm from the 'Gastelu'..." Foster answered, babbling, while he got on his feet, rubbing his eyes and still not fully realizing where he was.

"From the ship that was calling its people all night long?"

"Yes! Did they leave...my companions...and they left me?" he added, stammering.

"Now that I think of it, they asked for someone named Foster. Are you Foster?"

"Yes, I am Foster!"

"And me, who told them you had gone with the others ...chasing women!" Don Erico said with an indifferent and bestial burst of laughter.

"And the ship?"

"It's probably far away...a ship waits for no sailor!"

"Please, give me some gin!" Foster mumbled, feeling his pockets in search of some money.

They went to the bar, where Erico served him up a big glass of gin.

"I was a sailor, too!" he told him. "For many years I sailed in the 'Hapag'—and more than once the ship left me behind and I shipped out again on another!"

Foster, who was stiff with the previous night's cold, was able, with the gin, to stop his teeth from chattering; and after steadying himself with another glass he was going to head for the harbor.

"Don't leave, it's really snowing hard!" Don Erico warned.

"It doesn't matter! The ship could still be there!" he answered.

"It would have blown the whistle again!" the proprietor replied.

Nevertheless, Foster went down to the docks to search the bay, enveloped now in the snowfall's mist but he only found hulks tied to their shackles, trade ships and a wool dealer or two arriving late to their ships. The "Gastelu" wasn't anywhere to be found; by that time, certainly, it would be heading out of the eastern mouth of the strait, heading for Africa, and then Europe, to the Mediterranean, on its long nautical days. From everything he had heard, that was its last trip; it was too old and they had prohibited it from sailing. Surely some shipowner would buy it in order to break it up and take some advantage of it...his hardened heart sunk as if it had been stabbed...

If he didn't meet up again with the "Gastelu" in some other port in the world, or if they broke it up, which was more likely, what would happen to the money that Martin had hidden up high in the foremast, next to the top, underneath a lantern? Who would be the lucky owner of that small treasure for which he had committed the most vile act of his life, when he didn't pass the glass of water with the medicine to his companion in his moments of agony?

It was shortly after having crossed Abyss Pass in the channels, when Martin felt bad and called him to reveal the place where he had hidden his savings from the years of sailing on the freighter "Gastelu"; money with which he intended to retire in his home village, in the interior of Pontevedra, where his elderly mother still lived, for whom now those savings would be. In the Vigo Harbor Master's office they knew her now because of the stipends that they were accustomed to sending her; Foster could have left the savings there; but if he had some time available, it was preferable for him to personally hand them over in the village. It was his only—and last—wish!

From that moment a slow but inexorable shadow began to arise from within him.

"What could it be?" he asked himself. "Could I be that way, that evil?" He had diligently cared for Martin during his sickness; but after the revelation, something doubtful began to obstruct all of his actions with the sick man. He avoided him and even suggested, plainly, the desire that he should die right away and stop dallying...Why did he want him to die then? For the money on the mast? No! He couldn't be that wicked to keep that money, which the other man had saved for himself and for a poor old woman!

Well...he would see what would happen with that money. He would take some of it to the old woman...because there was quite a bit and there was enough for the two of them.

He trembled upon thinking, for the second time, that evil thought. Was he that wicked? Now then, if he were really that way, so evil, and only now did he realize it under those circumstances, before that proof of Destiny, why not keep all of the money and retire once and for all from those old ships of doubtful routes and even more dubious cargos, to where the scum of the ports would come to rest? Money was everything in life and there was his opportunity!

And that is what made him hesitate so much, during Martin's agony, at wanting to hand him the glass of water with the remedy that he so desperately asked for! That glass of water which could mean a little more life! Who knows? Perhaps an entire life...because who was to know God's plans?

However, he delayed in handing over the glass of water with the medicine, as if some invisible shackle had stopped him, mooring his feet...

Until Martin himself realized his friend's intentions...and it was then that the lightkeeper turned that strange glare upon his wicked companion. It was his last one, at the moment of death; but its brilliance flooded the cabin, impregnated the walls and later, did not let him sleep...

With that splendor of fright and fear, that look had passed on to eternity, had remained in the atmosphere like one more breath of pain in the face of human wickedness. A rarified air began to surround him everywhere since the day of Martin's death; now outside turning the rudder or scuffing the paint in a storm; it was always there filling him with a strange anxiety.

And in that cruel hour of abandonment, while he finally witnessed the departure of the "Gastelu" toward other seas with its small treasure hidden in the mast, the atmosphere had become even more rarefied, in spite of the snowfall, whose white petals, innumerable, came to touch him, as if someone from far away were trying to recognize the man...surprised that he could suddenly change himself into another man, so much and in such a way...

Foster wandered through the port like a ghost looking for another ghost...and little by little he began to realize—with horror—that the mariners' superstition was being fulfilled by him and that he himself was the one carrying that other ghost inside.

The loss, abandonment, lack of money increased his remorse and made an impression on his years. Depressed, he kept the secret and he asked no one nor did he communicate anything about the strange event with the coffin for which he so feverishly searched...the circumstances were so agitated that he was completely unaware of the place where his companions had left it. And then, the drunkenness...well, the drunkenness had been the reason for everything else...

Where was Martin's body? Had it mysteriously slid down the snowy hills, returning again to the sea so that it would never let him live in peace? Had his soul already incorporated itself into his, splitting it in two and tormenting it, while his body remained upon the land or wandered the depths of the sea?

He stealthily searched the cemetery, but no one gave him any clue. Don Erico, the bar owner, didn't know anything either. Everyone was unaware of the mysterious incident.

Life became distressing, intolerable for him. He wandered like a beggar from door to door, lighting fires in the mornings at cantinas and bars for a piece of bread or a glass of brandy. After a while, he couldn't even continue to carry out these miniscule domestic chores and he didn't have the alcohol to sustain himself.

One dawn they found him frozen inside a small cave that erosion had formed in the cliffs located on the outskirts of the port, on the east side. He had the characteristic grimace of those who freeze to death, and his open eyes, staring, looked intensely toward the east, toward the mouth of the Strait, on whose horizon the masts of those old vagabonds of the sea are lost, that pass by the port or pull in only because they have to repair some damage or drop off some sick person...

What they call "St. John's summer" unexpectedly occurred and the haggard austral sun increased its calories for a few days, melting the thick snow cover that past storms had formed. One fine day, on a street at the edge of town, on the road to the cemetery, a strange dead man's chest appeared, painted green, with its cadaver frozen inside. The discovery touched the authorities; the police carried out investigations, autopsies; but no one could find out anything for certain.

Only Mike, the half-crazed baker's son, tried to say something when he came across the coffin that they took from the morgue to carry to the cemetery. He held his hat in his hand to accompany it, and tried to say something. Then he held up five fingers, swayed like a sailor, insistently pointed to the coffin; but no one understood that with his mime he meant: "Five mariners and a green coffin".

Cururo

I

The riders galloped through the night on a plateau whipped by snow, pelted with hail, beaten by the wind. Five sheep workers rode on dark, tall and tough horses, followed by eight dogs that trotted in pairs alongside the hoofs of their masters' mounts.

That group of men and beasts moved like a strange shadow through the stormy night. Black ponchos fluttered above the shining rumps of the horses, keeping time with the gallop, like flags from a strange squadron, and the whole group seemed to be another mass of shadows that undulated with the wind's howls, among muffled notes, frozen gusts and shuddering pressures of the storm that made strong bodies tremble.

Suddenly, a shred becomes detached from the fleeing group. It is a rider. He turns his horse back toward the trail already taken and quickly takes off. His movement is so unusual and he pulls out of there in the opposite direction with such conviction, that it seems the whole group turns around with him, and the four riders who continue galloping in the distance only resemble the true shred of the entity that is this man, who has turned around as if challenged to attack the ferocious night, slashing the swells of snow, water and darkness...

This strange rider is Subiabre. He begins to retrace three hours of intense galloping over the highest meseta, the one that protects the three houses of "Section 13" of the "Baja" ranch on Tierra del Fuego from the wind. He is traveling without dogs. The reason for his unexpected return is a sudden distress, a remorse for having abandoned the most cherished dog in his life as a sheepman, now dead in a valiant effort to save a flock during that day's shift.

So tender are the memories that assail him, so impetuous is his regret, that a deep affection overtakes him; but a gust of wind and snow hurts his eyes, and something that might have become a tear disappeared inside of him, a bitter distress painfully fills his chest until it almost bursts. He grits his teeth, takes a tighter hold of the reins, sinks his spurs into those powerful flanks and cuts through the storm like a ghost.

Oh, "Cururo"! What a great dog he had lost! He was certainly worth more than all the thousands of sheep that in obedient flocks took the course that his clear and powerful barking pointed out in the Fueguian countryside.

"Cururo" had been everything in his life. That co-worker meant more than the world to him, now that he had no one.

Coarse, solitary men, tamed by the tough caresses of the frost, by sharp icicles; cured of all their humor by the strong pampa winds that whip unraveled threads into knots and those knots into weapons...these men love their dogs as life itself, and not only because tenderness has forgotten them, but because those dogs are unique in their intelligence, and their proximity to primitive life has taught them that at times a dog is better than a man, at least he doesn't change as much.

The jet-black horse, strong-backed and vigorous, galloped erectly. The man, with his black Castilian blanket serving as a poncho, began to dream about the past. Night and the storm fell upon them, soaking their bodies and troubling their souls.

At the end of the wind-swept meseta, in the "Three Orphans" ravine, "Partiera," his other old dog, would still be howling and scratching in the snow, trying to find "Cururo". And he, as a man, naturally more ungrateful, had abandoned them...but that gust of snow and wind had arrived just in time; now he returned to look for him, to help old "Partiera" in the fraternal task that he had already begun on his own account. He would no longer cross that meseta until he found "Cururo"; he would not leave him, forgotten, as he had done, to become fodder in the springtime for birds of prey...

Spring! The time when the Fueguian plains convert their snow cover into threads of silver that shimmer toward the lowland meadows; when cadavers appear intact and, afterwards, after being gnawed on by young eagles and hawks, show their bones, bleached by the sun! It was in that season when the good dog became part of the man's life.

And, like a line full of ups and downs, Subiabre began to remember as in a dream the life of his great dog from the day he found him as a puppy, clambering among the blades of grass, out in the open country, like one of those rodents indigenous to the island, the "cururos".

II

It was a Sunday afternoon, charged with light and idleness, full of life.

After lunch, existence on the ranch became monotonous. Some ranch hands wearing those wide, rope-soled peasant sandals that make your whole body relax, were playing "taba"; others were sleeping on their work clothes on the bunks, listening to tangos wailing from phonographs or accordions conjuring up memories of the brothels in Río Grande or Porvenir, of the nights in which they spent all the money saved in years of tough work on drunken sprees, women dressed in red and wild laughter. Finally, others got skinned playing "monte" and "truco".

Subiabre, foreign to the heavy wheel of destiny of those men, saddled up his special horse, "Tostado", took some riding gear that the gringo Mac had entrusted him with, and set out with an easy gallop toward the furthest post of the ranch.

In the region known as "Twenty-three", at the beginning of Río Chico out near the mountains, lived Mac, a lone outpost overseer, a gringo whom the war had left somewhat broken, sometimes half crazy, and who had the custom of tossing down a few bottles of gin or whiskey that made him forget his solitude from Saturday afternoon until Monday.

Aside from this weekly interruption, Mac was a good post overseer who lived without illusions, among his dogs, horses and sheep, the dull existence of those solitary beings who from post to post watch over the enormous flocks of "soft gold" on the vast plains of Tierra del Fuego and Patagonia. Alone, their entire life alone, with a glass of alcohol at the end of the week to endure such a tough existence.

Subiabre, at a quickened pace, was ascending the smooth hills which in lengthy extensions announced the mountain ranges in the eastern part of Tierra del Fuego.

The trail wound among the black shrubs that covered the horse up to the front part of the saddle, and there, at the end, squeezed through to the very crest of the hill that opened up a door from which one could contemplate a marvelous vision of nature. With a sudden depression of land from the pinnacle itself, a valley splits open that advances kilometers like a sea of green until it runs into the colossal blue foothills in the distance. There, in that valley next to Río Chico, which hushes its waters so as to not disturb the peace of that solitude, the red-roofed house of Post Twenty-three rises up.

In that gap at the top, Subiabre stopped his horse, and man and beast began to view the vast, green immensity like some kind of hope. They smelled the breeze that the valley exhaled, and then, with long strides, they began to descend the hills in the direction of the outpost. The sun caressed their bodies and the countryside with the tenderness of caresses that are from time to time given lavishly. Everything in the plain was now flowing in golden light. An enthusiasm of life ran through the yellow-green savannah of pasture grass. In the distance, suspended by rays of light as in an oriental fantasy, guanacos crossed placidly with cadenced rhythm in caravans of graceful silhouettes. More closely, they saw the chicks of caiquenes, their little brown bodies dotting the ground like seeds, running crazily around the females who were flapping their wings as if they were broken, to attract attention to themselves, pretending to be injured in the face of their chicks' enemies. Their feet, more astute, hid their golden-plumed chicks, and then they limped, dragging an extremity that seemed to be broken, with the object of throwing man or enemy off the track, really the same thing, to save their tender offspring.

Subiabre dismounted to lift up a fallen sheep and was ready to mount up again when he saw that from the hollow left in the ground from a horse's hoof a little bird, something like a canary, came out, spines bristling like a shrew, ran toward him and began to peck ferociously on his thick boots; the big man smiled with his serene face and with curiosity went to see what it was that such a brave bird was guarding; he bent down even with the ground, fanned away the meadow grass with his hands and discovered in the slight darkness at the bottom of the hole three poor little featherless chicks sitting on some fragile blades of grass.

"This is motherly love," he thought, and continued his way to the post in the middle of that valley that was like a song of life, like an immense embrace by the sky to the earth, by the earth to the sun.

Some swans sailed up the river, their whiteness moving along. At the edge of a blue lagoon rose-colored flamingos were dozing. And suddenly, something strange moving along the ground stopped his vision: a black body spotted with white was creeping along without direction. He moved closer to see it and met with a month-old sheep dog puppy, who whined while hiding himself in the grass, just like one of those small rodents who populate the Fueguian pampas: the cururos.

Surprised by the find, half a league from the post, he looked all around without finding a trace of the mother, in spite of the fact that he knew of no instance of a sheep dog giving birth far away from the houses.

How did that puppy, who had scarcely opened his eyes, get that far? Without being able to answer that, the man followed the trail toward the post. The dog had stopped whining and remained curled up in the white saddlebag under the warmth of a protective hand, of a tranquil ruggedness.

"Brave pointer," said the strapping youth, smiling at the puppy, "you should never head out too far without first taking a look at your provisions, especially if you're new...because our intentions always leave us in bad shape! You will be fine," he continued, "you have a sharp nose and prominent eyes, and that tells me you will not fail! I'll take you to 'Partiera's' kennel and when your legs get stronger you'll head out with him to learn your job. What would you think if I call you 'Cururo'? Do you like it?...It's a little ugly, eh? But when I spotted you, you looked so much like those little rats with no tails! Besides, to us folks it isn't the name or the looks that matter, but your conduct and actions!"

So from that afternoon on, the man bound his life to that of the dog...And the encounter was to impress him forever because of the tragic surprise that awaited them in the outpost's house.

A desolate peace enclosed the modest hut of Post Twenty-three. Next to its stack of black firewood was a small stable for the emergency horse and a corral made of rough planks for his troop of horses; everything was placed next to the trail, and without the environs being really tamped by human movement, there was flattened grass, some yellow paper, a tin can or a pan full of holes denouncing the proximity of a dwelling. Such are these posts, lost on the Magellanic plains, sprouting out of the pampa itself, without color or trace of human life. When they appear at the foot of a hill, it amazes one that people live inside, and upon seeing the overseer, who comes to the threshold to invite you with rural hospitality to rest a while and to eat a meal, one wonders how a normal man could put up with such extreme abandonment and solitude.

Subiabre was approaching the threshold. From inside the kennels, sheltered behind the house, the dogs began barking.

Man is known by his dogs and by his horses.

The gringo MacKay closed them up so that they would not get worn out running around when they spent a few days without work. Mac was neither bad nor good with his dogs. They responded, likewise, with an equal normality in their work. They always got fed at mealtime, and for a sheep dog one caress is worth as much as the daily

The sheepman tied his "Tostado" to the rail, removed a leather strap, loosened the cinch, and removed the saddlebag. He placed little "Cururo" in the hollow of his large hands and strode toward the outpost's house...

Suddenly he stopped short; next to the pile of firewood, stacked in the shape of an Indian hut, he saw four puppies just like "Cururo", thrown on the ground with their heads smashed, as if some monstrous being had killed them by thrashing them against the sharp sticks of dry oak.

What a strange thing! There was no doubt that poor "Cururo" had miraculously escaped the barbaric extermination of his siblings.

He felt giddy, then clear, he thought about Mac, then did not. It couldn't be, the gringo wasn't so brutal and he also knew the value of those fine puppies. Sometimes, it's true, when he got drunk, he was hit by attacks of madness which had no consequences beyond an attempt to get up from the bench where he was drinking and fall at the foot of the same bench, moving his hands and stammering a nasally "Fire!" and other shouting in a guttural English, all of which ended with his snoring...

The now heavy silence continued to hang above the post house. The small bodies were covered by the firewood's shade which the sun, now beginning to set in the west, was extending. Everything was quiet, not even a breeze passed by to rarify the dense mysterious atmosphere. Soured inside and out, Subiabre moved toward the door; he pushed it open with his big fingers and entered the room that served as the kitchen...nothing! Mac wasn't there. Everything seemed in order within those six drab faces of the dwelling, made of thick rough planks, displaying that unpolished cleanliness of bucket water and a scrub-brush with sand.

The youth inclined his left ear with an instinctive gesture, accustomed to adjusting himself in order to perceive faraway noises on the steppes, and he heard an agitated, weary breathing coming from the next room.

"Mac!" Subiabre called in a loud voice, which in the middle of the silence sounded like a loud blow that didn't even echo. He then pressed his ear to the door of the room and heard more strongly a low breathing, intermittent, like a scratching sound. He pushed, and something like a body flung on the floor stopped the door with a particular softness...

This disturbed the sheepman's habitual serenity, and bothered by so many mysterious airs that did not suit his toughness, he moved forward resolved to finally come across the object in question.

The encounter was rough! A body always has a spring, an instinctual muscle that raises it up, places it at once in a defensive position before the unexpected, and at times, the more surprising the attack, the stronger the defense; but in other fights..., in those in which the body is out of any danger and on the other hand the being's moral fibers tremble, in those calm collisions not a single muscle moves forward on its own account to the idea, to the thought that keeps inflating itself with unknown, dreadful lights, like a huge bubble of water and soap, whose element, the air, creates it and destroys it...

That is how Subiabre saw everything. Mac the gringo was in the deepest stupor of drunkenness, with a beastly alcoholic face, his square jaw hanging and projecting like a cadaver's, and in his mouth, and in the gross crease of his lips, a sickening and repugnant, diabolical, beastly grimace, something like a smile stopped by a paralytic attack, which showed extraordinarily yellow and rotten teeth like those of a dead seal. His legs were opened and one of them hung down from the edge of the cot in such an independent position that it seemed to be detached from the odious body. And farther, thrown against the door like an old sack, the body of the mother dog, strangled, trampled...

From between Subiabre's eyebrows sprang forth a penetrating look that advanced like a gaff with which rubbish and destitution are stirred up with the hope of finding something of value to save, and finding yourself before a heap of poverty such that you do not dare to rub against for fear of augmenting the pestilence.

The man continued looking, motionless in the middle of the room, next to a bench that had fallen in the fight. From their height his eyes finally passed over those bodies, over that whole scene, like the beacon of a lighthouse moving over the ocean's surface on stormy nights, sweeping away shadows, until they stopped a moment, without expression, on the detail of an obscene postcard, nailed up by itself in the middle of the gray wall, and the sheepman slowly left the house...

Outside, the Fueguian night began to spread out its long, dark robe.

With a stern gesture Subiabre grabbed the saddlebag, mounted the horse with "Cururo" still in his arms and headed out on the trail without looking back. Some tucuqueres and owls crossed the rider's path and the moon had halfway crossed the starry bulge of the sky when Subiabre unsaddled "Tostado" in the horse corral of the ranch.

"Cururo's" life on the ranch continued anonymously, unknown to everyone else, but very well known by his master.

For a while he stayed in "Partiera's" kennel; then, when he was bigger, he had his own.

At the end of an autumn in which Subiabre returned from a long drove to Río de Oro, he found that "Cururo" had become half trained and his eyes shined with joy upon realizing the incomparable spirit of this pup who had grown like a weed.

Commenting later in the kitchen, the other sheepmen divulged all of the mischief "Cururo" had gotten into while his master was away.

"No one less than 'Futre' himself found him one afternoon driving a flock that he had amassed in camp Eighteen!" one of them said.

"And all that in spite of the fact that you locked him up tight so that he wouldn't get spoiled before it was time, working orphaned and without a master!" another sheepman answered trying to justify himself, because Subiabre had entrusted the care of the dog to him, and he added—"But, it was impossible to put up with him, he's really lively. It's a good thing the foreman didn't think he was so bad; it seems as if the pup has really impressed him, because a few days ago, when we were all heading out for a roundup, he told us, laughing, 'Subiabre's pup is going to be good!' The other afternoon I was passing by the pasture of the select sheep, and I saw that he had them completely rounded up. He had them coming and going next to the fence, walking them all around the pasture; then he scattered them and rounded them up again. He really worked independently, and the dog who works independently from the time he is small won't mess up a flock even when he becomes hoarse in his old age."

"That's the way it is," Subiabre replied, satisfied, "but there's no reason to send them out to work so soon; they become hard to control and demanding."

"Cururo" really was lively. His master and the flock constituted his only pleasures; at the sight of the first one, he ran and jumped with joy; before the second he calmed his spirits, intelligently channeled his energy and rushed from point to point like a piece of elastic, grouping, pushing, finally holding the ductile mass of sheep. Like a triumphant general before the vision of his army he was exalted; the isolated sheep didn't interest him, he looked at them without expression.

Apart from that, he was a rare, solitary dog. When his master was away and they disregarded the kennel door, he would leave and wander the countryside; in his veins ran perhaps the blood of some stray dog to whom his tragic mother gave herself on an afternoon of loving on the pampa...

Those who rode the countryside found him from time to time hanging around the far limits of the ranch walking along the beaches, running and sniffing the winds that came from beyond the Páramo, from out in the Atlantic...

The day finally arrived to take him out on his first drive, the definitive consecration of a sheep dog. That is not some kind of game or party, but the ultimate, decisive proof of true physical worth of having to withstand for an entire day the pull of continuous, exhausting efforts.

That day "Cururo" revealed himself before the astonished eyes of the sheepmen. It had to do with rounding up a field of seven thousand sheep in ten thousand hectares of poor, broken land, sown with creeks, matted grass, enormous patches of thickets; there still remained hidden some low-lying areas, treacherous seams of icy slush.

Subiabre worked the point with his "Cururo" and his good "Partiera".

In a roundup, the leader's duty is the toughest and most responsible. One has to work and gallop strongly along the contour of the whole countryside, following the fences that never seem to end.

"Partiera" did his work and watched over that of his quick companion; he did not pardon him any carelessness and even nipped him more than once in the difficult task of uniting small groups of sheep and driving them through the valleys toward the plains of concentration.

In the late afternoon, when the lowland area was becoming populated with thousands and thousands of sheep that were arriving in small flocks from everywhere, driven by the shouts of the sheepmen and the barking of the dogs who were now running with their red tongues hanging out, the restrained congratulations of the sheepherders fell upon the great "Cururo" and his lucky master.

Subiabre, followed by his horse, went toward his "Cururo" and emotionally embraced him, with that affection that sheepmen have for their faithful companions of work and of suffering. The poor animal was panting. The man took him in his arms and put him on his saddle, just like that afternoon in which he found him clambering on his trail, just like one of those little animals from the Fueguian steppes.

The existence of "Cururo" continued to be famous, full of triumphs, until the tragic day of his disappearance. Death had had its eye on him since the day he was born. His elegant, vigorous figure, with black and shiny fur, spotted with slender patches of white, traversed the countryside of Tierra del Fuego with his happy note for only a very short time.

How that noble dog had shown himself on his last day! His life was not extinguished slowly like most vulgar existence, but instead, in his last moments he outdid himself, lost himself in an explosion of light.

It was a day in the heart of winter, white and blue with ice. The overseer who crossed the northernmost countryside of the ranch advised the second foreman that the entire flock had moved toward the northwest seeking shelter from the wind, which in those days had blown violently, dragging heavy snowstorms with it. That being the roughest and most oppressive part of the country, the sheep in search of protection had been covered by those characteristic piles of snow, great caves of soft, treacherous covering, in which they would perish if they were not taken out in time.

Sometime before noon on the tragic day, five sheepmen with ten dogs arrived from the ranch to work at that task, in the rugged land that began at the foot of the end of the meseta that Subiabre was now crossing.

Climbing up and sliding down the hills, the sheepmen advanced. Under the most confident of the horses' steps there was at times a depression hidden by the snow that made the animal fall suddenly with his rider on his back; the man dragged himself over the unsteady surface with his poncho in one hand and with the other pulling the horse, which came out by virtue of slaps and tugs.

After a tiring struggle, they reached a hill near the flock, and from there any advancement with the horses was impossible.

From a distance could be seen extended heaps of snow in the form of giant white whales, run aground on a strange beach, covered with whitish dunes curved by the swirling of the strong winds.

That day, the heroes were the dogs; the men were virtually worthless, impeded by the snow.

"Cururo" saw a flock penned in at the bottom of a low area and took off rolling and slipping down the hillside.

The sheep, already foreseeing their destiny, had grouped themselves in that giant hole, squeezing together until they could squeeze no more, giving each other warmth and eating each other's wool. In the middle of the packed group, many had fallen, others were dead, trampled by their companions.

The dog glanced around intelligently and found no possible opening. He moved the flock a little, changed its position, and at once took off at full speed to cross the length of the ravine.

After covering a long distance he returned and made the flock advance toward where the hills narrow into a difficult pass. He even pushed the sheep by biting the backs of their legs and made them file out through lost paths toward the higher, freer part of the countryside.

Two or three sheep remained at the bottom of the ravine, lost from view by their companions, and stupidly refused to budge, making the dog work harder than he did with the whole flock. Disgusted, he left them, lost among the hills, and went to guide the saved flock.

That was a feat. The dog had done the job by himself. "Partiera", meanwhile, was steadfastly working hard, while the master was dragging himself almost uselessly among the scrub trees.

Whistles extended stridently over the calm of the snowy countryside. Subiabre called his dogs.

Farther away the "Oh, oh!" of the sheepmen was heard as was the clear barking of the dogs driving the sheep through the low-lying areas.

Reunited, Subiabre, "Partiera" and "Cururo" descended to the area where the fence and a small hill had packed in a huge quantity of windblown snow. From far away it seemed like a great white ridge; a ridge that, covering the whole fence, had risen up with a gentle contour to the level of the hill, covering it, too, and making the hollow level.

To the eyes of anyone who was not a sheepman, that rise could hold no interest; but Subiabre recognized a large number of small holes that appeared through the snow cover and "Partiera" and "Cururo" began to sniff next to a halfway squashed shrub that resisted the weight of the snow, forming with its twisted branches a hole the size of the mouth of a beaver cave.

And that's just what is was: a gigantic cave, a cavern whose interior held more than two hundred sheep.

The animals sustain themselves several days in caverns that the snow has slowly formed over their backs, licking and eating each other's wool. They breathe through small holes formed through the snow by their heated breathing, but then they begin to fall and to rot away, or they succumb, crushed by the layer of snow that finally cannot resist the thinning produced by the heat of the bodies inside.

Subiabre inspected those little holes again to verify the strength of the cavern when he heard a bark like an echo reverberating through faraway ravines or coming forth from the depths of the earth. And he understood! The brave "Cururo" had jumped into the interior of the cave, through the opening where he had been sniffing before, in search of the sheep. "Partiera", perhaps because he was old or because he was prudent, fortunately had not followed his impulsive companion.

Subiabre, foreseeing the imminent misfortune, ran toward the opening and sticking his head in as far as he could, with two fingers in his mouth he let loose with the characteristic calling whistle of the sheepmen, one long and two very short ones that ended like a cadence. Next, slashing with his knife, he began to widen the hole. The hard crust destroyed, his strong hands desperately began to break up the snow.

He called, whistling, and to the sharp whistle a kind of shriek answered, like the chilling laughter of solitary foxes who follow riders on gloomy nights, and a muted sound, like a flattening of clouds, gripped the man's heart and made "Partiera" raise his ears...the snow cave had collapsed.

Subiabre and the other dog heard at last a murmur of brief, heavy sounds, just like the "Hu-hu!" of pigeons in heat or like the guttural murmuring of certain mutes, low and trembling; it was the flock's agony, the death rattle of the sheep, that tender animal that does not know how to cry out in pain even in death.

And after that slight sound, that soft prelude of death that was ceasing within the smooth core of the cavern, followed a howl that went straight to the man's marrow; Subiabre felt that his bones or his flesh became out of sync. "Partiera" howled and inclined his head along the ground, digging his paws in the snow with such force that it was as if a formidable lashing were trying to blow it away.

It all happened in an instant. Dog and man looked at each other: "Cururo", the companion, had departed, driving his last flock to eternity...

His last yelp perhaps was not for him, but for his flock that was also lost under the snow cave.

III

The wind on the meseta continued to grow stronger, blowing in gigantic gusts. Howling over the smooth plain without an edge or an obstacle to tear up augmented its fury and unleashed it in circular blasts of air and snow.

The other four sheepmen had gone on to find shelter in some faraway outpost or they were probably about to arrive to the ranch. Subiabre stopped remembering! He stopped his horse to tighten the harness; he dismounted, fixed the saddle padding, adjusted the leather pads under the saddle that had slid with all the heavy galloping, gave his horse a caressing slap on the neck and mounted up to continue on again like a shadow through the night and the storm.

He finally arrived at the edge of the meseta and began to descend, carefully, with the attention required by the treacherous shadows, with the reins firm, alert to the sitting motion of the horse, who could tumble at any moment.

He left the horse hobbled and again crossing the snow-covered hills, he cut in the direction of the collapsed cavern.

He found "Partiera" still in the same place, feverishly scratching the snow and vigorously hurling it behind him. He took off his heavy poncho and began to help the dog, who had already made a deep hole in the place where "Cururo" seemed to emit his last yelp.

From the time the man arrived the work was to continue for an hour, when "Partiera", stopped scratching, having sensed the proximity of his companion's body. He then increased the momentum of the search, digging powerfully at the snow until he grazed with his nose the body of the fallen dog. He was immobile, ears motionless, his eyes strangely fixed and wide-open over that body. He opened his mouth as if to bite the air and from his big mouth a strange-sounding bark escaped. It was the voice of the dog, bewildered before the mysteries of death...

The man was no less astonished. He, too, called out. "Cururo!" he said, and his voice, like the dog's, was the knock without answer at the closed doors of death.

Subiabre entered the excavation. He took out "Cururo's" body, put it on his shoulder and with the beloved bundle on his back he headed toward his horse. "Partiera", his head bent downward, followed his footsteps. The wind seemed to stop its snorts, the snow became thin and fell lightly, accompanying the strange procession. The night was ending and with it, the storm. From the east the morning light began to drive away the swirling snow. The unusual entourage was silhouetted against the snowy steppe. With his rough hand, the man caressed the head of the body that fell lifeless over his heart. "Partiera" walked behind.

"Oh, beloved 'Cururo', how much your life resembled mine!" the sheepman murmured. "Why did you end it so soon? Is mine also to end soon?"...

And Subiabre began to relive his life. From that day they kicked his father off the ranch for being too old, for being useless. He had already broken every bone in thirty years of killing work in the service of the foreign company.

The poor old man, having collected his last month's wages, grabbed his wife and train of kids, made up a bundle of their small amount of old clothes, let out a bitter sigh toward the countryside where he had suffered so much, and headed off on the trail...a trail that destiny was beginning to darken...

But he, the little Subiabre, born and raised on those plains, child of those lands, lay to one side of the trail, huddled up next to some thicket. No! He would not go to the city, which was like the death of everything! He loved those extended plains and mysterious mountain ranges too much, with all his heart!

And he saved himself from that kind of death. Looking after the cooking pot for the overseers, bringing the horses into the corral until, finally having become a man, he became a new sheepman on the ranch, to continue, and repeat, his father's history...

He had been exactly the same as his deceased "Cururo" had been! Some day he, too, would end his life on a treacherous path of cruel destiny. "Dog and man are just about the same in these lands!" he thought.

Were not his companions perhaps other innumerable, anonymous "Cururos" who drove flocks of "soft gold" in the vast Magellanic regions?

"Yes, they were no more than that!"

And Subiabre, tightly embracing his dog's body as if he were hugging his life, sat down on a pile of snow, hard and cold like the hearts of the owners of that land.

Water and Moon Torture

A beam of moonlight again revealed the sinister coarseness of the cell, and the shackled woman in the corner could not contain the trembling produced by the intermittent passing of light through the little window of that improvised prison.

December nights in the Strait of Magellan are very short. After a livid, enchanting twilight that lasts until almost midnight, the darkness begins to stretch out indecisively, but it has still not finished painting shadows over the earth when already the tenuous splendor of dawn appears in the east, which will quickly emerge full and radiant with its bejeweled light.

The prisoner had suffered for some time now that subtle torture of moonbeams, which appeared and disappeared in a sky speckled with profound brightness and tufts of clouds, ashen and dark, like the bearded faces of the seven artillerymen with which the ferocious Cambiaso had begun the revolt in the incipient penal colony.

That spectacle of tenuous lights and shadows in the helplessness of the cell was a subtle torture and sometimes a painful fright for the young woman.

People exist who are so especially sensitive that they suffer even a change of color; they are agreeable when they fill their eyes with green or blue and feel anguish when grey flattens them, yellow irritates them or red wounds them. There are those who are harmed by the arrival of day or night, before light or shadow.

Cambiaso's prisoner was neither one nor the other, she was something more: a ruptured sensitivity. She passed from the most absolute impassiveness with which she contemplated the execution of an Indian or white man in "El Peral", to the most intense fear caused by the noise of the very shackles that hindered her beautiful, white legs. She remained at times in a superhuman or subhuman state, her mind floated among sleepiness, bewilderment and a proximity to madness. Only when the tyrant came into the cell, with his face of a squeamish mouse, at first sight beautiful, but then unpleasant because of his roguish, evasive eyes and the exaggerated length of his head, accentuated by the Greek-style military cap, only then did she gather together all her disperse qualities, her damaged strengths and rise up erect, with a magnificent will, to refuse the amorous demands of the god and master of the destroyed Magellanic colony.

His exaggerated donjuanesque self-love had saved the prisoner from certain death. Irresistible lover, abductor of women all through the country: one in Santiago, another in Petorca, another in Ancud, a fourth in Valdivia and a fifth one who had come following him hidden in the sloops until Punta Arenas, this guy considered it unacceptable, based on the merits of this past, to take by force that little French girl who had fallen into his hands.

He had sworn it to himself in his bitter solitude as an angry man: he, the banished lieutenant Cambiaso, converted now, by his own disposition, into a general, king of cards and drink, who had overthrown and burned alive the governor, shot, hanged, and knifed all enemies or anyone he believed to be an enemy, would not call himself such if he did not conquer, by pure love, the little French woman; "my firefly", as he had lovingly nicknamed her with certain irony upon feeling himself intimidated under the irascible glow her beautiful eyes emitted when he visited her at nightfall like a vassal.

She was always a mystery in the colony. It was said that she was of French origin. She could have come hidden—they said—in the frigate "Phaeton", a warship of that nationality that came to take possession of the Strait of Magellan and that dropped anchor on September 22, 1843 to fulfill its mission, when the Chilean flag had already fluttered for a day on the steep banks of Puerto Hambre, hoisted up by the expeditioners of the schooner "Ancud", sent to these lands by the far-sighted President Don Manuel Bulnes.

Other commentaries had her appear as shipwrecked, possibly from that brig also with a French flag, run aground on the southern coast of Campana Island of the Duke Wellington Archipelago, some of whose saved crew members headed into western Patagonia, from where, many years later, only one returned, half-crazy, skinny, old-looking and ragged, bringing tales of marvelous cities. The French woman lived under a kind of tutelage of that old crazed man whom she called "my uncle", sometimes with a certain slyness.

She soon caused trouble among the seven hundred inhabitants of the colony; she became something like the terror of the fat wives of the big-moustached artillerymen and the cause of many quarrels among the unmarried.

The young men of the colony who had seen her on snowy days come up the main street, which departed from the little pier, and climb the sharp gradient that served as a sidewalk, supported and cut straight by a wall of oak posts, spoke dazzled by the whiteness and the contours of her legs.

"She strides like a 'chara', she sinks her foot shod with high-top boots in the thick layer of snow, almost a meter deep, and so that she doesn't get wet, she lifts her skirt up to her knees and oh delight!, no one knows whether the snow or her skin is whiter or if her leg or life is more beautiful!" they exclaimed when, after becoming bored with playing cards, the travels of the little French woman were obligatory conversation, which put an unaccustomed note into that waste land of civilization.

Don Benjamin himself, the governor, more than once stuck his honorable head out the window of the governor's office, the imposing building with three balconies that rose up in the center of town dominating the drab settlement, in order to contemplate "madame", as they also called her. She would cross the open courtyard that served as a small square, her slender figure emerging, fitted well with an elegant jacket with a high neck, with the wide skirt that she gracefully raised from time to time upon going around the puddles, thus showing the fine laced boot modeled on her beautiful leg.

She was not very miserly with her gifts; but among those removed from her favors was the handsome conqueror and brilliant "General" Cambiaso. This was the motive for which the tyrant, since the night he had her detained, since he was besides decidedly resisted in his love, joined to his useless entreaties the cruelty of making her a forced spectator of his horrors.

The young woman was taken near the "Peral", the "pear tree", a thick oak trunk where the executions were carried out, and whose name had been given, in a figurative sense, because of the macabre fruits that hung from it each time a new victim was going to swing from the log.

Since the night of November 26, in which the Magellanic Nero gave himself the satisfaction of destroying the colony by fire and she was saved from dying burned in the jail, by the intervention of Nicanor García, named at that time "general of the brigade" by Cambiaso, from that night and during two weeks she had witnessed the most horrendous scenes: scorched bodies twisting in the pyre raised up in front of the "Peral", shot at close range, hands and fingers cut off. In the human carnage there were whites and Indians, men and women.

The English sailors of the "Elisa Cornish" and the North Americans from the "Florida" were shot after they seized the ships and a great booty where nine bars of gold figured in.

Almost everything had been razed by the strange, devastating madness of the rebel leader. Everything that had opposed him disappeared, only one opposing being remained, the one who was both the weakest and the strongest: the beautiful, young French woman or she who was supposedly of that origin, since nothing certain about that was known.

Cambiaso made a law for his subjects. The strangest thing about this law was its procedure and its sanctions.

In this strange statute, for each offense, or better said, for each of the tyrant's wishes, there was an article; but as with all statutes, this one also had a fundamental gap in order to satisfy the capricious will of he who had created it: there was no article in which the case of the French woman was considered; in his arbitrary law the rebel leader had not contemplated the crime of refusing his desires of love.

For that reason the woman had a more violent shudder when she heard the steps of several men who approached her cell. Up until then he had come alone bringing her food and his repugnant insinuations of love. She had become accustomed to resisting him, and after two weeks in prison she was almost indifferent to the sound of his steps. She trembled upon thinking that the tyrant had become bored with the procedure and now he had ordered them to get her for who knows what kind of outrage or torture. In those instances death did not matter but the manner of dying certainly did. A bullet would have been a pleasure.

The chains that took the place of bolts resounded and four artillerymen with big moustaches came into the cell. Two of them knelt next to the woman and with steel cutters carefully broke the shackles that tightly held her small, round ankles. The other two men took her by the arms and led her out of the cell. It was past midnight.

The hour had arrived.

The journey was made in silence. The woman did not seem to be aware of everything that surrounded her.

The sky was a deep, dark blue, sprinkled with stars and speckled with white clouds that moved quickly, pursuing each other, forming and breaking up strange caravans through which the moon crossed navigating, sometimes breaking them up with its diamond prow.

A white light floated above the rubble of the destroyed colony, giving the impression of a strange enchantment underneath the clear night, a spell that every so often interrupted the gloomy shadow of some large wooden ramshackle house that remained standing.

The sea of the Strait was crossed by a brilliant route, a trail of little mirrors moved tremulously by the frozen western wind, which came from combing the spine of the Brunswick Peninsula to ripple the sea.

Near the "Peral", at the base of which shined a crust of human blood extended over the ground like the bright skin of a sea lion, was an artillery cannon. Next to it three men were conversing, from which stood out the fine, tall silhouette of the ferocious Cambiaso.

"Strip her!" the tyrant said when the artillerymen and the woman were at the base of the cannon.

"No! No! For God's sake!" she shouted, struggling violently.

The two men squeezed her against their stout bodies, where she became imprisoned, breathing with difficulty.

Then the artillerymen approached and began to loosen her fine clothing, fulfilling the order of he who now looked beside himself, like someone possessed. That was the instant in which everyone feared him, since he no longer seemed to be a man, but rather the devil himself. He extended his head like a feline, with brilliant eyes, eager for cruelty.

Suddenly, from the dark group of men broke forth a vision. A vision that all of them contemplated wide-eyed. With marvelous, swollen muscles and breasts, the totally nude woman appeared, like a siren who had leaped from the sea's foam.

Sixteen eyes turned toward the vision; sixteen glassy, animalistic, feverish and crazed eyes became fixed upon that beautiful skin and then they rolled toward the body's curves, forming one palpitating, graphic shape, with all the supreme breath of the spirit made reality and the anguish of the poor and miserable human condition.

The eight jackals became eager and indecisive. The moon shined way up above and its powerful beams embellished the female's contours with cold, white light.

The woman straightened up, her head defiant, as if she were not embarrassed by her nudity. It was not a fragile and delicate loveliness but a powerful beauty that rose from the soles of her feet and enveloped her whole body.

The men became still, as if petrified. The graceful movement of her head troubled them a little and then they seemed to revive. Their moustaches moved like wounded antennae. It was a supreme moment. Cambiaso understood the danger, and suddenly, desperately, he shouted, "To the cannon with her!"

The artillerymen, surprisingly trapped in their subconscious, moved like beaten beasts, held the woman in the air, stretched her out on her back on the wide cannon with her head toward the carriage and tied her crossed feet on the projection of the cannon's mouth and her arms around the cold, bronze mass. The victim seemed to be somnambulistic; she closed her eyes and leaned her head on her beautiful shoulder, waiting for her destiny.

Then, from a nearby barrel, one of the artillerymen took a bucket of water and approached the cannon.

"Now!..." one shouted, and the bucketful of water fell like a broad whiplash on the white body, which cringed, shivering.

Cambiaso, surrounded by his entourage, looked undauntedly at the spectacle. The one who had given the order approached the woman's ear and said, "My general says that as soon as you say 'yes' he will end the punishment and you will be treated like a queen; in the meantime, this will continue until no water is left in the whole colony!"

The victim did not answer; the buckets of water continued with brief intervals. Her body, stretching and cringing, shined like a mother-of-pearl Christ, a pagan, strange Christ, a woman-Christ, beautiful and helpless.

Now the cruel tyrant could call the crucified woman "my firefly". An enormous firefly, made of water and the moon, phosphorescent and magnificent, palpitating, with pearls of light that ran to hide themselves among the shadows of harmonious curves.

This was the missing article in the curious code: the woman who refused the loving desires of Cambiaso was to suffer the water and moon torture. The water will punish her body, the moon with its whipping will penetrate her soul!

The woman resisted the first bucketfuls of water. Even though they were cold, she would have preferred them to be continuous, like a shower or a river, since she really suffered more when the moon skated over her body, with its infinite ski of light showing her to the eyes of her sensual executioners, than when the tongue of water covered her.

Then she felt as if the bucket of water would skin her all at once. After that it seemed to her that she was coming completely apart, in a slow inanition.

"Enough!" Cambiaso suddenly shouted, and he quickly moved toward the cannon.

The beautiful body had become pale and stiff with cold. After observing her for a moment, the rebel leader exclaimed: "She's dead!"

By the tyrant's orders an artilleryman brought a sailcloth and covered the victim's body without untying her from the cannon.

"I never would have believed it!" Cambiaso exclaimed, distressed, and he continued; "I never intended to kill her. When I was a boy I stuck a puppy into a tub of water for hours on end until it died, trembling, in my hands. I thought she was going to resist more. Well, tomorrow we will give her a burial more worthy than the others."

But when the artillerymen went the next day on their master's orders to get the body they almost fell over backwards when they saw that it was not on the cannon, upon which only the untied ropes hung...

"You mean the poor woman suffered besides a horrible outrage after being killed?" I asked the almost one hundred year old tiny lady who had just related to me a shortened and barely-coherent version of this strange story of the old colony of Punta Arenas. "Or perhaps," I continued inquiring, "she fainted on the cannon and was only unconscious when they thought she was dead, later fleeing by her own means from her terrible executioners?"

"These poor eyes that no longer see have seen so many things that nothing surprises me!" she responded with her muted and unsteady voice. "I know of people thrown in the sea who at the bottom have broken the cables that tied them to dead weights and they have come out walking with their own feet on the beach! They say that not long ago, in the Big Strike and in the one at Santa Cruz, men were shot by the score, and that afterwards, at night, some came out scratching from underneath the earth and got to the mountain, running to take shelter. Sometimes the hot coal melts the snow and doesn't go out!" the old lady finished as she lifted, with a still-agile gesture, a strand of silver hair that had fallen over her eyes. Over her small, blue eyes like two bright spots of sky, in the depths of which still seemed to burn among the cinders of blindness, tenuous and faraway, some live coal of the past youth of this old woman who could well have been the heroine of the story about the colony.

Tierra Del Fuego

Defeat rode just behind those three riders who crossed the Páramo with a fast trot.

The last exchange of shots against Julio Popper's forces had taken place on the shores of the Beta River, and the rich gold prospector's enemies, some seventy adventurers from every nationality, had disbanded, completely defeated because of the heavy casualties suffered.

Some fled toward the Carmen Sylva chain of mountains, a range that Popper himself had thus christened in honor of his Rumanian queen. Others were swallowed up by the vast grasslands of China Creek, and a few ascended the mountains by MacLelan River, a refuge for horse thieves and for the last of the Ona Indians.

Only Novak, Schaeffer and Spiro fled along the southern coast of Tierra del Fuego, hoping to hide themselves behind the dark hillock of the San Martin cape. They still had a few bullets for their rifles, and Novak, a cartridge belt full of .9 calibre bullets for his long-barrel Colt, the only one the three of them had.

This scant ammunition was the only thing that still gave them courage in their desperate situation, in spite of the fact that with them they would not have been able to sustain a prolonged exchange of fire. Everything else was total defeat, weakness, annihilation, as much within their hearts as fugitives as outside of them, in the desolation of the Fueguian steppes.

"You have blood on your pantleg," Novak said, with a strange tenderness in his voice, pointing to Schaeffer's right leg.

"Yes, I know," Schaeffer answered coldly, his bluish eyes staring at the overcast sky like a bird who stretches out its neck just before taking off in flight.

"Bullet?" Spiro asked.

"No, guanaco turds!" Schaeffer uttered with rage.

"Let's see," Novak said, checking his horse's trot.

"What?"

"The wound," the German ex-sergeant replied, still with a certain something from the superior who is preoccupied about the state of his troops.

"It's nothing...let's go on..." Schaeffer uttered with a slight cordial indication, spurring on his horse.

Cosme Spiro cast a wary glance behind him and spurred his horse even more, putting himself out in front of the trio.

Old Schaeffer, like a wounded bird, again lifted his head toward the sky. What tormented him more than the sharp pain of the wound was the flow of his blood; because every time he steadied his foot in the stirrup to support his body in the rhythm of the trot, he felt a liquid wave gush from the wound, a wave that oozed down his leg toward his foot with a chilling warmth, all the while soaking the inside of his boot.

With his right hand placed on his old German sawed-off carbine, placed across the front of his saddle, he tried to lessen the pressure his foot placed on the stirrup in order to maintain the rhythm of the long strides; but it was useless, the tepid wave surged with an exhausting regularity, insidiously sliding along his skin until it formed a puddle inside his boot. It was then that Schaeffer stretched out his head, like a bird, not to send up a prayer but to let fly a flock of curses to the heavens and to his God, for having dragged him into such a wretched situation.

"Who ordered me to get involved against Popper," the old man asked himself, "when the Rumanian treated me like a compatriot and me being as I am a Hungarian lost on these shores?"

From time to time, like the warm, insidious waves of his flowing blood, fleeting memories sprang forth in his mind about his fate with the gold prospector who got rich in the Páramo. In any circumstance pain and death patrols bring life in that way, in fragments.

He remembered his first encounter with that drunken officer in the Punta Arenas bar whom he almost confused with, because of the uniform, a lieutenant in the Austrian-Hungarian army...it was none less than Novak himself, who was at this very moment trotting by his side as a fugitive with the same defeat behind him! Popper had made him the commander of his personal escort, uniformed in the Austro-Hungarian military style, the same as the rest of his police force in the Páramo, whose weapons and uniforms commanded respect among his workers and the Indians who were beginning to become aware of the significance of armed forces.

On that occasion the commander of Popper's escort had paid with some strange coin that the bar owner didn't want to accept without first having weighed it on a scale for gold. There were exactly five grams of this metal, minted on the back with a big "5" crossed through with the word "grams", and with a trimming that said "Southern Gold Panners" and on the other side, "Julio Popper —Tierra del Fuego—1889".

That strange coin was a surprise for him, since he found himself without a cent in the port of Punta Arenas, where he had arrived after having uselessly dredged along the coast of the Strait of Magellan, arriving at the gold-bearing placers when others had already left the holes alone. He spoke with Novak on that occasion and the reputation of the rich Rumanian who had people call him "the King of the Páramo" attracted him. Encouraged by the escort leader, he joined his army; but as with everyone who pursues gold's brilliance, he did so with the secret plan of making himself as rich as the master.

In the lugger "María López" they cut through the waters of the Strait bordering Tierra del Fuego on the Atlantic, and arrived to the Páramo, a gigantic breakwater that extends a dozen kilometers into the sea, protecting with its stony arm an extensive bay, San Sebastián, where the ocean rises and falls more than ten meters, laying bare kilometers and kilometers of clay beaches bordered by dunes and coastal thickets where the Fueguian plains, covered by extensive pasture, have their beginnings.

The whole region is known as The Páramo, and there, Julio Popper, who was the first white man to cross over the island from the Strait of Magellan to the Atlantic Ocean, had discovered virgin gold deposits of dust, scales and nuggets. But the common wooden trough, the pan and the jig were not good enough for the lucky gold prospector. Observing the tremendous difference of level of ten or more meters that the tides produced, he managed to take advantage of this cosmic energy: he had tunnels dug, seven meters below the level of high tide and he invented a wooden mechanism that he placed inside them; when the sea rose, he enclosed the water inside these tunnels with solid flood gates and when it receded, he released it from its prison, and regulated its force in such a way that it revealed all the gold-bearing material accumulated by his dozens of workers.

The performance of these devices was so extraordinary that Popper christened them with the name "Gold Reapers". And it was for a good reason; the sowing produced almost a half a ton of gold per year, and with that cosmic bull subjugated to the yoke of human ingenuity, Julio Popper was able to boast of having been the first man to have "plowed and harvested in the sea".

But the audacious Rumanian's reapers produced only for their inventor, and the greedy adventurers who accompanied him in his travels with the hope of becoming as rich as he, began to look with envy and rancor at the master who took possession of all the placers without leaving a piece of land where any of them could prosper on their own.

One day several of them deserted because news arrived that in the Cullen River and in the Alpha, Beta and Gamma streams they had found other auriferous alluvions almost as rich as those in the Páramo. There the individual pans and jigs could make more than one gold prospector prosper independently, instead of being subjugated to Popper's yoke, like the sea that washed his gold.

"The King of the Páramo", however, did not allow the deserters to give him competition right in his face and he began to harass them with his armed forces so that they would abandon those parts and leave them for his own excessive ambitions. Other events came to aggravate human conflicts in that remote shore of the planet: taking advantage of the absence of the master, who had gone to Punta Arenas, a group boarded the lugger "María López", anchored in San Sebastián Bay, and fled, taking twenty-four kilograms of gold with them.

But the sea not only helped Popper harvest gold but cared for him like a jealous guardian, more faithful than men: upon sacking the "King of the Páramo's" storage vaults, they carried off all the liquor they found, which resulted in misfortune for them. On the open sea a storm came up and since they were all drunk, celebrating their flight, they didn't manage to maneuver the sails and the lugger capsized, carrying all of its crew into the ocean's womb, sunk forever along with the twenty-four kilos of gold as an eternal example for the "King of the Páramo's" subjects.

Upon returning to his domain, Julio Popper did not turn out to be conformable with this exemplary action of his faithful ally the sea, and he took it out on those who washed gold in the three streams, saying that they were to blame for being a den of bandits and thieves that he would have to punish with a harshness even more exemplary. And so he did, and he hanged three or four individuals from the posts which marked the boundaries of his property, placing a sign on them which read "Lasciate ogni speranze vol ch'entrate", the phrase from Dante that warned humans that they were to give up all hope upon passing over the threshold to Hell. Neither the Ona Indians nor the adventurers of the Beta stream knew Latin; but for them even more eloquent than Dante's language were the clean skulls of the skeletons upon which eagles sat, gorged from their feast.

This was, in short, what awaited Novak, the German, Spiro, the Italian, and Schaeffer, the Hungarian, for having crossed over to the gang of rebels instead of defending the property of the one who had confided in them. Especially the faithful Novak, commander of his personal guard, who had personally led the last resistance of the seventy combatants of the Beta stream. This was also the cause of Spiro's constant furtive glances behind their backs, although by now they were quite well-protected by their companions who followed their movement.

Schaeffer curled up his toes as much as he could inside his boots to calculate the blood that had trickled inside, and as if at the same time trying to avoid that calculation, he stretched his numb body, lifting his gaze one more time from his foot to the sky, now a cruel gray that was crushing the Earth.

The Carmen Sylva mountains diminish when one approaches the east coast of Tierra del Fuego; its spurs break down into smooth hills covered with underbrush, shrubs and rosemary, foliage appropriate for hiding. Then the range rises up again in the knoll of cape San Martin, whose cliff, falling straight down to the open sea, closes the San Sebastián Bay, preventing passage along the beach, from where one sees the great breakwater of the Páramo like a dark, static wave, petrified in the open sea.

Upon taking refuge along this oasis of protection, the cavalcade diminished its fast trot a little.

"Let's stop to see that leg," Novak said, and addressing Spiro he ordered with an authoritative voice: "You, walk over to that hill, and stay there to let us know if you see something."

In a small clearing of the pampa surrounded by thickets of black shrubs, Schaeffer dismounted and established for the first time the importance of his wound. The bullet had passed through the muscle in front, from one end to the other; but, fortunately it had not hit the bone. Because it had passed through the muscle at an angle, the wound served as a drainage duct, which took in the blood from the damaged tissue on the inside and shed it through the lower hole. Overall, upon steadying the foot in the stirrup to support the body in the up and down motion of trotting, the muscles compressed the wound and drained the accumulated blood in those warm insidious waves that made Schaeffer stretch his neck and head like a cormorant.

With his pants down, the old man looked at the entrance and exit of the bullet; he was helpless and pale, with a quivering in his upper lip which became more and more visible. But he contained the trembling by biting his moustache, like oxen do when they grasp a bunch of grass between their lips. His face was naturally red and swollen, with a somewhat upturned and alcoholic nose, on whose tip almost always hung a drop of suspicious liquid. The same in his eyes, where there was always a moist luster, as if an indifferent tear had gotten stuck in them.

When the old man leaned back onto the pampa, Novak saw that pale face, bluish eyes, with a hieratic radiance as if a hidden youth wanted to appear to him. He untied the canteen from his saddle and gave him some water. Schaeffer, opening his lips half-way, drank a little; but all the while retaining a piece of the bitten moustache as if it wanted to take root in him. Novak took off the blue and red kerchief from around his neck and, tearing it, closed up the holes the bullet had made and with the rest bound the wound. Schaeffer's paleness increased and he closed his eyes. Novak saw his nose twitch, the upper lip quivered again and the juvenile brilliance was accentuated in the withered face of the old man. But in a while Schaeffer half opened his eyes and looking around a little frightened he silently uttered:

"I thought I was done for..."

"You're better," Novak said with an accent of cold consolation, "but we better get out of here to a safer place...you've lost a lot of blood and I don't know if you can move."

"Just leave me here...if I recover, I'll follow you; if not, I'm already too old to continue with the fast trot like that."

"The horses are almost spent. I don't think we can continue without giving them some rest. We should spend the night around here and leave tomorrow before dawn."

Novak whistled harshly, and Spiro began to come down from the hill where he was watching.

"Schaeffer is bad, I don't think he can continue on horseback," he told him.

"So?" Spiro uttered, with a kind of cruel and unpleasant smirk. He was an average individual, chubby, with a round, fat-cheeked, spongy face with black and shifty little eyes that fluttered like two flies moving over recently kneaded bread.

"We'll look for a place to be able to spend the night more safely, and we'll see tomorrow where to head with fresh horses," Novak added.

"Don't screw yourselves up because of me," Schaeffer uttered, lifting himself halfway up on his elbows. Then he looked at his leg and saw that the bleeding had stopped a little. He tilted his head, and from the ground his eyes scrutinized Novak's face, with its square, salient, long and angular jaw, like his whole gigantic body, topped with some blond locks of hair underneath his greasy leather cap. There was a physical soundness in that scaffold of bones and muscles, and the face, somewhat childlike, had a certain air of pride and control.

In turn, Spiro looked at Schaeffer's wound, blinking as if something bothered his vision. Suddenly the three men looked at each other; that is to say, Spiro and Novak looked at Schaeffer, and the latter, from the ground, took them in with one glance. Then the eyes of all three looked away, as if they had slipped; but they all focused again on the bloody wound. There they were bent over and staring at the flesh through which the bullet's lead had passed, perhaps thinking that instead of a leg, it could have been one of three fugitive hearts.

"Don't worry about me...just go on," Schaeffer repeated with a firmer, but also colder, voice.

Spiro and Novak looked askance at each other, mutually scrutinizing.

"We'll have to look for a place to spend the night as far away from the road as possible," Novak said again.

"If you want I'll look around here," Spiro said in a low voice.

Novak, from his height, seemed to pierce him with his grey eyes.

"No," he told him, "my horse is in the best shape. You stay here and take care of Schaeffer; I'll go and come right back."

Spiro blinked his two "flies"; he looked at Novak and a cunning smile crept along the grass to the German's heels.

"Okay, go..." he said.

Novak mounted and left, at a swift pace, crouching over his horse.

The slow half-light of the Fueguian twilight began to flow from the opaque sky, making Schaeffer's face even more pale and accentuating Spiro's whiteness. The latter looked at Novak until he had disappeared among the hills and then he turned his eyes toward Schaeffer; the old man continued nodding off.

"I'm going to look over the hill, to see if anyone is following us," he uttered with a velvety voice, as if he didn't want to wake him.

"Don't worry about me," the old man answered, surprisingly awake. "Just grab your horse and get out of here!"

"It's just that..."

"What, just what? Novak's not coming back, catch up with him."

"You don't think so?"

"He just beat you out."

"Why are you like that, Schaeffer? You don't think he'll be back?" And with a voice as silent as the nightfall, he added, "How can I leave you lying here? You would die of hunger and cold!"

"I'll shoot myself before that happens." And he added, coldly: "And hand me the carbine just in case...don't be afraid, it's for just in case you take off; I'll need it then."

"Take off, you say?"

"Don't pretend..., you're just itching to follow after him."

"No, Schaeffer, I'm not going to hand you the carbine..."

"Why not?"

"You could do something stupid...you have to hold on until the end...you don't think Novak will return?"

"Why are you so worried about Novak? Worry about yourself!"

"It's because sometimes, you know Schaeffer...the circumstances ...if you knew when you were going to die, you'd kill yourself first."

"Just go, and leave me the carbine...Novak isn't coming back anymore to be able to hand it to me..."

"He's not returning, you say, Schaeffer? No, no,...he's returning all right! I'm not giving you the carbine, you could do something foolish before it's time..."

"Then let me sleep!" the old man said, complaining somewhat, and he settled down, leaning on his good leg.

Even though they are short, November Fueguian nights are still intensely dark, especially when the curtain of clouds that darkens the Earth is drawn across the sky.

He awakened when Novak shook his shoulder, asking him about Cosme Spiro. He was nowhere to be found, he had fled, and while on one hand he had left the sawed-off carbine next to the old man, on the other he had stolen his horse, saddle and all.

*   *   *

Novak had found a good refuge among a group of volcanic rocks near the coast and that same night he led Schaeffer there. The pile of rocks had formed a kind of cave, where the dung indicated that the guanacos used it as a cover during bad weather.

"It's all the same...if he had stayed or taken off like a coward!" Schaeffer said, commenting several days later to Novak about Spiro's flight.

"It isn't the same," he replied. "The sooner you discover a traitor, the better."

"I doubted you," the old man said sparingly; "But with Spiro I was sure that he would take off, you could see it in his face. I'm not kidding, the only thing that bothers me is that he took "Molly", and without my mare, what will I do when I recover?"

"We'll see..." Novak uttered.

After a short time Schaeffer had recovered quite a bit from his wound. On a rock from the nearby beach, Novak had found a crust of marine salt, and bringing it in order to roast the birds he hunted, it also served to disinfect the old man's wound which, with the help of the coastal sun and air, was healing up.

"I wonder why this guy is so worried about me?" Schaeffer asked himself more than once, without suspecting that the military training of the German ex-artillery sergeant drove him to save the man wounded in the fray. Fritz Novak carried the soldier inside him, and if he organized the uprising against Popper, it was because the latter had acted like a feudal tyrant with his troops, of which Novak was commander.

On the other hand, the abused life of Schaeffer, from his distant infancy during which he had to abandon his "Puztda" to emigrate to America, had left him hardened before the conduct of his fellow man. For him, all men were more or less the same, especially those who went running madly after gold nuggets. From each one of them he could just as easily expect something bad as something good, all depending on the circumstances in which they found themselves. That's the way life had taught him, and that's the way it had to be. That's the way he was, too; he never considered himself better or worse than the others, and for that very reason Novak's conduct intrigued him. Deep in his heart Schaeffer considered more logical the behavior of Spiro, who fled the danger, leaving him his carbine so that he could kill himself, but stealing his horse which could serve him as a reinforcement in his flight.

However Novak, the hard and sometimes cruel commander of Julio Popper's armed forces, had set him upon his horse and carefully leading it by the halter so that he would not lose blood, led him to the cave among the rocks. He still remembered the seagulls' cry and the cormorants' caw which, in the middle of the night, led them to the coast. The next day Novak found out that the cries came from a rookery: between the cliff with which the pampa ended and the line of high tide, an extensive stretch of volcanic rock rose up, where millions of seagulls had scattered their nests, laying their eggs in the holes made in the tuff by the action of glaciers. With the kerchief he wore around his neck, Novak carried a good provision of eggs that he undertook to boil in the pot for both of them. These seagull and cormorant eggs, at the height of egg laying season were Schaeffer's definite salvation.

"Perhaps that's why he hasn't gone yet," the old man thought, "because he found food!"

One morning Novak hunted a guanaco with her recently delivered "chulengo". They roasted the little one, as tender as lamb, and from the mother guanaco they made "jerky" which they dried on the rocks in the marine sun and air. Life was beginning to be easy for the two refugees on the other side of cape San Martin, so appropriate with its cliff that fell straight down to the deep sea, preventing all passage along the coast.

Little by little Schaeffer was dragging himself outside the cave to defend—by lashing out against the birds of prey—the guanaco meat that from time to time fell under Novak's good aim. He gathered shrubs to make fires and attended to other chores of the cave while Novak went out to provide the dispensation, nothing difficult during that time, since the Fueguian springtime was at its most abundant apogee.

Great bustards and caiquenes, the latter as big as geese, began to arrive by the thousands in their long migratory flights from the North, to brood in Tierra del Fuego and later, with winter's arrival, to return with their coveys to milder climates. Rose-colored flamingos and different varieties of ducks also populated the ponds and rivulets that slid through the pampas, among the smooth, low hills of abundant, tall meadow grass.

Like the butterfly who abandons the useless cocoon in which he was a chrysalis, Schaeffer's spirit was appearing from his bitter mistreatment and finding that life in those barren plains was not all that bad. Both men did freely whatever they felt like, exchanging only the necessary words in order to live in good company. Tierra del Fuego was also transforming itself in harmony with their spirits, coming out of winter, which is also a hard road underneath the thick crust of snow and ice. The meadow grass, the only grass whose metabolism allows it to live underneath the snow, had resurged again for the consolation of guanacos, swans, great bustards, ducks and caiquenes. On the coast, seagulls offered up eggs that were the size of those of chickens, but speckled with brown and blue, like delicate flowers on the dark volcanic rock, and even herds of seals began to inundate the rookeries and sand dunes with their pups recently born in the birthing lairs of Cape Horn.

But from time to time, in the midst of those days of placidity and idleness, Novak and Schaeffer suddenly lifted up their heads from among the rocks of their refuge and looked around like a pair of suspicious seals. They always feared the King of the Páramo.

Besides, they knew that was not going to be eternal; that winter would come to humble the land; that one day caiquenes and great bustards would undertake their return flights to other lands and even the guanacos would make themselves more scarce. And them! Where would they go? To what place? With what wings?

"Little snail, little snail, come out of your shell!" Schaeffer would say every time the weather was good and he was able to place his wound out before the eternal healer of the land.

As soon as he could walk, using his carbine for a cane, he headed for the beach to deeply breathe the sea breezes. One morning he took a long walk toward the north, across the dunes that run along the pampa before the cape's escarpment rises up. Another promontory rose up between the pampa and the sea, in the middle of the wide beach of sand dunes and crushed stone, like a solitary medieval castle, with a thicket over its top and shrubs and coastal flowers descending like vines along its sides. In order to test the healing of his leg he headed there and began to climb; from its summit he could make out the faraway jetty of the Páramo, and toward the south, the sandy beach that waves slightly until it merges with the distant Cape Domingo rock. The South Atlantic disappeared toward the Antarctic regions like a gray-green plain and the pampa, with yellow-green plains, toward the blue mountain chain of Carmen Sylva. The dunes festooned these two immensities with gray, and in turn foam lined the dunes with white, as waves came in like roses to defoliate on the wide stony beach.

Suddenly, upon drawing his vision in from the oceanic plain, his eyes stumbled on another whiteness like the frame of a ship run aground in the middle of the grayish beach. The form of the structure seemed strange to him, and upon observing it better, he discovered it to be the skeleton of an enormous whale, bleached in the open air.

He looked again toward the confines of the Atlantic Ocean, where the whales' domain was, and again he drew in his vision as if following the cetacean's route up to the framework of bones embedded in the middle of the gray-stone beach. Then he looked at the contour of the pampa, the clayey wall with which the shelf of the pampa became elevated toward the cape, the dunes like a quieter sea and the promontory under his feet. "My bones, too, could have been tossed like this on this last shore of the world!" he thought, with a certain annoyance, and he started back.

*   *   *

A human breeze, which for a long time had not renewed their hearts, was little by little invading the life of those two men in that remote corner of the eastern shore of Tierra del Fuego.

Often they would go together to hunt the single-skinned seals that arrived with their pups from the southern sea. Their hides served them as overcoats, and the meat of the young ones, killed by a single blow to the snout with a stick, served as food.

While the brooding advanced, the edible seagull eggs became more scarce and the gulls more dangerous in the defense of their nests. While one man bent to collect eggs, the other had to constantly swing a whip or a stick to defend himself from the furious flapping of wings hurling themselves in flocks against those who were stealing from them. There were thousands of birds who adorned the skies with the movement of wings and with chattering, and on occasion they became so threatening that they had to suspend their collecting and place themselves back to back to be able to defend themselves, lashing, from the pecking.

But the great bustards and the caiquenes replaced the seagulls in abundance; they also arrived by the thousands, and among the pampa grasses nests overflowed with fifteen, twenty or more eggs in each one, the caiquenes eggs the size of goose eggs and those of the great bustard, the size of hens' eggs with the same taste as those of the barnyard birds. The caiquen was easy to hunt, since it allowed you to approach on horseback, although not on foot.

A piece of jerky shared next to the fire, the horse which commonly served the two of them, everything was cordially bringing closer together the life of these men. In other moments they wandered together, crossing the beaches and cliffs with that permanent instinct of the gold prospector whose eyes are never idle at the sight of rocks, clay or sand.

"The other day I spotted a whale skeleton on the beach near the cape," Schaeffer said, deliberately, "and I'm beginning to think about bringing some of the ribs to make a wind block in front of this cave, and we could also secure them at the entrance, with some hides on top; neither the wind nor the rain could get through."

"That would be good, but do you intend to spend your whole life in this cave?" Novak said.

"As long as there is something to eat I think we're better off here..."

"I don't plan on ending up like an Ona Indian underneath a sealskin tarp."

"I think we have to stick around here."

"What for?"

"To look for gold."

Novak raised his head; it was the first time since they had been there that the word "gold" was mentioned and it even surprised him that Schaeffer had said it.

"Maybe so, but in other places on the island. Popper has taken possession of this whole coast and he even intends to continue on further to the south with another expedition on his own...to think I protected him from the first time we crossed over the island killing Indians! And now hiding myself like a mouse so that he doesn't hang me from his posts!"

"We never should have gone against him! One must always howl with the wolf, never against the wolf!" Schaeffer uttered, poking the few remaining coals among the ashes stuck on the rock.

"I howled enough with the wolf, commanding his armed forces so that others could clean his gold for him. In two years almost a half a ton of gold in nuggets and dust! And finally so that he could say to me: this is your pay as squadron commander, tossing some coins at me that he himself manufactured!"

"They were solid gold and were worth what they weighed, not like the ones that governments make."

"But who authorized him to mint coins on his own and to pay his people with them? And his portrait on the mailing stamps that he invented? And his arbitrary laws and that uniformed militia as if he were a real king? Who gave him that power?"

"You yourself...you liked to command soldiers like when you were a sergeant, to give them uniforms so they could call you 'commander', and you felt like a general," Schaeffer told him, smiling sarcastically.

"I did it so that the Indians would respect us."

"After the Indians, it was our turn, so that we would work for him without reclamation. You helped him in that shitty mess because you thought he was going to give you a good cut; but because he didn't give it to you, you went against him and got me caught up in it. And to think that we screwed ourselves with the very stuffed figures that you invented!"

Schaeffer was referring to the picturesque stratagem used by the Páramo King to show his "army" to be much larger than it was, to the aborigines' eyes and to the groups of men who always marauded around the Páramo, attracted by the greed of gold. Novak himself had made some straw mannequins: dressed in the militia's uniform and secured to the horses' saddles, they were led by the halter in single file by one lone rider along the borders of his property, each with a wooden carbine slanted across its back. From a distance they seemed to be real cavalry soldiers, with the advantage that a bullet could pass right through their hearts without knocking them down...

"It seems like those soldiers are sick...why are their faces covered up?" someone said, who observed them from a distance and who later came to work in the Páramo's deposits.

Then Popper had masks painted on them and he placed them among tufts of pampa grass. Schaeffer smiled bitterly upon remembering that many times, under the "commander's" orders, he had to lead the mannequins by the halter, making them trot so that they would appear to be more lively.

What bothered Novak the most about his memories was that the very dummies he had invented had later served to defeat his forces in the Beta Creek scuffle. Knowing the trick, he had neglected his front and reinforced the rearguard; but instead of straw men, Julio Popper in person and all of his men had charged from the front, while the mannequins surrounded the flanks from a distance. His men, confused, didn't know how to face up in good form and so disbandment and defeat took place.

The next day Schaeffer saddled the horse that served them both and headed for the beach to put into practice the idea of a shelter from the wind and rain made of whale ribs.

When he approached the bones, the horse began to snort, mistrustful of that strange and so-white skeleton, and then, when they got closer, it refused to budge. When Schaeffer spurred him, he jumped to the side and almost bucked him off. He got down, tied the hobbles and moved toward the skeleton.

Even more impressive close-up was the size of those bones, which still maintained intact the shape of the great cetacean, which must have been at least thirty-five meters long. The head bones resembled a gigantic Roman chariot, the thorax the frame of a ship, and the tail vertebrae a monstrous serpent that was buried in the sand.

Schaeffer walked around for a while inside the arcade stretching his arms up above, calculating, amazed, at the animal's dimensions, in spite of the fact that the vertebrae were half buried in the gravel and sand. He looked at the ribs one by one and leaving the inside of the skeleton began to shake them in order to get what he had proposed. They were very firm; but one of them ceded to the tremors on its side, the sharp edges opened up a hole until, by hanging on one side, he succeeded in pulling it out. The old man dried his sweat after the task and sat down on the same rib, putting it on the sand like a curved bench. He thought about resting a while and then would drag it to where the horse was hobbled; he would lash it to the cinch with his halter if he couldn't lift it over the front part of the saddle, and he would drag it to the cave. One on one day, another on another day, so that he could build the shelter.

He contemplated his leather jacket thrown on the ground. He had removed it to work on the rib; it was threadbare and had lost its dark brown color; it seemed more like a piece of his own skin, also discolored and cracked from the inclemency of those barren lands. "Not to be able to take out your own ribs," he thought, "and renew them!"

Suddenly his eyes stared like those of a cat when it spots a mouse's tail; he rubbed them hard, as if trying to wake up from some vision and, silently getting up, also with feline movements, he cautiously approached as if hypnotized by what he saw on his threadbare coat. It was black sand that had shot out of the bottom of the hole when he had detached the whale bone with a jerk.

He took it between his trembling fingers and sifted it; almost without believing his eyes, his fingers recognized the "fierrillo", the characteristic black sand, in the vicinity of which gold is generally found. All the abandonment of that isolated region became for Schaeffer the most beautiful and attractive place on earth.

Caressing the "fierrillo" in the hollow of his hand, he moved closer to the hole from where it came; sand and gravel had covered it up again. So then he began to scratch with his hands, as if wanting to open up a road through the heart of the earth.

When they got to the bottom, his hands stopped as if they had taken hold of the world; his fingers carefully felt underneath the ground, recognizing there the velvety smoothness of the "fierrillo", magnetic iron oxide, the black sands that made the compasses go haywire on the Nassau fleet, the first ships to drop anchor on the other side of Cape Horn.

Schaeffer sunk his hand in as far as possible until he touched the edge of the vertebrae from where he had pulled out the rib, and he began extracting the stimulating material as with a pan. He dumped some of it into the palm of his hand, and with religious respect began to remove it, as if his hand were a tiny jig. He meticulously examined up to the last grain of sand, but...there was no gold, it was pure "fierrillo". With a benumbed gesture, as if he didn't even want to let those sands escape, he half-opened his fingers and let the sand slip through, which was blown away by the breeze. All around him the place became forsaken again, the beach became more gray, the sea hostile with its harsh whitecaps, and the sky, in spite of the flashes of light that the wind opened up, harnessing clouds up high, was an unmerciful eye contemplating that reality.

But Schaeffer continued digging, now with his knife, then with his fingernails, like a frightened mole trying to take refuge. He stopped only to dry his sweat or when he was exhausted; he took advantage of those moments to again sift the sands in his hand; but, proving his failure he threw it again, uttering with discouragement—"pure fierrillo!"

In the middle of the afternoon, because he wasn't hungry and he didn't realize that noon had passed by he began to remove another rib, with the same result; now exhausted and enraged, he tried another, a smaller one. The sun, always moving between clearings in the sky and cloud banks, like man's spirit, illuminated and darkened the place's environs.

Tired, with his nerves torn to shreds, he sat down again on a rib placed like a bench. He felt an emptiness similar to that which he felt the night the bullet passed through his leg. He looked at his leather jacket, as wrinkled as an old rag, like he was, inside and out. But recovering, he got on his knees to dig again, as if life depended on it.

The gold nugget of the sun also began to sift down into the black sand of night, when its last lengthy rays meshed with some even more yellowish little lights on the palm of Schaeffer's hand. They were scales of gold, which by the puff of his breath had remained free from the shadow of the fierrillo on his wrinkled skin.

He looked at it, motionless for a good while, until the drop of suspicious liquid that always appeared on the tip of his nose swelled and fell, dissolving on the scales of gold. He rubbed his eyes, not to keep from seeing visions, but because they were crying, and it had been many years since those eyes had cried.

The sun, hiding itself, also left huge gold nuggets at the edge of the horizon's jig: they were golden heaps with which the Fueguian twilight lit up its ever-changing phantasmagorias.

But Schaeffer didn't see the sunset; for him the sun continued in his hand, it was its same color, that of the most coveted and malleable of all metals.

*   *   *

If Julio Popper had invented his famous "gold harvester", subjecting the bull of the sea to the yoke of his ingenuity, nature, in that desolate shore of Tierra del Fuego, had also fabricated its own harvester.

It was a natural phenomenon of Tierra del Fuego, since while gold nuggets and scales are dragged along in other places by rivers, where they tear them away from their quartz beds, on the Fueguian coasts they are dragged along by the force of waves where they are rooted up as much along the shore of the ocean bed, the extensive sandbank of the Atlantic, as from the jutting rocks at high tide.

By some phenomenon of geological upthrust, also characteristic of the eastern shore of Tierra del Fuego, the sea had shifted, leaving the skeleton of the whale embedded in the middle of the extensive beach. But before that, who knows for how long, the scaffolding of bones, ribs and the cracks in the vertebrae had played the part of a curious gold-cleaning wooden trough.

With the providential find, the two men's lives suddenly changed. The first nuggets and scales served so that Novak could go down to the port of Río Grande, toward the south, to obtain tools, the same kind that had been abandoned with the disaster at Beta Creek. He also stocked up on food and tobacco in order to vary what nature was offering them. His horse and a Malvinas pack horse for Schaeffer served to transport this load.

But the human breeze began to move away again from those hearts...

"According to the custom, your cut is one-third," Schaeffer said, when with the tools brought by Novak they organized the work in common and divided up the first proceeds.

"Why?" Novak inquired, surprised.

"Because I found the deposit..."

"You call that a deposit? A few whale bones that have collected a little gold thrown to the beach by the sea!"

"Be as it may, it's mine. I found the skeleton and the bones and everything below the bones pertains to me. The rest of the beach can be all yours and we can work it half-and-half, but not this. It would be beautiful," Schaeffer continued with unusual loquaciousness, "if tomorrow you came upon a gold nugget in your path and with me behind, you would have to share it with me. Would you do it?"

"That's not the same."

"It is..."

Novak looked him up and down. He was almost six-foot three and his square face, with a protruding chin, with his dark eyes, infantile, made a sad, pensive grimace.

"I know what you're thinking," Schaeffer uttered with a smile that was somewhere between mischievous and cruel: "to me, who saved your life, you pay me this way! I can return it to you, take it back if you want, but that's the way gold is divided up."

"Life isn't taken back, even less so for a bum like you!" Novak shouted, with more bitterness than anger.

"Yeah, it's true, it's not to be recovered, but gold is."

Novak thought about leaving, and he would have done it if military regulations had not taught him to reflect on a given situation first. One never completely abandons the camp to the enemy that way. It was what Schaeffer would have loved, to remain alone with all that gold! He stayed, but that breeze never returned to refresh their hearts. Now they spent little time together in the cave that Schaeffer had fixed up with a good wind and rain shelter, just as he had thought up, with the whale ribs and sealskins on top. Like two suspicious animals, they spent all of their energy, from morning until night, in the work of panning gold. They looked at each other, distrustful, even in the task of carrying water for their jigs, and only out of necessity did they exchange any words under the sealskin awning, among the rocks.

After each day's work, on a scale they had built with two little sticks, strings of guanaco nerves and two saucers from the dried skin of the same animal, they split up the gold in the proportionate parts decided upon by Schaeffer. If at times the old cordial breeze came to blow toward those men, it was soon sent away by the counting of gold on the scale.

In a few weeks the surroundings were completely excavated, disturbed; the skeleton taken apart vertebra by vertebra. Not a handful of sand or gravel remained that had not experienced the slanting, seesaw motion of the jigs, when Novak exclaimed at the end of one day, "I'm leaving this place; this isn't going to produce any more."

"Right, it's done," Schaeffer agreed.

They both stood there a while, amazed at all of the gravel and sand they had excavated at great depth, and the way they had taken apart and moved the heavy whale bones.

"We almost covered the whole beach," Schaeffer uttered as a last commentary before they walked away.

That same afternoon, in the cave, they weighed all of the gold they had acquired.

"There must be almost a kilo!" Schaeffer exclaimed, his eyes shining with greed, weighing the leather bag in his hand.

"It wasn't half bad," Novak said, putting his underneath his guanaco and sealskin bedcovers.

Schaeffer, on the other hand, put his bag of gold into one of the large pockets of his leather jacket and slowly went out under the awning of seal skins that covered the whale ribs.

Every time they divided up the gold after each work day, Schaeffer did the same thing. He left the cave, lingered a while on the pampa and then returned, again taking the dark leather bag from his jacket, and letting it fall ostentatiously on his bedcovers, the fringes of which mingled with Novak's in the narrow cavern under the rock.

Notoriously, the caiquenes and great bustards had already begun to gather in great bands on the flat, grassy terrain. One morning both men contemplated with a certain discomfort how one of them suddenly rose up and, forming a great triangle with three males up front as guides like three suspension points, began their migratory flight toward other faraway regions; they had already raised their chicks among the Fueguian grasslands and they carried them off, announcing with their ancient instinct the coming of the first autumn snows.

"We have to leave along with these caiquenes!" Novak said.

"Where do you plan to head?" Schaeffer asked, coldly.

"North, where they are going...life is there."

"But they came to look for it here," the old man said, smiling down.

"I'll cross the Strait of Magellan and in Punta Arenas I'll take the first boat that sails; I'll head north, along whatever side it may be."

"I'm going to go to Río Grande. I'll also try to leave this island; it's good here now, though," Schaeffer sighed.

*   *   *

A heavy silence seized the two men the night before their departure. They ate together, as they had done before, a piece of jerky and some matés. It had been a long time since there had been caiquen or seagull eggs. There was something between them that prevented their talking; nor could they get up and go together to the miserable fire that was more ash than fire, like the embers that remain from "mata negra", a useless shrub, with weak, hollow branches, and an extremely dry and porous heart like cork; but which nevertheless survives on the Fueguian plains.

With the crepuscular half-light they silently went in to go to bed, like every evening, under the stone cave. In a while, the old man snored placidly; on the other hand, Novak could not get to sleep.

Dark thoughts began to wander through his mind; they came and went, with each return accentuated their darkness. To get away from them, he began to retrace the steps that carried him to that distant corner of the planet. He remembered them as all men remember in the darkness, watchful, taking long strides in the past over risky obstacles, illuminated here and there by memory, with hidden reasons that carry it along to wander through the heavy sea of oblivion.

He had come from Europe as an artillery sergeant in charge of a battery from the Krupp firm, which was to compete with the Schneiders and other armament firms in the outskirts of Buenos Aires for a contract from the Argentine government. He always had a somewhat infantile imagination, as warring strategies often are, and on that occasion it occurred to him to cheat so that his cannon and his projectiles would surpass the competitors. At night he managed to moisten with kerosene the targets that corresponded to him. The next day, in the test before the military authorities, his projectiles not only destroyed the objectives but also set the targets on fire.

A compatriot tempted him, offering him the position of administrator of the Las Heras ranch, on the Argentine Patagonia, and he came to the south to militarize cattle raising. The ranch was very modest and did not compensate for Sergeant Fritz Novak's ambitions. He imagined himself living like a king in his domains, like the administrators on the big establishments of the English companies were really doing. But he was a German, and the Germans have always moved behind the English in their colonization.

During that time something occurred on the coasts to the south of the ranch where he was working: a seal cutter sailing in front of the low, extensive shelf of the Patagonian coast, in search of the eastern mouth of the Strait of Magellan, was surprised by a storm and thrown to the beach of the cape that Magellan named Eleven Thousand Virgins. The shipwrecked men, upon digging a well in search of water, found that that slime contained abundant particles of pure gold. The shipwreck's misfortune suddenly became good luck and the news of the discovery spread throughout the world. The eternal adventurers who look for the precious metal arrived from all corners of the earth. "Steep Trench", which the place was called because of the high walls with which the pampa was cut short on the Atlantic shore, became an improvised camp overnight where individuals of every nationality came together. But one of them, because of his knowledge and audacity, stood out from the rest; he was the Rumanian engineer Julius Popper, "Don Julius", as they began to say to him once they encountered his personality. Popper was on the shores of the Yang-Tze when he heard the news about the gold, and like a swallow from Salang he immediately undertook the trip from millennial China to virgin Patagonia.

Sergeant Novak also left his ranch and undertook the short trip from Las Heras to "Steep Trench". This place gave up quite a bit of gold, but not so much that they then began to defend their property with bullets.

Julius Popper lifted his sights over the Strait of Magellan and his engineer's eye made him see that the eastern shores of Tierra del Fuego, which faced "Steep Trench", were of the same geological formation as Patagonia.

He looked for the most audacious and determined among those adventurers—and for that reason they paid back the accuracy of his selection with rebellion—and organized with them an expedition to Tierra del Fuego. They were the first white men who, without mercy, crossed "Onaisin", as the Ona Indians called their country, leaving behind, as a sign of a first contact with civilization, the bodies of those aborigines.

With the experience gained at "Steep Trench", Popper organized, as soon as he discovered gold in the Páramo, an armed guard, in whose command he placed the German ex-sergeant Fritz Novak, who had been predestined for such a lofty position.

What had he gotten out of all this? Only a life full of sudden changes and dangers because of protecting the boss! Because no sooner did he have an armed force, than Popper became, as he himself proclaimed, the King of the Páramo. And he, Novak, who was like a second-in-command, now hidden among the rocks like a mouse!

A clear image of the Rumanian surfaced in his mind: a wide forehead, a bluish-white face, red moustache and beard, a straight, somewhat Roman nose, green snake-like eyes that looked with cutting indifference. An imperious voice completed the grandness of his elevated, robust figure.

It seemed that he could still hear that voice, accompanied by his flashing eyes, when he chastised his troops, in front of which Novak stood square-shouldered, like a perfect commander. "Soldiers: the two major forces that move society are hunger and imprisonment, like the piece of meat and the collar in front of a dog; we are no more than that, men—the need to eat, to defend our lives, to procreate in the belly of women...hunger obliges man to eat and prison makes him work so that he doesn't steal his food! So that we will always find the basis for all effort at the bottom an empty stomach! But man should surpass himself and only in that can he find his own salvation! Look at that flag that invincibly elevates the white of justice that guides our arms and the blue of the sky that protects your steps! The heroic deeds that elevate you will outlast all material riches!"

Whether they understood or not what he said, like the Latin phrases with which they hanged the deserters, the fact was that everyone, including him, felt dominated as much by the presence as by the harangue of that man.

"Of course," Novak thought in the darkness, under the rock, "it was a good philosophy for him: heroic deeds for some and for the master the riches above which they had to rise in order to win heaven! Scoundrel!" he murmured to himself, when he recalled the final scene in which he unsheathed his sable after the vehement speech and in unison with his troops answered the master's harangue: "We have lived with you, we will die if you die."

He repeated the "chorus" created by Popper himself and that he had to teach to the soldiers so that they could repeat it in a chorus as an oath to the boss..."We have lived with you, we will die if you die...." He sighed deeply, in anger and compassion for himself. He had been nothing more than a poor fool who served to terrify others more foolish! The Rumanian had managed him like one of those straw figures that he himself fabricated to deceive Indians and raggamuffins! Did life have to be that way: hunger and prison so that man didn't steal his food and that he had to work, to produce? Was there at the basis of all effort an empty stomach?

Deep in the night the west wind began to blow with force; its wide whip tore through, howling between the edges of whale bones at the cave's entrance and a loose sealskin between the cetacean's ribs began to dully resound like a drum.

Schaeffer woke up slightly with the resounding, moaned and turned half-way over in his bed of animal hides; in a while he continued snoring.

"Life was the same everywhere!" Novak told himself again in his silent language among the shadows. "Had he not served—just the same as in Tierra del Fuego—in another, larger army that from time to time also helped contain a hungry people from taking a mouthful from the rich by striking and shooting them? There had also been, on other beaches, commanders of great armed forces controlled like straw men by some skilled masters who fabricated great speeches with which to deceive the people! How simple things were all of a sudden: a piece of bread and a collar to teach a dog how to behave! What more was man? How had he not seen it before? How had he not discovered it with the simplicity with which Popper said it? He had to admit that the guy was sharp, intelligent! He had dominated nature, putting it to his use and he also dominated men in that way for his own enrichment. Except that for the sea, he employed his pure genius and for men, gallows and puppets: of straw and of flesh and bone.

And the Páramo's gold was the same as everywhere else! They ran after the yellow metal because it fed you without your having to work or falling into jail, it bought love and power. One had to see how they changed, before and after having it in their hands...hadn't that old miser snoring at his side perhaps demonstrated it? His fingernails had scarcely dug a little gold and he became a little Popper indicating to him his meager portion! He had saved each of their lives so that on the next day they might treat him as they had done.

Suddenly he stopped criticizing the others and his mute speech turned against himself: hadn't he also run after gold? Hadn't he perhaps on some occasion shot Ona Indians in order to cut off their ears and sell them to the cattlemen who began to settle on the pastures of Tierra del Fuego? He had received a silver pound for every pair of ears! He remembered the massacre scene on the hillsides behind Cape Domingo. And he had gotten involved in the party of Indian hunters—he remembered it as if justifying himself—because someone had proposed it as an adventure when he was drunk in a brothel in Río Grande. If not, he wouldn't have done it. The Onas, with their women and children, were returning from the beaches of the cape, loaded with cormorants and penguins, when they attacked them mercilessly and without risk from the cape's rock. Four or five had fallen from the bullets of his rifle. One of them was a girl; he remembered her beautiful nude body because as she ran her guanaco cape had fallen away; but he had not seen her face, which he didn't dare to look at when he cut off her ears...he cursed himself again for that act, the darkest of his life, that he hid in the depth of his conscience and for which he had to get drunk for several days with the same silver pounds.

Schaeffer stopped snoring and a rough deep breathing continued its rhythm in his tranquil sleep. Novak turned his face in the darkness trying to see that of the old man, but he only glimpsed his shadow below the rock. That was the way the Ona Indians lay after that massacre, like heavy shadows dumped on the grasslands...he trembled again upon remembering it, but he trembled even more when he realized that his mind continued watching askance the shadow of Schaeffer, who was breathing tediously, asleep...what if that old miser were nothing more than the shadow of a man? Maybe he was worth less than an Indian! Sure, because Indians were human beings too...Schaeffer had said on one occasion that in the black plans of Popper, we would come after the Indians. And the scoundrel had rationed the gold just like Popper...! The gold that was right there, now, within reach of his hand...he could take it from him. The old man was weaker than he, and if he resisted...okay...what did it matter, if he were less than an Ona, scarcely a shadow breathing under the rocks...!

Novak looked for the knife he had put under his pillow of hides, he unsheathed it...there was no reason to see his face; better than when he cut off the Indian girl's ears...he remained pensive, with the handle in his hand; it was somewhat bothersome to have to coldly decide in this way...he had heard say that born criminals killed with anguish...with a kind of inevitable dizziness...but not him; he was serene, tranquil, he was not a born criminal. He slowly raised the knife...

The wind again shook the sealskin over the whale ribs, like a torn drumhead, and whistled among the stones. Novak held his dagger up high; he didn't see the old man, but he heard his breathing, tedious from time to time. No, he was not a shadow, but a living being, asleep and sighing, just as he found him that night lying on the pampa when he left that cursed Spiro in charge of his life...his life, which he had saved, leading him along on his own horse, stopping up his wound...his life, which he would now take away from him because of gold...he slowly lowered the blade of the knife in the shadows until he touched his own forehead; he touched it two or three times as if pounding on a doorhead, calling or looking for something lost...then he rubbed his eyes in the darkness as if clearing away a spiderweb in order to recognize what he had just found and he pulled the knife away from his forehead, making an apathetic cutting motion in the light shadows.

"What's going on?" Schaeffer uttered, sitting up suddenly on an elbow, half asleep.

Novak froze in silence and breathed as if he were asleep. Only the resounding of the sealskin flapping on the whale ribs answered, which was what had awakened Schaeffer, and the wind with its eternal psalmody among the stony hollows. The old man gave another half turn and continued snoring as before; after a while, another snore was heard at his side, placid and long, like the noise that the rhythmic oars of two rowers make over a smooth surface.

They both got up early the next day to saddle their horses; they amicably split up the equipment and set out toward the Carmen Sylva mountains.

"I'll cut toward the port," Schaeffer said, when they were at the trail that led to the south, toward Río Grande.

"I'm going to Río de Oro," Novak said, pointing toward the northwest with a bold arm gesture, and he added, while they shook hands good-bye—"Take care of your pouch, it's all you have in life!"

"It is life...," Schaeffer uttered with his parsimonious coldness.

With the long strides of their horses they separated; defeat was no longer mounted on their haunches.

Shortly before disappearing in the first spurs of Carmen Sylva, Novak launched a fine, long whistle of good-bye. Schaeffer turned halfway in his saddle and indifferently raised his arm, answering the last salutation.

With slow strides he followed the southern trail that weaves among gentle pampa hills. Having traveled little, he stopped his horse, and like an old fox he turned only his head toward the mountain range. He looked attentively a good while; then, striding along the shelter of the hills that hid him from anyone's sight coming from the range, he turned his reins in the direction of the place they had just abandoned.

When he arrived to the environs of the mount of stones where they had holed up, he surveyed the faraway mountains and, dismounting, dug into a small abandoned "cururo" cavern. He put his hand in the gallery dug by the little rodent, then his whole arm, at once extracting a leather pouch tied up with guanaco tendons. He untied it, and his eyes shined with pleasure upon contemplating the gold nuggets and scales inside.

"Your best hiding place will always be the earth!" he murmured. He tied it up again, and carefully guarded it in the pocket of his jacket. Then, from the other pocket he took out another leather pouch, exactly the same as the one he had just dug up, untied it, looked inside, and while he emptied it in the air, he exclaimed, with a broken laugh— "Pure fierrillo!"

And the wind spread across the pampa that shadow of gold whose presence only indicates gold's proximity.

He kept the empty pouch with which he had pretended to carry the gold in front of Novak, mounted up, and taking a short cut continued in a trot in search of the trail that led to Río Grande.

From the south a large band of caiquenes came working the sky with thousands of dark wings; when they passed over his head, one of them broke away from the flock and like an autumn leaf fell upon the pampa grass. Four or five hawks appeared at once and began to flutter around the exhausted wild goose. Two or three fell straight down on the old solitary bird, which defended itself the best it could with its large gray wings and yellow spatulate beak. The birds of prey, in spite of their number, retreated cowardly, looking at their victim from a distance with fierce reddened eyes. Then they all returned to the task together and among a cloud of wings and peckings they killed the old straggling caiquen.

Schaeffer, who had stopped to contemplate the unequal combat, got down from his horse and went in search of the dead caiquen. He took it and tied it by its feet to the straps of his saddle.

"Nobody knows who they are working for!" he said to the hawks, who looked at him with impotent rage, waddling with their claws and shaking their raised crests.

He mounted up and with a slow trot he guided the reins toward the south, while toward the north the flock was disappearing, like a piece of the Fueguian pampa fleeing the coming cruelties of winter.

On The Horse of Dawn

To Professor Humberto Fuenzalida

It passed like a fireball in the distance, expelling something dark and formless under its belly, and stopped only when it got inside the corral.

All of us left our lunch in the small dining room of the ranch and ran to see what was happening. Fortunately, it was only a question of the leather straps of the saddle and of some furs that in the crazy race had slipped down to the animal's pubes. The reins were also split by the trampling and the foamy sweat demonstrated that the dark chestnut horse had galloped a long way.

"Who was riding this horse?" asked Clifton, the Second Administrator.

"The accountant left with it this morning," responded Charlie, the campañistas' foreman.

"Where to"?

"To Ultima Esperanza, and to Puerto Consuelo I think he told me."

"Isn't this 'Broken Head'?" the Second inquired, looking the steaming chestnut up and down.

"That's him," Charlie replied.

"And why did you give this animal to the accountant?"

"There was no other...the herd had already been released to the open field when he came to look for a horse...and I wasn't going to round them up again just for him."

"Why didn't you give him your spare horse and you take this one?"

"Everyone has his own drove of horses—I don't like just anyone going around disturbing my horses..."

"Mister Handler isn't just anybody...he is our accountant, and besides, it was your own nastiness to have given him this animal, knowing how it came away from its last taming session...okay then, leave at once to find out what has happened to the accountant!" Clifton ordered energetically.

"No! I'll go!" I interjected.

I went in to quickly eat some chops, changed the chestnut for another horse that a foreman provided me, and leading it by the halter I took off after the trail of Alfred Handler, the accountant of the "Las

Charitas" ranch, located on the southeast shore of Toro Lake in the Patagonic region of Ultima Esperanza.

On the trail I couldn't help but think of the meanness that it meant to have given Handler, the ranch's accountant, an animal like "Broken Head", a product of the campañista Charlie's last taming. He had been a good horsebreaker in other times; but now that he was old, with his shoulders and legs re-knit, he broke horses more with the handle of his whip than with the strap. In this way the chestnut had ended up with that name precisely because he had broken its skull with whip handle blows, not being able to break it with his legs. But the most serious thing was that the horse acquired the dangerous habit of rearing and tumbling, that is, he would stand up on two legs and hurl his body backwards trying to crush the rider.

The old horse tamer had not only gone bad with the animals, but also with his fellow man, since every time someone was thrown by a horse a malignant smile blossomed on his lips, and his satisfaction of giving the worst animal to the least expert range rider was poorly disguised.

All of that drove me to intervene to go look for the accountant; I didn't trust Charlie, who was very capable of taking the same horse and making him mount it again just to see him fall another time.

Besides, I liked Handler. He was a man who was too cultivated and delicate for the rough environment of Patagonia, and I had known him in his good times, when he arrived as an assistant to the accountant at the "Cerro Guido" ranch. I say his good times, because just as the Patagonian lakes descend to the sea less sparkly each time, Handler's mind was seemingly suffering the same descent, because of his affection for whisky, some said, or from his readings with which he became involved for days and weeks, said others. What is for sure is that after having been an excellent accountant in the greatest ranches of the Society, he became one at the smallest, at this "Las Charitas" ranch, with some fifty thousand sheep, and named for the abundance of ostriches that breed on its prairies.

On crossing a streamlet, I could see the fresh tracks of a horse that had come and gone, which convinced me that in reality the accountant had traveled toward Puerto Consuelo on the south shore of Ultima Esperanza Bay, where at times he had to deal with business related to shipments of leather and wool. No sooner had I verified the tracks than I spurred the horse and galloped decidedly in that direction with the other horse drawn behind.

*   *   *

The long November afternoon was declining when the rarefied oak woods that characterize the coastal region of Ultima Esperanza indicated to me that I was approaching Puerto Consuelo.

Little by little the shadows began to wrap up the branches, giving them that impressive animation that trees certainly contain in their saps, but do not succeed in transmitting to their leaves' tranquil palms. I became a little alarmed, not so much because of the nocturnal uncertainty but because I still had not come across any major signs of Handler.

Soon the hill appeared, some six-hundred meters high, on whose slope is located the famous Cave of the Milodón, an opening more or less eighty meters wide, by thirty high, by two-hundred deep. On that same southern slope other smaller caves are found, and some three kilometers east is one almost half the size of that of the Milodón.

The place becomes a little strange here; possibly because the fire that destroyed the surrounding oak forests left only black twisted skeletons, at the feet of which new sprouts now appear, dramatically embracing the spectres of their ancestors. However, in front of the wide mouth of the cave of the Milodón the fire had respected a wooded fringe that gave to the place a mysterious air of a millennial garden.

I stopped to inspect the surroundings, and not finding anything at first sight, I decided to search the smaller caves, beginning with the one located farthest east. With a brief gallop I was at its entrance; I got off my horse and entered it, shouting. I lit some matches, but the shadows were so thick that the light turned back upon me, flashing in my eyes. I went into that hollow as far as I could, but found nothing there, either; the same in the others of lesser size.

I headed then to the cave of the Milodón, ready to examine it more meticulously. Seen from a distance, the oval entrance, with some projecting crags, resembled the big mouth of a great black toad that blended with the body of night.

Just after entering, after having left the horses tied to an oak tree, I uttered a long shout, calling Handler. Sometimes your own voice gives you security in the darkness; but this time it would have been better not to have shouted, since a faraway and dreadful shout answered me from deep inside the cave. Tightening my nerves I remembered the phenomenon told to me by some sheepmen who on a day of bad weather had taken refuge there: a person seen at a distance inside the cave seems to be situated hundreds of meters away when he is not more than ten. Also, some deformation of the voice could occur, returned by the echo through the millennial acoustics, and the hanging stalactites would not be free from that strange effect.

I conquered my fear with another shout, which rebounded less strangely in the hollow of that prehistoric threshold, and this time, after the echo another shout came forth that, even though it made me shiver again, allowed me to recognize in it, full of joy, Handler's accent.

I finally found him in the depths of the cave, behind a low mound of rocks, seated next to a small fire.

"What do you say, Handler!" I shouted to him, stumbling toward him.

"Hey!" he replied, and with a vague gesture invited me to sit down next to him while he scooped up pellets of dry dung to feed the fire.

"I've been looking all over for you," I told him, and added anxiously—"has something serious happened to you?"

"I don't know...no, nothing..." he responded with a voice somewhat detached from reality, with that disturbed quality with which people in dreams speak.

"We were alarmed because your runaway horse arrived to the ranch houses....

"It must have escaped, I don't know..." he said with that same hollow accent. I looked around, trying to find the cause that I suspected of that strange state the accountant was in; but I couldn't see any liquor bottle. Handler was somewhat dipsomaniac, and sometimes the whiskey brutalized him so much that on more than one occasion we found him splashing in the mud formed by the thaw in front of the small dining room; but this time he proved not to have drunk a single drop of alcohol.

The small bonfire continued fighting weakly with the cave's thick walls, outlining Handler's thin face and making his silhouette dance confusedly on the rocky wall, from whose roof stalactites hung like huge phantasmal tears. The accountant was a man some fifty years old; graying hair, tall, thin, with noble, fine traits, with a grayish-blue sparkle in his eyes, and a convulsive grin, somewhere between kind and sad, on the right side of this thin lips.

"Let's get out of this cave," I told him, gently grabbing his arm.

"What for?" he replied. "Wait a little bit, I have to tell you something!"

I sat down next to him with my legs crossed like travelers do when they rest on their heels.

He picked up a good handful of dry dung from the ground, and then another and another, throwing them on the fire. It was a very dry manure that didn't seem to be from either guanacos or horses; it was more like a brown soil, and its smoke also smelled like burnt earth.

It gave off a sudden radiance and the shadows took refuge fantastically among the bases of the stalactites; but a band of the most dense tatters of shadows began to flutter all around us, emitting little guttural shrieks as if they were confused words that sprang from the rock itself. I cowered, seized with a certain fear, and I confess that I stayed there only because I saw Handler's impassive expression; he seemed to receive with pleasure the flapping of those huge black butterflies that screeched like little rickety bellows.

I became calmer when one of those horrible monsters lit upon Handler's shoulder, since what we were dealing with was bats. The tiny flying mammal looked at each of us with its tiny black-ember eyes; it rubbed its little snout like a miniature condor who cleans its beak with the edge of its wing, and it stayed on the accountant's shoulder, blinking at the fire's light; the band again pushed in close to their nests among the stalactites.

Handler looked at the small animal, sitting like a tailless mouse on his shoulder, then at me, with his absent air, and his convulsive grin changed into a vague, sad smile. He let his hands drop on his knees with a skeptical gesture, and he spoke to me with a faraway, lost voice, while he intently watched the fire, as if it were another tongue communicating something to him, half-opening remote shadows of the past.

"It was when the immense cold wave came," he began saying, always with his broken accent. "We still had not learned to articulate; our language was no more than those guttural shrieks of the bats; but we understood each other perfectly, and what the lips did not say, our hands, our eyes, our whole face expressed...

"Of fire, we only knew what the volcanoes belched forth and what from time to time lightning hurled, sowing destruction. But we didn't know how to make it to warm ourselves, and then the cold wave prevented us from living in the meadows, where we would pick greens and catch a sleeping or sick animal or two. Otters and mice were our favorites because we could kill them with stones or sticks, gulping them down raw. Or else we followed the tracks of the great sabre-tooth tiger, secretly picking up the carrion that he didn't eat...

"The cold wave pushed us to these woodsy areas. Many of the small animals perished, and the strongest ones also took refuge in the forests. Among them was a small horse, golden like the light of dawn, which at times we corralled in the narrow valleys in order to eat it.

"In the meadowlands, women and children belonged to everyone, and all of us cared for them. But when the ice arrived and with it hunger and cold, each man separated with a woman to live alone. I brought my woman to this cave; I put two stakes marking the entrance, and I demolished with a club anyone who crossed the threshold.

"In the sun-filled prairies I used to meet with other men, joining them in cornering some animal; but when the cold wave hit, I took refuge in this cave; I could no longer see other men without hating them.

"Among the animals was one very large one that, like us, ate plant shoots. It had a thick skin covered with scales like little white stones, through which red bristles came out like the afternoon sun. When it stood up on its hind paws, leaning on its short, thick tail as if it were another paw, it reached with its long snout to the very heart of the tallest trees, where it found the most tender branches to eat, and in this way seemed to be another, more alive, tree that moved from branch to branch...

"One day I beat one of these large animals with a stick and brought it to the cave. I made a stone fence, enclosing it, and I brought it branches and grass so that it would stay peacefully in captivity. When I got hungry I killed it with club blows and with the edges of stones I skinned it, carved it up and ate it raw. I had many flocks of these great animals, one after the other, enclosed in the cave, which I divided into two parts, one for them and the other for my woman and me.

"In that way I resisted the cold wave for quite some time. The woman had a baby and we wrapped it up with thick furs to keep it warm, but it died from the cold. I made a little niche in the stone and I buried him so that he could accompany us for a while there. After a short while the woman died too. I made another niche and buried her beside the boy, so that she wouldn't be so alone..."

Handler's voice was moved to pity like that of a child, and his upper lip began to tremble with the cold. Then he raised his hand to his forehead and covered his eyes from the firelight. The bat was like another small shadow taking shape on his shoulder and only its tiny eyes continued to blink sleepily in the reflections. Then Handler took his hand away from his face and taking some more handfuls of dung, he threw it on the flames. They fluttered again, making the shadows dance, and on the wall, on the east side, two open niches could actually be seen; one of the sepulchers was smaller than the other.

"From here," Handler continued, "I could see the great white wave held back on the other shore of the sea's arm; but in reality it was advancing inexorably. From time to time the great wave's crest cracked, launching a deafening thunder, and the ice wore away more of the forest.

"On one occasion in which the thundering increased I headed out, running, in search of other men who might accompany me, but when I approached other caves they came out with their clubs and chased me away just as I had done with them before. Oh, how I missed the gentle look of my woman and the boy's little hand...!

"One day the ice thundered so much that the woods filled with shouts, howls, neighing, and the bellowing of frightened animals. I tried to leave the cave, but an avalanche of terrified beasts came this way, along the slope of the hill; many of them followed the hill above, but a group of them, upon seeing the cave's mouth, came in here...I still remember the small golden horse, like the color of dawn, which galloped toward that corner, followed by the great sabre-tooth tiger and then by the shaggy giant, the swamp otter and others.

"Time ran as inexorably as the thundering of the ice, which crumbled like gigantic planks. Animals and birds continued invading hills and woods with their frightened cries. But a colossal stampede resounded more strongly than the others, and the cave darkened with a more cloudy light...

"I tried to lift up my chest, but my heart, like a frightened mouse, climbed into my throat...the cloudy light became condensed between the wall and the stone fence, in which I domesticated the large animal...and it was precisely one of them that had darkened the cave, since it had escaped from the fence and remained with its gigantic body vacillating between entering the cave, terrorized by the stampede, or running headlong toward the open country.

"Other ashen masses followed the first and they began to come down upon me...I fled to the deepest corner of the cave, but the roar of the sabre-tooth tiger stopped me. Stuck next to it, the little golden sorrel neighed in terror; but, strangely, the roaring puma made no move to sink his claws into it and to eat it up; they were both as frightened as the great swamp otter, which meowed like a bundle of nerves, or as the hairy giant who coughed mutedly, as if it were the throat of the cave itself, stopped up by the fugitive herd. In the midst of the tumult, mixed in with the thundering of the ice, the clear neigh of the little sorrel could be heard like a luminous clarion in the gloomy darkness...

"Is it the glaciers that rumble? No, because they don't croak that way! It is the ashen mass, it is the great animal...his large snout is what croaks and moans that way, subdued like a ruined trumpet from the final judgement...the others also bellowed pitifully and they advance, move toward me more rapidly and inexorably than the ice itself...

"Everything is confused: stampede, thunder, roar, swamp otter, cavernous coughing, ululating of the hairy beast, ashes of ice and forest, bird, fish, plants, neighing of the little horse of the dawn...

"An enormous paw, yes, an enormous paw...ashen, advances and advances until it sinks into my chest. Ay, but suddenly a flash of lightning supervenes! Its light crosses the ancient meadowlands of sun where the plants are juicy and round fruits hang...the flash of lightning flies and in one jagged bolt illuminates all happy life from the past...forests that shake like loose hair in a storm...I am the tenderest of plants, the sound of water and wind! The wind, the wind, which now uproots me and carries me off through the air...what will become of me? Will I return again to the branch of some woods from which no wind can carry me away? Or will I go away definitively transformed into an errant gust of wind?

"The guttural bellowing, the last neighs of the horse of dawn are fading away, crushed by the ash...the last lightning with its last luminous bolt now liberates the woman...from the stone wall she silently slides toward me, as if she wanted to accompany me...she smiles with sadness because she is coming to tell me good-bye...I draw closer and ask her—'How is the boy'? With a vague gesture she responds that he is fine...then the boy is okay! But wasn't he dead? How can a dead person be okay? Do they live? Was she dead, too? I approach and graze her ashen smile with my lips...how cold they are! They are like the meadows when the ice advanced, like a dead plant...now I know, she is pretending to be alive! Her smooth, frozen woman flesh is lying! What does she want from me if she is dead? I break away from the ash that the thunder and lightning leave, but I don't know where I am going! Perhaps some eternal, errant gust of wind will take me somewhere else where my life can take root again! But if I bloom again will I remember what I lived before? I should! Because if not, it would be better not to resurrect, because oblivion is the only thing that is truly dead."

Handler stopped his disconnected harangue...he looked up toward the roof covered with hanging stalactites, as if the entire cavern were crying perpetual, nocturnal, millennial tears. He turned his graying head like a more living and ashen stalactite, looked for something among the shadows and not finding it, raised his hand to his forehead again and closed his eyes tightly. The bat stuck out its thin tongue, licked its snout with it, and with the edge of its wing wiped away something like a tiny tear.

"Let's go, Handler!" I said to him, frightening away from his shoulder the little animal who rose up like a humble condor, beating its two little umbrellas of black skin instead of winged plumage.

*   *   *

Outside, the November night was clear and bright. A full moon moved like a great round diamond among cottony clouds, which blended in with the eternal snow of the tall sharp peaks northwest of the gulf of Ultima Esperanza. Up above, the Southern Cross glided toward the Magellan Nebulae, which like two gigantic udders nurtured with milky brilliance all that portion of the orbit.

We mounted up and undertook the return trip to the ranch. We went silently, one behind the other, trusting in the sure gait of our horses. From time to time, in some turn of the road, the moon cast a shadow of Handler's horse, interweaving it with the hoofs of mine...

Past midnight we arrived at the peninsula of Toro Lake, whose point is cut off by possibly the shortest river in existence, since it is only thirty meters long and its current joins Maravilla and Toro lakes together.

A stream in a lowland area stopped our horses' pace, where they began to drink. The tops of the oak trees opened up a bit more there, letting the moon shine through, twinkling on the water and the horses' lips, and the water fell like broken crystal when the horses raised their heads to savor it.

A cloud of mosquitos rushed preferably upon Handler, and he nervously slapped at his neck, snatching them by the handful. Just then I saw that his hand shined in the moonlight like a bloody limb.

"You're wounded!" I said, coming closer.

"I don't know..." he replied, looking at his blood-stained hand.

The mosquitos insisted on forming a ball at the back of the accountant's neck and a tiny stream of blood began to trickle down his neck, under his shirt.

"Let me see it," I uttered, spurring my horse.

Under his hairy skin at the base of his neck he had a stanched wound, but with the biting of the mosquitos and his own slapping he had detached the coagulated scab and was bleeding again. I covered up the wound with a handkerchief to protect it from the mosquitos that continued pestering us until we left the wooded area and came to the gentle hills that give way to the open Patagonian pampa.

The lake shore became lower and flatter and treeless, which allowed the silvery light of the water to spread to the pasture with a rare luminosity. This moonlight reflected by the silver plain of the lake and the grassland acquired even more charm when we entered into an extensive field of "paramelas", shrubs covered with small, thick, yellow flowers, which reached up to the horses' gambrels. This paramela along the shores of Toro Lake is a curious plant, with a strong perfume, whose leaves and stems many times replace tea and herb, although they say when you drink too much of it, it produces headaches and hallucinations.

The silver of the lake turned into pure gold when we were right in the middle of the field of paramelas. The blooming bunches, upon being trampled and torn to pieces by our horses' hoofs, exhaled their attractive perfume, which was encircling us, just like the golden light that made us imagine we were walking through the meadows of the moon.

Suddenly a group of ostriches got up from the ground, a big male with his five females, and began to run, swerving across the plain with their speckled plumage. Handler kicked his horse with his heels and headed in pursuit of the great birds. Much faster than the horse, they crossed over a hill, on whose summit Handler pulled up the reins.

With slow strides I continued waiting for him; but on seeing that he remained on the hill like an equestrian statue, I decided patiently to go get him. He was riding a brown sorrel, and when I approached I noted that both man and beast had joined the aura of that night of magical beauty, in which the paramelas gilded the face of the earth with a more vivid light than that which our dead satellite reflected.

The impressive stillness of the man and beast instilled respect in me. Both of them were enraptured, contemplating the vast landscape. It was as if they had arrived at the end of a long ride and glimpsed the frontier of a spectral world whose border they dared not cross.

In their precipitated escape, the huge birds had made other groups of ostriches get up from their nests, and they began to join each other on the side of a nearby hill, observing, curious as always, those who had come to disturb their nocturnal peace.

"How good it is that you have come," Handler suddenly said to me. "Because this way other eyes can contemplate what mine see."

"Because here," he continued, "are the first seven hills that arose from the sea. At that time we still did not exist on the land, and on its shorelines, among algae and grass, were those who were the first to tread upon the meadows from the first mud of the world.

"From the swamps, light rose up in their small brains for the first time, and their thin tongues hit upon the first terrestrial tastes. They naturally left their huge eggs to hatch in the sun, and one day in which the father star cooled off a little, they did not know how to defend their origins. The eggs did not germinate and those great species perished."

"What are you talking about?" I asked him.

"You mean you don't see them?"

"Who?"

"The dinosaurs! The dinosaurs!" he exclaimed in jubilation. "There they are on their first hills from the sea!"

"They're ostriches that you flushed from their nests," I informed him, pointing to the ostriches who traveled with gigantic strides on the slope of the other hill, ever hurried along by their huge males whose high, elastic necks moved, undulating like arms that waved meaningful signs at us.

"What a shame that you cannot see what my eyes see!" he replied with sadness.

"Come on, Handler!" I said to him, calmly taking one of his reins and turning him toward the trail that led to the houses of the ranch.

In a while we had begun a good gallop in order to arrive as soon as possible. Upon leaving behind the country of "paramelas" and their intoxicating perfume, the violet light that precedes dawn invaded the vast meadows, rapidly displacing the enchanting reflection that the moon was still emitting from the nearness of its setting. Like a slow throbbing, that violaceous splendor passed, and the crude light of dawn plainly revealed all of the contours of the Patagonian nature. The early morning breeze shook the grasses, awakening them, and a more glorious diamond replaced that of the moon, while horizontally striping all of the earth.

*   *   *

We had just sat down to eat in the small dining room of the ranch, three days later, when we saw Handler suddenly become intensely pale; a sudden trembling shook him, and he collapsed, holding on to the edge of the table.

All of us got up to help him so that he wouldn't fall to the floor and, at once, we set him in a chair. The Second Administrator, somewhat bewildered, quickly tried to open his teeth with a spoon handle and to give him water; but one of the foremen stopped him, warning him that he could breathe in the liquid and drown.

"His heart is beating," Clifton uttered, after having listened at his chest.

In that distant corner of the earth no one could think about a doctor and so what we did was loosen his clothes as the only aid and we left him in peace.

Three days had passed since the night in which Handler's hallucinations made me suspicious of his judgement, harmed perhaps by the blow he received on his head at the base of the cranium. But the strange thing was that during those three days he had carried out in a normal fashion his duties as accountant; of course we never saw him other than at meals, and during them he spoke prudently of routine things, and he certainly never referred to his accident, nor did he return to his fantastic stories. Neither did any of us allude to his fall from the horse, maintaining the discretion that ranch hands always use in these cases.

"The soup's getting cold!" the Second Administrator advised, sitting down to serve us from the head of the table, since he was the highest authority there.

Although no one felt like eating lunch in the face of our sick companion's unconsciousness, we sat down, more to accompany our unapprehensive Second Administrator. But our first mouthfuls of soup were interrupted by a weak complaint, like that of a new calf, which the prostrate accountant began to emit.

Little by little the deathly paleness was disappearing and he came back to life, which flourished in his eyes with a gray sparkle. It was life, and we really felt relieved after those long minutes in which we saw it disappear from our friend's face.

Handler got half way up in the armchair and began looking at us one by one as if recognizing us after a long period of forgetfulness.

"What happened to you?" the Second asked.

"The horse threw me..." he answered, raising a hand to the nape of his neck, and while he looked strangely all around, he added: "But, where am I? I...I fell from my horse in front of the Cave of the Milodón..."

"That happened on Tuesday and today is Friday," the Second replied, as he stopped slurping his soup.

"What?" Handler asked, surprised.

"You fell off the horse on Tuesday," I interrupted. "The animal, a runaway, arrived at the ranch and I went to look for you until I came upon you inside the Cave of the Milodón. It was already nighttime when I found you...don't you remember? You were building a fire inside the cave!"

"It can't be...I remember that the horse got frightened by the sight of the cave, reared up on its hind legs and hurled itself backwards...I felt a blow here on my head and that's all I knew ...until just now when I woke up thinking that I was still in that same place."

"That happened three days ago," the Second insisted; "in the meantime you have been working in your office and have come to eat with us every day."

"Working...? Me? In my office?"

"Yes, you."

"No, it can't be. What did I do? What did I say?"

Handler leaned his head to one side as if looking for something that he had left behind. He closed his right eye with a bitter convulsive grin and hid half of his head as if a painful shadow had fallen over it. During those three days he hadn't shaved, and the tip of his graying beard, next to his hair that was now somewhat white, accentuated that impression of a man fallen half way into the past.

"Pardon me," he uttered, "I don't know anything that has happened to me after falling from the horse."

"It would be better if you ate some warm soup," I told him, when I guessed that the Second would insist on knowing more.

But Clifton understood, because when we got up from the table to go to work, he said to me: "Don't go out today, stay in the auxiliary dining room accompanying Handler."

We settled into the small room in the employees' house with the accountant, and it only took one match for the stove, already prepared by the houseboy, to offer us a nice fire. Handler left and returned shortly with a bottle of whisky and two glasses.

"First let's have a drink to clear out the cobwebs," he said, smiling for the first time.

"Thanks," I said, "But it would be good to clear up this mess first and then drink."

"Okay," he said, reluctantly setting aside the bottle and sitting in the other armchair, in front of the stove in whose interior the fire now sparked cordially, "but it seems that it is you who has to clear everything up for me," he added.

"Really, Handler, you don't remember anything about what you have done during these three days?"

"Nothing! I assure you! My last recollection is a kind of difficult tumult that came with the blow to my head upon falling from the horse...afterwards, nothing; until I began to awaken with a confusing sound of waters...it was your voices in the small dining room, and when they became clear, your faces came to me...but I swear to you that I thought I'd still find myself on the ground in front of the Cave of the Milodón."

"And you don't remember the trip we took in the night until dawn?"

"No."

"Nor what you told me."

"No."

"Good grief, they're like three days not lived!"

"Really, during those three days it seems like I haven't lived either!"

"So you mean you were in another world from the moment I found you next to your fire in the Cave of the Milodón?"

"My fire?"

"You had built a fire with dry dung when I found you, and in its light you told me a strange story."

"Yes, that ground has a meter and a half of a layer of millennial manure...according to Rodolfo Hauthal, a paleontologist, it corresponds to the 'Gripotherium Domesticum', a prehistoric animal that the interglacial man of Patagonia domesticated, enclosing it in that cave as if in a huge stable...but what could I have told you with respect to that?"

I narrated to Handler as authentically as I could everything that he had told me, just as I have tried to do now.

"It is simply fantastic what you told me," he said, when I had finished.

"What I have re-told you," I corrected, "since I have done nothing more than return to you your strange story."

"Quite strange!" Handler exclaimed, "but stranger still because in this case of amnesia that the blow to the head seems to have produced, what I told you in such a state totally coincides with the excavations that Hauthal did in the Cave of the Milodón at the end of the last century!"

"In effect," he continued, "this researcher found there two empty sepulchers and human remains of the prehistoric man who inhabited

Patagonia...these remains were underneath the layer of dung, next to those of four animals until then unknown to science and that pertained to other different orders. By the skulls that they found, other bones and pieces of hide, one of those animals was the size of a rhinoceros and resembled an anteater more than a sloth. Hauthal proved that the troglodyte killed this huge edentate, tore it into pieces and ate it raw, since he still did not know how to use fire. The skulls, which can be seen in the Platte Museum and the pieces of hide in the ones in Santiago and Punta Arenas, reveal that they were killed by club blows and that that primitive man used stone knives to cut up the gigantic

"Lehman-Nitsche and Santiago Roth studied and classified Hauthal's findings, among which were the remains of a gigantic hairy beast, a type of armadillo of great size and a feline that was bigger than all of those known up until then.

"But what most called to the attention of these men of science were the remains of a small horse, which is now known by the technical denomination of 'Onohippidium Saldiasi'. They even found the hoofs of this curious animal, one of which still contained the last phalange with its cartilage, and a crown of hairs from its birth. It was a fine coat of a bright yellow color. There is no doubt that it dealt with a remote ancestor of the horse, which became extinct in Patagonia, leaving only that trace...that of the horse from the dawn of life!"

"And what do you say about the vision that made you see huge dinosaurs in the common ostriches?" I inquired, now completely captivated by the revelations Handler was making to me through his scientific knowledge.

"Ah," he uttered, as if trying to pry into his memory. "The giant reptiles that in other times dominated all of vast Patagonia, which you know is an ocean bed from which seven geological upthrusts arose! The wise Englishman Huxley made the notable discovery, later confirmed by Scope and other men of science, that these ancient dinosaurs are the intermediaries between certain reptiles and certain birds; these last ones were of the family to which ostriches belong, the largest of our living birds," the accountant finished, while the fire, although hidden and domesticated between its steel walls, continued fluttering wildly.

The Hen Who Laid Eggs of Light

"Not the hen!" shouted Oyarzo, the head keeper of the lighthouse, moving between his companion and the small beanflower-colored hen that jumped cackling from a corner.

Maldonado, the other lightkeeper, looked at the head lightkeeper out of the corner of his eye, a look in which desperation and anger were mixed.

The sea and the land have been battling ferociously for more than fifteen days on the stormiest point in the southern Pacific: Evangelists Lighthouse, the most elevated and solitary of the small islands that mark the western entrance of the Strait of Magellan and upon whose bare back the lighthouse tower and its beacon rise up as the only light and hope that sailors have to escape the ocean storms.

The fight between the land and the sea is almost permanent there. The Andes range tried, it seems, to raise up some big walls, but in the combat of centuries everything has split up; water has penetrated channels, has even reached the wounds of the mountainous fiords and only the fiercest of fists closed tight in hard, glaring rock like at Evangelists Lighthouse have remained striking the sea.

It is a black, defiant island that rears up to a great height. Its sides are smooth and sharply cut. The construction of the lighthouse is a heroic page of the courageous sailors of the Lighthouse Inspectors of the Magallanes Naval Station, and the first person to scale the promontory was an anonymous hero, like the majority of men who confront that nature.

They had to hoist brick by brick. Even today, the brave lightkeepers who watch over the most important beacon of the southern Pacific are totally isolated from the world in the middle of the ocean. There is one single, fragile path going up from the sea to the summit; it is a rope ladder that in mariner's slang is called the "cat's ladder", which remains hanging at the edge of the sinister cliff.

Provisions are hoisted up from the launches that tie up at the edge by means of a winch installed at the top and driven by manpower.

A revenue cutter from the National Armada periodically leaves from Punta Arenas to cross over to the western lighthouse, providing them with supplies and acetylene.

The most feared assignment for these small but tough transports of the high seas is Evangelists, since when there is bad weather it is impossible to approach the lighthouse and to lower the whaling launches that carry the provisions.

Like a warning for those sailors there exists, some miles inland, the renowned port of "Forty Days", the only refuge in which ships have been during the whole time riding out the storm. Sometimes a cutter, taking advantage of a lull, headed out at full speed to fulfill its expedition, but upon sighting the lighthouse, the storm broke out again and they had to return to the sheltered haven of "Forty Days".

This time the storm lasts more than fifteen days. The storm outside, in the elements, in which the raised mass of rock trembles, seems to complain when mountains of water unload themselves over its smooth sides; while inside, under the lighthouse tower, in a human heart, in a brain badgered by the surges of big raindrops drumming on the zinc roof, in a sensibility punished by the whistling howl of the wind tearing up the tower, in a hungry, weak man, another slow and terrible storm is developing.

It was the second time that Oyarzo had saved the miraculous—and only—hen from the desperate impulses of his companion. The hen had begun to lay exactly the same day she was going to be sacrificed!

The lightkeepers had exhausted all of their provisions and reserves. The launch had been delayed a month now and the storm was not abating, certainly bottling it up in the port of "Forty Days".

As if by a miracle, every day the hen laid an egg which, mixed with a little water and salt, and with the meager ration of forty beans allotted to each man, served as precarious nourishment to the two lightkeepers.

"Take your forty beans!" Oyarzo said, handing the ration to his companion.

Maldonado looked at the tiny pile of beans in the hollow of his hand. "Never," he thought, "had his life been reduced to this! No"— now he remembers—"only once did the same thing occur in the St. Felix Lighthouse, when he lost two years' worth of pay, also converted into a pile of beans, in a poker game as it passed from his hands to those of his companions!"

But that was only two years of his life and now these constituted his entire life, the salvation from the claws of the subtle panther called hunger, which in its rounds came closer and closer each day to the lighthouse.

"And this Oyarzo," he continued in his weak-minded reflections, "so tough and so loyal!" He had thought of rationing the small quantity of beans very fairly and at times even gave him a few more, giving up some of his portion. Even the hen had its portion: he gave it to her a little warmed up with milled shells and grain so that she wouldn't stop laying.

Every day and every night that they spent under the constant clamor of the rough sea, death was nearer and hunger sunk its livid claws a little bit more into those two beings.

Oyarzo was a tall, bony man with straight hair and a dark complexion. Maldonado was shorter, thinner and in reality, weaker.

If it had not been for that big man, the other certainly would have perished already, with the hen and all.

Oyarzo was the wise craftsman who prolonged those three existences in an intelligent and dauntless struggle against death, which was now slipping through the crack of hunger. The hen, the man and the man! The energy of a few small beans that passed from one to the others! The miraculous egg that day by day lifted the last bits of strength of those men to light the beacon, the safety and hope of sailors who ply the wretched route!

Maldonado began to become obsessed with one firm idea: the hen. He was weakened, and the hunger, after eating away his insides like a slow, piercing fire, began to erode his conscience as well, and some sinister lights, that he tried in vain to extinguish, began to rise up in his mind.

He firmly arrived at this conclusion: if he could satiate his hunger just once, he would die happy. He wasn't asking for anything more.

However, he did not dare to think or to arrive to where his instincts were pushing him. No, he was not capable of killing his good companion in order to devour the chicken!

"But what the hell!" he said and he began to tremble and turn around, frightened, as if someone had pushed him to the edge of an abyss.

The ocean continued to envelope the lighthouse with its harsh thundering, the rain continued with its incessant beating against the zinc and the roaring of the wind made the tower tremble, in whose heights the beacon continued to be lit every night thanks to a hen's egg and the toughness of one man.

Ocean storms are never steady, they take a breath every four hours. One night in one of its culminations it grew so severe that it could only be compared to the end of the world. The thunder of the sea, the howling of the wind and the surges of rain that let loose on the roof, shook the mass of rock so that it seemed to become detached from its base and cast off to navigate through the storm.

The storm inside also reached its climax.

Maldonado made his way stealthily among the shadows, knife in hand, toward Oyarzo's bunk, where the latter, because of his mistrust toward his companion, carefully guarded the miraculous hen.

Maldonado had not clarified his intentions very well. Distressed because of hunger, he advanced toward something confused and black. He had not wanted to stop himself very long to determine against whom he was going with a dagger in hand. He was simply going to get hold of the hen; once it was dead there would no longer be any recourse, and Oyarzo would have to share the snack with him; but if he intervened like before...Ah! Then he would raise the dagger, but only to threaten him.

And if Oyarzo attacked him? Oh, hell, here it was, again, that confusing and dark thing against which he was going to confront, reckless and blind!

He opened the door, cautiously. The head lightkeeper seemed to sleep profoundly. He headed trembling toward the corner where he knew he would find the hen, but in the instant he was going to pounce on her he was knocked over by a punch on the nape of his neck. Oyarzo's heavy body fell upon his and with a rapid twist of the wrist he made him let go of the dagger.

There was hardly any resistance. The head lightkeeper was very strong, and after totally dominating him, he tied his hands behind his back with a rope.

"I didn't intend to attack you with the knife, I only carried it to threaten you in case you didn't let me kill the hen," said the lightkeeper with his head lowered and full of shame.

The next day he was tied to a heavy oak bench with his hands still behind him.

The head lightkeeper continued working and fighting against hunger's claws. He made the batter with the egg and beans and with his own hand he went to feed a portion to the man who was tied up.

The latter, with his eyes lowered, received the spoonfuls, but in spite of the hunger that was devouring him, he felt this time a bitter distress when the food passed down his throat.

"Thanks," he said when he was through. "Pardon me, Oyarzo!"

Oyarzo didn't answer.

The storm did not diminish in the ensuing days. The avalanche of water and wind remained the same.

"Untie me, I'll help you, you're making a big sacrifice!" Maldonado said one morning, and he continued desperately: "I swear to you I won't touch one feather of the hen!"

The head lightkeeper looked at his tied-up friend; the latter looked up and their eyes met, face to face. They were exhausted, weak, eroded by hunger! It was only an instant; the two men seemed to understand each other in the collision of their glances; then their eyes clouded over.

"I'll still fight alone; the moment will come when I have to release you for the last feast that the hen will provide for us!" Oyarzo said with a certain tone of prophecy and of doubt.

The words resounded like a whip in the conscience of the other lightkeeper. He would have preferred a slap on his face to that sentence loaded with his companion's scorn and mistrust.

But the miraculous hen laid another egg the next day. As usual, Oyarzo prepared the precarious meal. The last ration of beans was all that was left.

Once again he approached the prisoner with that scant portion of beans, lifted a half-full spoon, like one who is going to feed a little child, but when he tried to give it to him, the prisoner, with his head high and his gaze fixed harshly on his generous companion, emphatically exclaimed:

"No, I'm not eating any more; I won't receive a single bite from your hands!"

The head lightkeeper's face lit up as if he had just received good news. He looked at his companion with a certain kindness and suddenly smiled a strange smile, a smile in which kindness and joy were mixed. He put the plate of food to one side and, untying the rope, he said, "You're right, excuse me, you don't deserve this punishment anymore; Evangelists has two lightkeepers again!"

"Yes, once again!" the other said, getting up, now free, and shaking his companion's hand.

*   *   *

When the delivery of provisions was completed and the commander of the launch went to find out the latest events in the lighthouse, it surprised him a little when he observed some traces of struggle in the faces of the two lightkeepers. He looked hard at one, then the other; but before he questioned them, Oyarzo moved forward, smiling, and caressing with his rough hand the delicate head of the beanflower-colored hen that he protected under his arm, he said:

"We wanted to kill the hen who laid golden eggs, but she defended herself by pecking us!"

"You mean 'the hen who laid eggs of light'," the commander of the launch replied, possibly suspecting what had occurred, "because every egg meant another night of light for our ships!"

The Voice of the Wind

"Even the birds become wild beasts in this cursed land!" the overseer's wife said, shaking off the snow at the doorway of the hut.

"Another blind sheep running against the wind?" Denis asked from inside.

"This is the fifth one!" the woman answered and continued, "everything is going bad in this wasteland! For days you go around turning a knife in your hand without anything to kill; you frighten me when you stare at me so much and I see you go over the edge of your flaying knife with your fingertips. In springtime, it's the eagles who eat the newborn lambs straight from the mother's womb; in the summer, the seagulls who come from the ocean to the mountains to attack and eat the baby geese and in the winter these damn caranchos who peck the eyes out of the sheep to make them fall and then to eat them up."

The wind roared over the smooth, frozen meseta, lifting up a fine powder of snow two meters high, enclosing the horizons level with the land and forming a tempestuous sea, strange and ashen, whose waves disintegrated into a feathering of snow that blended into the misty distance. The little house on Outpost 22 of the China Creek ranch, on Tierra del Fuego, seemed like a small, desolate reef in the middle of that sea of floating snow.

Lucrecia put her hands up to shade her eyes and looked into the distance. Fighting in the furious surf, a sheep without eyes advanced against the wind, followed by a small band of caranchos. It walked like animals who are drunk after eating bad grass from the lowlands, stopping at times and at times running a short, paralytic race, as if it had stepped on fire.

The band of brown birds rose up from time to time from the ash-colored sea and enveloped the sheep with an endless number of wingbeats and then they disappeared again into the swells of the blizzard.

The carancho is a cowardly bird, but, hounded by hunger when the snow increases and covers up dead animals with a thick layer, it gathers in flocks and attacks sheep in this treacherous, cruel manner in order to devour them.

In storms sheep head against the wind until finding a refuge in which to take shelter. The storm and a strange night had fallen upon this sheep after they had pecked out its eyes, leaving two bloody holes in which the wind and snow swirled.

"Denis, leave the knife alone, please!" the woman begged.

"That's the last straw, that it's left to the caranchos!" the post overseer said, and he went out with the knife between his teeth to find the wounded animal.

Lucrecia came into the hut and closed the door so as not to continue seeing the painful spectacle of the blind sheep pursued by caranchos, which would then fall to the shiny blade of Denis's knife, that sharp "eskiltuna" blade that the gringo constantly caressed, day and night, with a strange pleasure. He would put the knife in front of his eyes, lower his head as if he were going to kiss it and, with a peculiar puckering of his lips he would softly blow on it and run the tip of his thumb along the edge; then he would affectionately slap it two or three times in the palm of his hand and carefully put it back in his belt.

The knife was for Denis like an extension of himself, an additional sense through which he received secret vibrations and pleasures. It was always with him during the day, cutting strips of leather, thinning rawhide straps, pulling out fine guanaco veins to use for sewing. At night he calmly rested with his company underneath his pillow, next to the wide belt where he kept his money.

"But who are you afraid of?" his woman would say to him. "We've been married almost a year, we live in an outpost where not a single soul passes by and you're always sleeping with your knife and your money underneath your pillow."

Denis didn't answer, turned his head away scornfully and began to whistle an odiously monotonous song.

Lucrecia was a sensitive woman; that's why she didn't put up with the things of that hard land; that's also why she abandoned that other life of prostitution in Río Grande, where waves of sheepmen, guanaco hunters and cowboys would descend to relieve their years of abstinence and solitude.

One night the drunken gringo Denis arrived, paid a huge sum to the owner of the house, "La Cinchón Tres Vueltas", for exclusive rights to Lucrecia, and the next morning he said to her, "Listen, why don't you come with me to Post 22?"

"Where's that?" the woman asked.

"Out there, in the heart of Tierra del Fuego!" Denis answered, and went on, "Look, I'm the campañista and the butcher for the China Creek ranch; I am bored with breaking colts and slaughtering and dressing animals and I want to rest. My boss has offered several times to change me to the outposts and now is the opportunity to do it. We'll go to number 22 where the pay is double, because it is a diabolical land, and after a few years, with my savings, we'll change our lives."

Lucrecia stared at him. He was a short, unexpressive, beardless man; his face dark and olive-colored, where two small brown and evasive eyes drowned; his body was somewhat chubby, a bit bulky in the buttocks, without that lean severity of most Fueguian campesinos.

She found him neither ugly nor good-looking; neither good nor bad. She, a prostitute fallen among the talons of the old famous women exploiter of Río Grande, nicknamed "La Cinchón Tres Vueltas" because of her voluminous corpulence and other exaggerations that her customers attributed to her, could not try for anything better than that dark campañista of English origin.

That same day the gringo Denis paid the price of ransom, bought a city suit and went to get married. At nightfall he left with his wife on the haunches of his horse, heading for China Creek.

The caretakers of cattle on the vast island of Tierra del Fuego and of Patagonia combat their main enemy, solitude, with whiskey and gin; but Denis had now carried off a new, esteemed element to combat it: a woman.

The man had attained happiness: a woman at an outpost. His WOMAN!

She was white, pink, a little taller than he and about thirty-five years old. A real marvel in a land of lone men where not even a wretched Indian woman remained, as in the old days.

He remained for entire hours fascinated, contemplating how she moved about the only room of the hut. He looked her over, up and down with his greedy eyes and suddenly he would emit a strange whinnying sound and throw himself on top of her.

It was the same sound with which he pacified his months of abstinence; that uncontrollable euphoria that at times disturbed him in the middle of the countryside and that weakened only when he drove his spurs forcefully into his horse, gave it a whipping and took off at a full gallop among the peat bogs, shouting like a crazed being.

Now, all of this had ended with the presence of the woman, who was there entirely to indulge him in pleasure.

In order to enjoy his new condition he half closed his eyes and evoked the current episode that happened on the ranch when some prostitute, en route from Porvenir to Río Grande, stopped to lodge in China Creek. The Second Administrator ordered two armed men to place themselves that night in front of her bedroom door; there, carbine in hand, they protected the woman who upset the hundred men of the ranch.

On one occasion, when an individual with a container of wine and gin came to stay with the prostitute there was almost a brawl in front of the woman's door. The Second had to impose his authority with pistol in hand against the group of drunks.

"Leave her!" they shouted. "Let one man be cashier and we'll pay her the same as we do at 'La Cinchón Tres Vueltas'."

But the joy of the first times was weakening, the ardor calming down, giving way to a progressive indifference that was invading those two beings lost on a meseta in Tierra del Fuego.

The overseers in these outposts generally get accustomed to the solitude. So that it doesn't corner them, they execute a series of actions that in other places would seem strange: they converse with their dogs and horses and open the doors so that the sun, wind and countryside can come in to keep them company.

This solitude, which a man endures facing nature, seems to increase or transform itself into an anguishing thing when in the middle of the immensity two beings who do not understand each other have to live together.

In Denis the sensation of solitude increased and in Lucrecia it became intolerable.

Besides, in the former a strange nostalgia for his job as a butcher was taking hold of him. Denis had been a butcher all of his life: a skillful butcher with a reputation in the cold-storage plants. He slaughtered with a surprising quickness and skinned the animals in rapid succession. He did his work with pleasure; he felt pleasure when he was looking for the sheep's trachea with the tip of his knife; pleasure upon ripping it open and seeing blood gush forth; pleasure when he put an end to the death rattle cutting the small hard vein that joins the vertebrae in the neck; pleasure when he turned the knife inside the ox's chest, looking for the heart so as to drain its blood; but when his emotions reached their greatest intensity was when he skinned and quartered an animal with decision. He seemed to be a doctor right in anatomy class; he cut following the fibrous lines of the flesh with mathematical precision.

After finishing the work of each animal, his face spattered with drops of blood, he would lick his lips, enjoying the taste of fresh blood mixed with his sweat.

Was Denis a born criminal, or had twenty years as a butcher converted him into a man who felt the need to kill on a daily basis?

Because ever since he stopped slaughtering animals to be transferred to the outpost, every day he felt something missing; he would take his knife and would, alone, make cuts in the air and skin imaginary animals.

In Lucrecia the fear of her husband's slaughtering mania increased from day to day, and she didn't escape from the hut just because she had found a horrible death on the frozen steppe. She felt relieved when Denis spent the day in the countryside, checking over the flocks, and somewhat frightened when the two of them were alone among the four walls of the hut.

Outpost 22 had, besides, a tragic tradition: a Scotsman had gone crazy and a Chilean had committed suicide by hanging himself from the ceiling.

The days when snow blocked the hut, life inside became intolerable. Denis didn't speak, he remained silent as if absorbed by an obsessive idea.

His wife caught him looking at her several times so strangely that she trembled.

Denis trembled too; it was a trembling that began in back, at the nape of his neck; it came from his head and pressed into his forehead, clouding his whole vision.

One day in which the maddening monotony of the falling snow worsened, Denis threw the knife toward the window and began to pound his fist on the table as if a severe pain shook him.

Days without wind and silent snowfalls followed the episode of the blind sheep. The solitude became more intense with the light falling of the snowflakes; at times it seemed that one could hear a light rustling in the distance, as light and subtle as the fluttering of a butterfly. Through the small window the closed horizons and a nearby and gray sky could be seen, all of which produced an interminable sadness.

Was that meseta cursed? Had the desolation, the abandonment of that landscape entered into the half-savage soul of that man, like an envenomed wind, corrupting him? Is that how the two previous overseers had died?

No, it wasn't just the desolation, the solitude, the white anguish of the snow! In that man's mind the idea of the crime had appeared, coming from whatever substrata and localized there in the nape with a sharp pain!

It was a kind of vertigo, like the attraction of an abyss. When he looked at her or passed by her, it was as if he were approaching that abyss; one more small impulse and—that's it! He would have killed her;

but he stopped himself at the edge of the precipice, trembling convulsively.

One afternoon he managed to take the knife out of his belt. The woman, unconcerned, had her back to him, doing some work in the kitchen; he raised the weapon up to a certain height and suddenly shouted ferociously and buried it with all his strength into the table.

"What's the matter with you?" the woman exclaimed, frightened.

"I can't take it, I can't take it anymore!" he said, sobbing.

He tried to flee, but the thought ate at him, followed him everywhere.

Underneath his breath he repeated these words all the time: "I can't take it, I'm going to kill her!", and the refrain had something spasmodic, anguished, that even shook his innermost fiber.

Another day, in a crisis, grabbing with all his strength at the edge of the precipice, he saved himself by rushing out and running like a madman through the snowy countryside.

A cold cruelty hardened him at times. "I'm going to kill her!" he calmly told himself; but then a tenderness that might have carried him to tears invaded him, changing him into a gelatinous trembling.

Finally, one night, he rushed into the precipice: while she slept, he killed her.

He carried the body to the horse corral, broke open the hard crust of snow and buried it.

He felt that the air was more bearable, as if an enormous weight had been lifted from him.

"Bah!" he said to himself. "She was like a sheep, only a little bigger!"

The days passed by without any great worry. Naturally, he went out to the open country more often...

He began to work harder; from day to night he crossed over the meseta and the adjoining lands.

The plain with its monotonous whiteness had become more attractive, and the outpost, a place where he couldn't be without a certain uneasiness. The reef in the middle of the sea of snow was little by little losing its warmth as a refuge and was becoming a hostile rock from which Denis constantly stretched out his flight toward the snowy plain.

He tried to ward off his anxiety by extending his head like a drowning man does out of the water; but one day something showed up that hit him directly and he wasn't able to continue deceiving himself: it was the west wind, that formidable wind that blows all year long over Tierra del Fuego.

Until he heard its howling he could continue with that "Bah! She was like a sheep, only bigger!"; but as soon as that cursed wind arrived from the west, his opinion changed radically: he had murdered his wife!

It began by listening to another noise within the sound of the wind. At first he tried to confuse it with the sound of a loose beam, with the creaking of the timbers of the hut, with the neighing of the emergency horse, with the barking of the dogs...but the noise was beginning to identify itself.

Normally the west wind had a great sound, powerful and howling, that crossed the steppe like a virile roar under which one could sleep peacefully without listening to the creaking of the house. Now, something like the sobbing of a woman came in the wind, which made Denis tremble.

The sobbing broke up and the wind began to chatter sounds that seemed to be imploring words; Denis tossed in bed without being able to sleep.

Little by little that plaintive jabbering was becoming clearer, and suddenly one night, Denis, crazy with terror, heard his name pronounced clearly:

"Denis! Denis!" It was the voice of his murdered wife.

The voice lashed underneath the door with every violent gust, as if trying to get in:

"Denis! Denis!"

The voice grew and the door seemed to give way with a push. Quickly, he leaped out of bed and went to open it, knife in hand. A furious gust of wind entered; he jumped backwards and brandished the knife as if to defend himself from a possible assault; but outside only the night and the storm reigned; the night with its dark wall of shadows and the howling wind.

He closed the door and, when a light vertigo gave him the impression that he was going to sleep, the anguished voice of the wind knocked again at the door:

"Denis! Denis! Denis!"...until a feverish drowsiness came to alleviate him with the milky whiteness of dawn.

The western wind abates in the early morning, disappears at midday and when the afternoon draws to a close it begins again, to blow with all its force at midnight. Denis's sufferings followed this same trajectory: drowsiness, anguish, and madness.

He stopped going out to the countryside, now weakened. Only when obligated by a major necessity did he leave the hut and he entered again hastily.

Outside he had the sensation that the sky opened up, that the vastness was an eye that harshly contemplated him, and he saw himself alone, weak, small and helpless: with that helplessness of inanition, in which man is a drop of water cast to the winds.

The dogs began to howl with hunger. One morning he went to find the emergency horse in order to flee, but it had escaped to the open country.

One night the howling of the dogs blended horribly with that of the wind and the voice that came with it. The wind did not diminish in the morning as usual and Denis lost the notion of night and day; he wandered like a pallid shadow inside the hut, wrapped in a kind of red mist.

The voice of the wind was like an enormous whip that struck him, the drone trepanned his temples, cut through his eardrums, got itself inside of him, drilled into him.

He was a human rag mashed by the prevailing wind, snow and solitude, on the hostile crust of the harshest corner of the island of Tierra del Fuego, "Post 22".

One night the storm grew worse. The wind arrived in swells and seemed to lift the poor hut up on its waves; the overseer, maddened, huddled next to the floor, clutching the planks, trembling and sobbing.

Suddenly everything became calm, a sepulchral silence surrounded the agonizing man and, when the mitigation began to rub against his shattered sensitivity, a voice rose up from inside the post:

"Denis! Denis!"

Cornered by the voice, with his last efforts, he went out into the storm and tried to run, like the sheep that one afternoon that approached the hut with blind eyes, followed by the wingbeats of a band of caranchos; but he couldn't, he staggered and also fell on the inclement steppe under the wingbeats of a band of words:

"Denis! Denis!"

Land of Oblivion

The farther we penetrated inland, the more the landscape became gloomy and disquieting. The sordidness of some passes disturbed the spirit and even the horses pricked up their ears, frightened by something that could not be seen, but that was there and just as alive as the bare rock.

Our path at times bordered the abyss, and before the sight of the river, thundering, running down there below in the depths, we—both man and beast—remained suspended a few moments, trying to lean against the vertigo. We were nothing then; we just stopped a little more in our stirrups, grasped the reins, and the horse, on its own, headed out, striding along with intrepid steadiness on the arid rock.

On a bend in which the chest of the mountain swelled, we saw the sea for the last time. And it was as if we had lost something... something that we would never again recover.

Now we understood the unpleasant disquiet that seized us as we were heading into the desolate landscape. The sea, although jealous and violent when one is in the middle of it, was from that distance an immense companion, a gentle plain of peace, whose vision instilled calm and, above all, that vague, indescribable sensation of hope.

There are landscapes, like moments in life, that are never erased from the mind; they always return to pierce us from the inside, each time with greater intensity. This one, in which we looked back at the sea for the last time, is one of them; there we turned our heads so as not to miss the last vision of that hope, and then we entered fully into that land of oblivion.

Our route, parallel to the Baker Range, was interrupted suddenly by a drop-off and to our surprise a grand valley stretched out before us, whose grasses, divided by the boxed-in wind, looked like the fine skin of an otter, cleaned by the breath of an expert. It was an immense slash left by a glacier in the heart of the mountain, one of those rivers of millennial ice, now gone, whose bed of slime made that meadow fertile.

We had to abandon the direction parallel to the river and turn toward the south, skirting this other dry river, in search of a descent. Only after several hours did the cordillera's backbone begin to bend and we were able to glimpse the depth of the valley that sunk down like a deep throat in the mountain. A sky without light scarcely allowed us to make out two things that increased our curiosity: the valley ended and gave rise to a thick wall of ice that intruded like a mountain wedge inside the valley; and below, at our feet, next to a boscage of dwarf oak and underbrush, on the summit of the first promontory that descended in the valley, could be seen an oxidated shack, small and dark, like something expelled and strangely kept in the most forgotten crevice on earth.

We descended and began to enter the plain whose pasture grass reached our stirrups. But the grim solitude of that place again overwhelmed us, that place whose vision from the peaks had been for a few moments an oasis of rest for our eyes. The grass grew abundantly and thick like a sown field; but not a single bird, nor a guemal nor any animal on the land interrupted that silence, through which only the buzzing of the trapped breeze came through from time to time.

We remembered having seen something similar in the hollow left by a gigantic glacier in Yendegaia Bay, in the Beagle Channel; but there man had carried along the rumor of life, and twelve thousand sheep grazed on the plains that also reached to the vestiges of the millennial ice.

We headed in the direction of the shack. The silence became more and more lethal and only now and then did the serpentine howl of the wind tear through the hollows of the valley; after that, that silence again...until...

A mournful howl shattered our nerves like a flash of lightning and the horses jumped in fear. We almost lost our stirrups; and by dint of reins and spurs, we dominated them, but, being as it is with animals, who get more frightened by the unknown, their nostrils twitched, their eyes flashed and their hoofs shook with a trembling that they never had facing the uncertainty of the abyss.

Slapping them on the wide part of their necks, we succeeded in calming them down; but not a minute had elapsed when the howl was heard again, this time less penetrating and acute, like the bleating of a sick or wounded seal. This time a few pulls on the reins were enough to contain the horses.

We stopped moving and waited. The silence weighed like the lead of the sky.

But in the moment we were going to continue making our way through the pasture, a strange animal appeared. It was a spaniel with a mix of whippet; but a whippet with a flat face, with lips like a sea lion and with a great deal of hair on its sides, stiff and long, like that of the fur seal. It was a rare and repugnant mixture, like that of hyenas, with such long front legs that they seemed to drag the body when it walked.

It came up right next to me and before it was able to pounce upon my horse, I prepared my carbine and pointed; but just then, Clifton, my traveling companion, took the barrel of the Winchester and pushed it aside. In that same moment a man appeared, too, from among the pasture grass and, taking the dog, if you can call it that, by one ear, he stood next to it.

Clifton approached and said something to him that I couldn't understand. The man responded with an unintelligible guttural voice, and pointed to the bottom of the valley, as if indicating the trail to us.

We moved on, with him behind us, always holding the dog by the ear, until we reached the edge of the hill on whose summit was the shack. But he didn't allow us to reach it; placing himself in front of us he uttered something again with his guttural voice, and as if threatening with the dog again pointed out the nearby mountain spur.

We took the direction that he indicated to us while he watched us from the side of the hill. As we were heading into the valley we heard the dog's chilling howl again; but the weird animal only came into our general area, since in the moment he seemed to catch up to us, another guttural howl sprang forth from the man, and the dog, rising up on two legs, threatened us around the horses' haunches, lifted up his snout and emitted his ululant bleating before returning to where his master was.

After a while, when we began to ascend the spur, we heard another, less acute but more profound, howl; we also shuddered deeply, but the man and the beast had stayed way back; it was the wind descending, howling, through the somber valley.

Then the first shadows of night began to ascend the spur after us and, little by little, everything was becoming dark and dense like a lonely heart; like the stony heart of nature disintegrating even the last human fragment in its millennial desolation.

*   *   *

Clifton, to whose small ranch in the Baker interior we were heading, never offered to explain or point out anything. He let things explain themselves and only rarely did he intervene to teach what he knew about the lake, the animal, or the mountain that we had just left behind. I don't know if he did this because of wisdom or temperament; the point is, in that way, one learned things better and did not forget them so easily.

When we had gone over the first spur of the valley and arrived at an extensive hillside in which the dwarf oak woods began, it became so dark that we decided to spend the night.

With his cordilleran knowledge, Clifton lit a good bonfire and we began to snack on the jerky that we kept at hand.

At the moment we were preparing our respective coffee tins he suddenly said to me:

"To what do you attribute the state of that man we met in the valley?"

Clifton always spoke cutting corners, as if someone had already developed half of the conversation and nothing was left save the conclusions.

"To a disintegration produced by nature!" I responded, trying to be precise, but on realizing that it had resulted in being pedantic, I succeeded in adding, as an excuse: "Once I spent three days on some rocks and when they came by to rescue me I was almost crawling like a crab!"

"I have also experienced what you call disintegration," Clifton continued, pronouncing that word as if he were chewing an insipid piece of burlap. "Nature first 'disintegrates' you and then 'integrates' you to her as one of its elements. In the first stage it would seem that you were going to disappear, some do perish, and in the second, you are reborn with a new vigor, so that perhaps nature selects and destroys whatever suits it best. All that occurred in my youth, on an occasion in which I spent three years alone on a sheep outpost on Tierra del Fuego, near Lake Fagnano. It was something like as if I had stopped being myself. I began by losing the habit of reading; the subjects in books seemed vain, insignificant, and I preferred the murmur of a leaf to the most profound thought of Plato. Then I stopped reflecting and almost stopped thinking. I was overwhelmed. It was cruel. Then I realized that the thoughts that had left my mind were being replaced by others, and I began to revive; but by means of a fundamental transformation of those faculties. With it, things began to acquire a certain mysterious value; for example, moss was no longer for me only a dark green herb that grew on the terrestrial crust, but something with more value that accompanied me in life like my dog and my horse. From the vague terror that the nighttime shadows began to produce for me, to the joy of dawn, of which I only had a presentiment in the song of the birds, everything was there, in nature, before which I lacked eyes, feelings, a mind, to see, listen and reflect upon.

"I had to leave that place and make a supreme effort to open a book again and light within me that flame which only springs forth inside the four walls of a house. If we could only carry Civilization to Nature and Nature to Civilization! Ah, you don't know what it means to find yourself with a hot stove inside four walls in the middle of these solitudes!"

I had known Clifton since my infancy in Punta Arenas; we had worked together on a ranch in the Fueguian east, and his life was like his talk: he would suddenly take the least expected path and he himself did not know where it would stop; besides that peculiarity of speaking as if what he knew, everyone else certainly had to know. That's why I had to stop him a bit suddenly to bring him back to the topic he seemed to have forgotten.

"And the man in the valley and his strange dog?"

"Ah! What happened to old Vidal is something more than a 'disintegration'!" he continued muttering with a certain irony, a word which for me too was now becoming more and more senseless. "As for the dog, I can't explain it. There is, in the Salesian museum of Punta Arenas, a reconstituted horse that has fur just like a guanaco, it is a true 'horse-guanaco'; but it doesn't seem possible to me that there could be a cross between a seal and a dog...that one could believe produced that offspring. Just like Lake Fagnano changed even my way of thinking, it could very well be that this nature here, where it seems to have changed even God, has transformed generations of dogs until it produced that strange 'pedigree'! Speaking of this, I remember having found on an island in the Moraleda Channel a bunch of rats who jumped in the water to gather shellfish and to fish, and they hung by their tails in the trees in order to hunt birds. Their tails had developed extraordinarily and their feet were like fins. How did those rats get there? No one knows! Just like no one knows how the Yahgan Indians got to the Beagle Channel! If the latter were tossed, in a canoe as they say, from Oceania to Cape Horn, then the former certainly could have come to the inhospitable island of the Moraleda Channel in a big paraffin tin thrown from the Corcovado by some shipwrecked sailor. Besides, there are men of science who attest that the sea lion, the sea elephant, the sea leopard, the 'dungungo' or sea cow, are descendents of their congeners on land, who 'disintegrated' and 'reintegrated' to the sea. It is not strange that through that forgotten valley sea horses gallop, because more than one person has seen them in the foam of the waves. Don't forget, either, that in this land there could be anything, since more than one German expedition has gone inland past Baker in search of the plesiosaur that could still exist here."

I saw that Clifton had completely forgotten the topic of conversation and in the vast countryside of his mind innumerable paths had sprung forth upon which he seemed to joyously rush in search of others, and still others that sprang forth from an inexhaustible sprout like branches in a forest. From that forest in which he was about to submerge, I made him come out again with another shove, this time somewhat rudely.

"That's all very well," I told him, "but you have forgotten to explain to me the case of the man we met in the valley!"

"Ah! Old man Vidal...." Clifton continued, "was a man who worked many years in Patagonia, with the ambition of becoming free one day to live on his own land; but, as you well know, there is not a single piece of good land in all of the extreme south of Chile that isn't occupied by the huge livestock societies.

"Vidal heard tell of a valley found by some cypress tree cutters in the interior of Baker River, and after recognizing it, he invested his savings earned in those years of work into sheep and installations for a small ranch of eight to ten thousand animals.

"With great sacrifices he succeeded in bringing the first flock to begin the operation. Pasture was abundant. It went well for him. He brought his wife, their four children, and with six or seven ranch hands and sheepmen he formed a small colony whose houses of red roofs looked like matchboxes in the middle of the extensive valley's pasture.

"It was what is known as the 'promised land'. He took the wool by mule through the interior of Baker and from there carried it to Aysen or Comodoro Rivadavia. Among his projects was that of exploiting the cypress on the north shore of the river, to build huge flatboats with which to take out his products to the Messier Channel, through which ships cut through from the Strait of Magellan toward the Gulf of Sorrows.

"He didn't get to build his cypress flatboats. If he had constructed them, perhaps he wouldn't be there now, changed into what he is.

"What happened was that the sun reverberated like never before in these regions; to such an extent that snows from the eternal crust of the Ice Age melted.

"Vidal was returning from the Baker interior where he had gone to leave a part of his wool harvest. When he got to the edge of the valley he found the most desolate spectacle: everything had been demolished! The pasture grasses were lying flat and upon it lay thrown, here and there, the bodies of his wife, his children and some of his sheepmen and ranch hands, putrid and eaten by a flock of condors that had taken possession of the valley. The houses had been torn away from their foundations and broken up as if they really had been the matchboxes they resembled from a distance. Most of the sheep had disappeared, and the remaining ones, along with the dogs and horses, also lay there, testifying to the magnitude of the catastrophe."

Clifton revived the fire with a stick and for a while remained watching in silence the fluttering of the flames, which with their dance of light and shadows shrank and enlarged the oak woods.

"The muleteers who accompanied him saw that he immediately lost his speech," Clifton continued. "But I was able to talk with him some time later, and even though he stuttered I managed to understand clearly what he told me. Now he seems to have completely lost his language and, as you saw, even his memory, because he did not recognize me today. Whether his reason is disturbed or not, the fact is that it has been impossible to get him out of the valley, where with the remains of some sheets of zinc he constructed that rusty shack that can be seen from up above, and he lives who knows how or by what means, moving around the area like a shadow, accompanied only by that strange spaniel.

"Did this man remain stuck there by the dagger of misfortune waiting for his last days? Is it the love for his wife and children, or for his vanished ranch that has definitively lashed him to the valley?

"We know nothing about what happens to souls beaten by fatality!" Clifton went on. "Vidal's attitude doesn't surprise me, when I have seen a fisherman, in the afternoons, take food to the sea and throw it among the waves, in the same spot in which his wife was snatched away one day. Every afternoon that man waited a while before tossing the food in the water, as if he still had the hope of seeing her appear; then with a renewed illusion, he would throw the pieces of bread to the sea and empty the bowl, by spoonfuls, as if he were really placing food in his beloved's mouth."

Clifton poked the fire again and became absorbed. The reflection of the flames rose up to his green eyes like a current of ignited water, which sometimes turned dark again, dimmed by the passing of some shadow. I respected his silence, but it became so long that I was afraid he had finished his narration. Would Clifton think, in his peculiar way of being, that I understood for sure the cause of the destruction of Vidal's ranch? I couldn't stand it any longer and I interrupted his abstraction.

"And what was the cause of what happened in the old glacier bed?" I asked him.

"Ah!" Clifton exclaimed.

And as I saw that he had not completely come to, I added, "A rising of the sea, perhaps?"

"No, the sea is very far away from here."

"Don't forget," I told him, "that in Ultima Esperanza the sea pierces the Andes Cordillera clear up to the Patagonian pampa."

"Yes" he responded to me, "but the bay at Ultima Esperanza is from a very distant formation, perhaps from the same source as the one which made the Strait of Magellan cut the tail of America and cross the Andean Cordillera to the Atlantic Ocean itself. Here, the case of Baker is an insignificant fact compared to those colossal prehistoric phenomena.

"What happened in the bed of this glacier was due to a flood that, from time to time, scourges the valley. Four years or more can go by without anything happening; but on the least-expected day a wave of water rises through it and covers it with several meters of water; then it descends, and if in the rising it didn't manage to flatten everything, it does so in the subsiding, since the vertiginous current goes away with the same impetus with which it arrived at the valley's mouth, which descends almost to the same level as the river waters.

"I have explained the phenomenon observing what occurs in some tributaries on the north side of Baker. There, when the winters are bad and the summers benign, alluvions and landslides are produced, with the uprooting of gigantic trees, oaks and cypresses that clog up the gorges where those rivers run, in this way forming huge dams that on one fine day break wide open and furiously overflow, raising the water level. Since the Baker River also runs between deep gorges and cliffs, these waters are going to flood with great violence all the valleys and narrow passages that are lower than their own level.

"This was what happened with the bed of the old glacier. The tributary that runs into Baker accumulated in its vicinity, during a long time, the material for its dams; some extraordinary thaw augmented the power of the waters, and on a given day they burst, leveling everything."

"No one has again tried to occupy the valley?" I asked.

"No one," Clifton responded, and concluded: "From the Strait of Magellan to the Gulf of Sorrows, among innumerable channels and fiords, there are many beautiful meadowlands like this one, and no one knows why they are abandoned. They are lands of oblivion!"

How The Chilote Otey Died

About nine hundred men met to deliberate on the peat meseta; they were the ones who remained of the five thousand who took part in the workers' uprising in the Santa Cruz territory of Patagonia.

They left their horses hidden in a depression on the hillside and set out for the middle of the high plateau that rose up like a solitary island in the middle of a calm, smooth and gray sea. The height of its ledges, some three-hundred meters, allowed it to dominate the whole vast pampa surrounding it and, above all, the houses of the ranch, a band of red roofs, lying some five kilometers' distance toward the south. On the other hand, no human eye could have discovered the meeting of the nine hundred men on that surface covered by extensive peat bogs tinged with small spaces of pasture grass. In the distance, toward the west, only the faraway blue ranges of the Patagonian Andes could be seen, the only geographical accident that interrupted that immensity's horizon.

The nine hundred men advanced toward the center of the bog and sat down on the hillock, forming a massive human wheel, almost completely camouflaged by the peat's dark color. In the middle was a brief clearing of pampa, where the tufts of grass moved like reflections of green steel.

"Are we all here?" one of them said.

"All of us!" replied several men, looking around as if they recognized each other.

Many of them had fought together against the troops of the Tenth Cavalry, which Colonel Varela commanded; but others were seen for the first time, since they were the survivors of the massacres at Río del Perro, Cañadón Once and other liberating actions on the shores of Argentino Lake.

This lake, embedded in a pass of the Andean spine, gives origin to the Santa Cruz River which crosses the wide Patagonian steppe before flowing into the Atlantic. In remote times, a sea strait right here, like the Magellan Strait today further south, united the Pacific Ocean with the Atlantic, engraving in its bed gigantic plains and mesetas that rise from the course of the river like colossal parallel steps, up to the high pampa. In these low-lying areas on the southern bank, a horse breaker, head of the revolt, nicknamed Facón Grande because of the gaucho knife he always carried at his waist, had success with guerrilla tactics, trying to divide the three squadrons that made up the Tenth

Cavalry. In the beginning, using bolas, lassos and knives more than the precarious firearms that were available, they held back Colonel Varela's forces.

The river itself, whose current prevented swimming across it, helped Facón Grande and his cowboys, field workers and horse breakers escape many times from the professional troops by their wading across it at crossings known only by the Tehuelche Indians and themselves.

"It looks like it's going to rain!" said a tall, lanky horse breaker.

Those seated around him raised their eyes toward a cloudy sky and set their sights on a more dense storm cloud that was coming, opening a way through the others like a big black bull.

"That shower will never reach here!" said a little man with a face blue with cold and with clear, watery eyes, wrapping himself up in his white course cotton poncho.

The horse breaker turned his dark, angular face, smiling mockingly upon seeing the little man who spoke so assuredly about the destiny of a cloud.

"So, it's not going to reach us...we'll see about that!" he replied.

"I'll bet you it doesn't get here!" the man in the white poncho responded, taking the bills out of his wide belt and depositing them on the grass, under the handle of his whip.

The horseman, in turn, took his out and placed them next to the others.

At that moment, a man of medium build, agile and strong, some forty years old, got up from the ring of men and headed for the small clearing of pampa. He was dressed with the characteristic trappings of the country men: spurs, colt boots, pants folded under at the shinbone, leather jacket, handkerchief on his neck, guanaco-skin hat with earflaps for the wind, and in back, at his waist, the long knife with a silver sheath and handle.

Facón Grande put his hands in his pants pockets and lifted them, clenched inside as if he were leaning on something invisible. He reared up a little, lifting his heels and acquiring more stature with a slight rocking motion; his face, grim, looked steadily at the ground. A gust of wind passed over the meseta with more force and the tufts of grass returned his gaze with their steely reflection. The nine hundred men remained waiting, so quiet and dark, as if they were other piles of peat, a little more protruding, in the bog.

Suddenly everyone moved at once and the circle closed a bit more around its core.

"Okay," that man said, stopping the balancing and settling firmly on the ground; "we all know the situation and there's nothing left but to add to it. Tonight or at the latest tomorrow morning the Tenth Cavalry will be in the houses of the last ranch that remains in our hands. 'Mata Negra', the traitor, will have told them what the only passageway left to us is, through the Payne mountains, to get to the border. They'll be riding fresh horses, the ranchers will have given them to them; on the other hand, ours are almost exhausted and will not hold us up much longer...they will surround us, and we will all fall, like baby guanacos. The only think left is to face them from the shearing barn of the ranch, so that the rest of us can reach safety through the Payne mountains."

The circle stirred around, somewhat confused upon hearing the word "us". Who were these "us"? Was perhaps Facón Grande, one of the rebel leaders who had initiated the revolt at the Santa Cruz River, also included in those who were to escape through the Payne pass, while others shot their last cartridge in the shearing barn?

A murmur, like another freezing gust of wind, crossed through the dark ring of men.

"Let's draw lots to see who stays!" someone said.

"No, not that!" another exclaimed.

"It has to be of your own free will!" exclaimed others.

"Who are those 'us'?"—one man inquired with cold sarcasm.

Facón Grande stood up on his toes again, gaining height, then leaned forward as if he were going to take a big step into a strong wind, and raised his arms to calm the air or as if he were going to grab the reins of an invisible horse. The murmuring human wheel became quiet.

"We, those who began this thing, have to end it!", he said with a darker voice, as if it had risen from between his feet, from the piles of peat in the bog. Standing up on his toes again, he looked above those who were seated in the foreground, and added with a clearer accent, "How many of us are there left from those who were on the other side of the Santa Cruz river?"

Some forty hands raised in the air above the nine hundred heads was the response. Facón Grande himself raised his, with the invisible reins up high, now seized in his hand as if he were going to put his foot in the stirrup of his imaginary horse.

"What do you think?" said the little man in the white canvas poncho, nudging the horse breaker who was sitting at his side and who had been one of the first to raise his hand.

"There's no other way...it is good what Facón has done."

"No...I was asking about the cloud," he said, gesturing toward the sky.

"Ah!" uttered the horseman, lifting his face, too, with a cold grimace of surprise.

Both saw that the black bull began to break up, unloading like a sprinkler over the plain in the distance. The shower advanced with its illusion of little shining arrows; but upon approaching the boundaries of the meseta it completely disappeared, leaving from the dark storm cloud only a clearing among the other clouds, through which a light passed that brightly lapped the wet pampa.

"It's nice to see it rain when you don't get wet!" the horseman said, slyly.

"Yeah, it sure is!" replied the man in the white poncho, as he bent over to grab the money won in the bet.

The men began to scatter around the peat bog toward the hillside where they had hidden their horses. The westerly wind blew more fiercely through the clearing that the storm cloud had left, and that bleak denuded plateau acquired a more desolate expression under the sky.

There were no good-byes. Those who departed toward the Payne mountain range did so with lowered heads, more grieved than happy to advance toward the blue ranges where their salvation lay. Facón's forty cowboys, also somber, headed immediately toward the fulfillment of their mission.

Suddenly, from the multitude in exodus toward the Payne range a rider broke away, and at full gallop moved in pursuit of the rearguard of cowboys. Everyone, from one end to the other, turned to look at that white canvas poncho flapping in the wind, as if it were one last look of good-bye.

"Another bet?" the horse breaker asked him, jokingly, when he saw him pull up at his side.

"It's just...that..." replied the man in the poncho, doubtfully.

"Just what?"

"I took your money, and you...stay behind, protecting me..."

"You're going to need it more than me!" the horse breaker replied, annoyed.

"He had to be a Chilote!" another of the cowboys uttered coursely under his breath.

The face with clear, watery eyes shrugged, blinking his eyes, as if he had received a violent whipping.

"Here's your money!" he responded with a harsh voice, and he added: "I don't need it either!"

"A bet is a bet, friend, take it and go quickly," another exclaimed.

"What's the matter with that man?" Facón Grande said, sharply reining in his horse.

"It's the money from a bet," the horseman explained to him. "We bet on a cloud and he won. Now it seems that he wants to return it to me as if I were going to need it. Have you ever seen such a thing?"

"I haven't returned because of the money," said the man alluded to, turning toward the rebel leader. "That money thing just came out of my mouth unintentionally...I have come back here because I, too, want to fight against those of the Tenth Cavalry."

Those who listened to the conversation pretending not to be interested, suddenly turned to look at him.

"But you're not from the other side of the Santa Cruz river," Facón said to him.

"No. I was a dairyman on the Primavera Ranch when the revolt began. Later I got involved in it and here I am; I want to fight it until the end, if you allow me to."

"What do you think?" the rebel leader discussed with his men.

"If that's what he wants...let him stay," several serious voices answered.

Before becoming lost in the distance, many of those who were heading on the road toward the Payne mountains turned one more time to look: the white poncho closed ranks on the rearguard of horsemen, fluttering in the wind like a big good-bye handkerchief.

*   *   *

At nightfall the men found themselves already entrenched in the shearing barn of the ranch. They adjusted thick bundles of wool tightly in entrances and exits, with the idea that between the cracks left they could aim their weapons toward a wide firing range. On the other hand, from the outside, it would be little less than impossible to shoot a bullet between the spaces of those unbeatable trenches of pressed wool. Sentinels allowed everyone to rest a little while the night wore on.

"You've got nothing to do with this," the horse breaker said to the man in the white poncho, when they had put some sheepskins next to their common trenches in order to lie down.

"I'm already well into the 'cueca' and I have to dance it well," he replied.

"Perhaps that 'he had to be a Chilote' got to you..."

"Yes, that bothered me; but I came determined to stay with all of you...I wanted to fight, too! Why not? And by the way, tell me, why do they look down on Chilotes around here? Just because they were born on the islands of Chiloé? What's wrong with that?"

"No, it's not because of that; it's because they're so servile...and they become suspicious when they have to decide about strikes, even though later they're the first in sticking out their hands to receive what has been gained...that 'he had to be Chilote' hurt me a little, too, because I was born in Chiloé."

"Oh, yeah? Where?"

"In Tenuán...my name is Gabriel Rivera."

"I'm from Lemuy Island...Bernardo Otey, at your service."

"Being from Lemuy, how did you get so far inland? Since those from Lemuy are only seal or otter hunters."

"There aren't too many seals or sea otters left...the gringos are finishing them all off. Even if you take your chances on this side of the Gulf of Sorrows, you still don't come out ahead, and the wife and kids have to eat...that's why one sets out for these parts."

"How many children do you have?"

"Four, two boys and two little girls...because of them one doesn't get involved just like that in strikes...what would they say if they saw me return with empty hands? Sometimes you even owe the money for the boat that you have borrowed from a relative or a neighbor! And you can't go around telling all this to the whole world...that's why we are a little suspicious about strikes...doesn't the same thing happen to you? Don't you have family in Tenuán?"

"No, I don't have any family. I came to Patagonia as a child. An uncle of mine who was a sheepshearer brought me. He died soon after and I was left here alone...whenever I remember him, I think of how he confused my mind with his Patagonia," the horse breaker continued, crossing his hands underneath his neck, and adding with a nostalgic voice: "He used to play the guitar and sing sad love songs and ballads from these parts...I remember the time he told me, 'It's a good life there in Patagonia, they eat roast lamb every day..., and they ride horses as big as the hills...' 'Where is Patagonia?' I asked him one day. 'There's Patagonia!' he responded, stretching out his arm toward one side of the sky, where you could see a blue and pink fringe. From that day on Patagonia was just that for me, and I didn't escape from its talons until he brought me here. Once here, what the hell!...the horses weren't as big as the hills and that piece of sky was always running on the same side but farther away!..."

"I worked as a sheepshearer apprentice," the horse breaker continued, "from ranch hand to fence runner. Later, because I loved horses, I became a horse breaker. I have earned good money taming colts, I'm pretty free, but...aside from the whores that you go to see now and then in Río Gallegos or Santa Cruz, I don't know what a woman is for someone, nor what a child would be like...what good is the money then if one isn't going to live the way God commands? Your heart turns inside out like those piles of peat: full of roots, but so twisted and black that they are not capable of producing one single blade of green grass...it's probably for that reason that you don't have much attachment to this life either, and so you plan things as if they weren't worth anything...it's all the same whether you end it under the back of a wild animal or in a scuffle like this one we find ourselves in. On the other hand, you should grab your horse and beat it for the Payne mountains...in Lemuy a woman and children will be waiting for you."

"Not any more, now! You want me to tell you something? I'm ashamed that no one from the group that cut out for Payne stayed behind!"

"A lot of them wanted to stay, but Facón convinced them that they should go. The fewer that fall, the better, he told them, and I think he's right. Ah! How we would have beaten the Tenth Cavalry and all the rest if it weren't for that traitor 'Mata Negra'!"

"I wonder why he started all this?"

"Hah!...who knows! The fuse was lit in the Huaraique Hotel, near the Pelque River...the troops attacked without any risk and assassinated all of our companions who were there...then we were annoyed, and with Facón Grande all of us from the open country began to fight, campañistas, horse breakers, cowboys and some sheepmen who were good with horses...we were winning when 'Mata Negra's's betrayal occurred, that son of a...he turned around and placed himself at the service of the ranch owners."

"All that is pretty well known," Otey said, with a quiet voice among the shadows, "but I wonder why the hell they don't settle things before the shooting begins, because afterwards no one settles them."

"Who knows!...well, some say it's the crisis that the Great War brought...it seems that the ranchers earned a lot of money with the war, but they wasted it, and now that bad luck hits, they make us pay for it...and everything was because of the petition...we were asking for a hundred pesos a month for the ranch hands and a hundred and twenty for the sheepmen...I wasn't even involved in the stoppage because horse breaking is done by contract...they were also asking for candles and maté for the outpost keepers, mattresses instead of sheepskins in the bunkhouses and that they would permit us more than one horse in our private stock...but it seems that there were still other things...in Coyle, men with several years' salary still unpaid and who had asked for the money retained from their guanaco hunting, were shot and the administrator stuffed away that money. Still others were paid by check with no funding and they got stuck turning circles in the cities. Colonel Varela realized all of this and at first was on our side; but the big shots made demands from their government, and in the newspapers they goaded the colonel telling him that he was incompetent and even a coward. Then the man had a grudge and asked for a free hand to suffocate the movement; they gave it to him, he returned to Patagonia and began the battle," the horse breaker said, ending his version of the strike.

With the first lights of dawn some beef jerky was passed around and, by turns, the men went to the machine shed on whose stove some had boiled water in a kettle for the maté. Above, in the attic for the wool baler, watching the horizon, a cowboy was singing a faraway "Vidalitá" in a low voice:

> More than a year away, vidalitá...
> I was from this land.
> Today when I found you, vidalitá...
> you had already spurned me.
> And that is what I call, vidalitá...
> being an unhappy man.

The tune was suddenly interrupted by a warning call from the other side of the roof that announced the arrival of the Tenth Cavalry troops to the trail leading to the ranch buildings.

Everyone ran to their posts, while two squadrons of cavalry, each with about one hundred men, dismounted in the distance, taking positions in a line of sharpshooters.

No sooner had morning broken when the first shots were heard from one side to the other. A machine gun began to stutter its bursts, destroying the glass in the windows and the troops from the open countryside began to close in around the shearing barn.

With an isolated shot one of the cowboys clearly knocked down the first cavalry soldier; while he was preparing his rifle to shoot another one, he uttered in a loud voice the well-known popular verse with which cards are dealt in the game called "truco":

> Coming from the corrals
> with flat-nosed Salvador,
> ay! Son of the great seven,
> there goes another petal from my flower!

Among bursts from machine guns, fire from rifles and long moments of very tense silence, the duel continued all that morning without any major ups or downs. Several soldiers had fallen already, without a single bullet having succeeded in getting through the subtle cracks of the thick wool bundles, behind which the cowboys were entrenched after having closed the big doors of the shearing barn, an enormous building of wood and zinc constructed in the shape of a "T" and surrounded only by holding corrals, cattle chutes and drying areas for the sheep baths, all made of posts and planks.

Both sides soon realized that the other was difficult to defeat. The one band, inside the barn, well entrenched behind the bales; and the others, professional soldiers, advanced slowly but inexorably in the line of marksmen, with technical experience in taking advantage of the terrain. Their objective was to reach the wooden corrals to better protect themselves in the attack but those inside knew their intent well and made them pay very dearly every time someone ventured to run from the open to reach that refuge. That person would fall, fatally knocked down by a bullet, and his audacity only served as a serious warning to the others.

Facón Grande had given the order not to shoot except when completely sure of the target, with the object of saving bullets, causing the biggest number of casualties and carrying their resistance to its maximum so that the fugitives had time to reach at least the foothills of the Payne mountains, where they would be completely safe. Another night fell with its own bale of shadows, placing it between the two bands of men. Both took advantage of it to cautiously take a breather, and with the dawn they renewed their stubborn duel.

Something unusual occurred on this second day: one of the soldiers, possibly maddened by the nervous tension of the prolonged standoff, rushed forward in attack, alone, with a fixed bayonet. Those in the barn didn't shoot him, but rather curiously opened the big doors and let him in; then they hurled his body through a window so that no one else would want to do the same thing.

But the tactic gave Colonel Varela a hint: those who were surrounded had few bullets, but they weren't yet completely out of them. It was what he had foreseen and he awaited anxiously to give the order of attack that would put an end to that obstinate duel in which now a third of his squadron had fallen.

The bugle call was heard like a shrill whinnying, giving the signal that the hour had arrived. The machine guns hurled their bursts protecting the final advance. Those who were inside didn't have a single bullet and other than their gaucho knives and skinning knives had no weapons to face that last charge. In heroic hand-to-hand combat, the death of rebel leader Facón Grande put an end to the prolonged action when there were still twenty cowboys alive, since very few had fallen in the shooting and the majority had died only in the final attack.

That same afternoon the rest were shot on the cement in the drying area of the sheep bath. They brought them out in groups of five, and Varela himself ordered not to use more than one bullet per prisoner, since their ammunition was also just about exhausted.

Gabriel Rivera, the horse breaker, and Bernardo Otey, with three other men, were the last to be led out in front of the firing squad.

It was halfway through the afternoon, but a low, overcast sky had transformed the day into an interminable dawn, ashen and cold. Upon moving toward the stone slab of the drying area, they saw the pile of their companions' bodies ready to receive the sprinkling of kerosene to burn them, the best grave that Varela had prescribed for his victims, while not leaving them for the recreation of foxes and buzzards. Among those bodies Facón's stood out, which the Colonel had ordered placed on top so that he could see it with his own eyes, since he had been the only rebel leader that would have finished him and his whole regiment off if "Mata Negra's" treachery hadn't intervened.

An intense cold forewarned a snowstorm. When the last five were placed in front of the firing squad that was to shoot one bullet into each one of their chests, the sergeant who was in command approached and began to attach, with pins, right in the area of the heart, a circle of white cardboard so that the soldiers could set their sights.

Once he did this, he stepped aside and from an equidistant place he unsheathed his curved sabre and placed it horizontally at the height of his head. He was going to lower the sword giving the signal to fire when Bernardo Otey slapped his heart, ripped off the white circle, and hurling it into the faces of the fusileers, shouted: "Learn to shoot, shitheads!"

The troop had a confused reaction. But at once they aimed the five rifle barrels toward one body, that of Bernardo Otey, who fell doubled over, mowed down by the five bullets that—like one—answered back his last curse.

But in that same instant, taking advantage of the fusileers' reaction, the other four men jumped and began to run while the firing squad prepared to load their rifles again with a bullet in the muzzle.

"After them!" the sergeant yelled, on seeing that while three of them ran along the trail, another, the horse breaker, took a great leap over a barbed-wire fence, fell astride one of the troop's horses, and shot off toward open country, hugging the animal's neck.

At first the sergeant shot his revolver a few times; but then he took one of the soldier's rifles and, kneeling in a firing position, continued firing at the horse and its rider stretched out on its back as they ran swiftly until a ravine swallowed them up.

The other three fugitives, on foot, were very shortly cut down by bullets, falling once and for all on the trail.

The unending dawn thickened its ash even more and a dense snow began to fall on the countryside, finally hiding the fugitive with its thick wings.

Well into the night, Rivera the horse breaker succeeded in giving his horse a rest. When he dismounted, both horse and man remained accompanying each other for a while in the middle of the storm clouds and the night. The shadows, in spite of everything, opened up their heart a bit with the light glitter of falling snowflakes.

His own heart breathed a sigh of relief, too, taking advantage of that dark atmosphere, and the recollection of an Indian superstition turned up in his memory: the eagle of the pampas must be hunted before it succeeds in screaming out, and if it does so, the storm will come to his aid...no sooner had he remembered it than he mounted up again and continued galloping on the wings of his guardian.

In one of those radiant daybreaks that follow big snowfalls, the horse breaker caught up with the mass of strikers when they had already found refuge on one of the wooded slopes of the Payne mountains, all of them safe and sound. Upon encountering them, the horse stopped by itself and the human wheel, as on the peat meseta, reunited around the horseman as around its axle.

The animal had stopped with all four hoofs spread wide, when a thin line of blood trickled from its nostrils and lips. It shivered upon noticing it and was then seized by a strange trembling.

Like a good breaker, Rivera knew that a horse that has been ridden to death does not obey either spurs or whip, but neither does it fall as long as it feels the rider on top. For that reason his account was very brief, and on finishing it, he got off the horse at the same time that the noble beast collapsed.

With the snow, all of Patagonia seemed to be a big white poncho that ascended the foothills of the Payne mountains up to the high towers that, like three colossal fingers, pointed somberly to the sky.

And in this way the memory of how the Chilote Otey died was conserved.

Submerged Iceberg

From out of the cabin on the pier a man in gray overalls approached and said, "Do you want to go to work on Navarino?"

"Navarino?" I replied, trying to remember.

"Yes, Navarino!" he told me. "The big island lying south of the Beagle Channel. They need someone there who can do a little bit of everything."

The proposition caught me on one of those days when one could set sail for anywhere, and in a moment in which I was wandering around the jetties as if I were detached from myself, like those remnants of clouds that remain floating above the earth after some storm and fly away with the first wind that comes along.

Something like a storm had also occurred in me: a storm of what still lingered in my mind, the image of a woman; and in my heart, drops of parceled-out shadow moved from time to time through my blood.

However, when I signed the contract, I didn't feel the joy of other times when I set my life on something. Being free and unemployed, perhaps I lost something upon abandoning that limbo of idleness and entered, not fully awake, into that dark purpose that made me accept the Navarino offer.

The pier at Punta Arenas, carpeted with snow, penetrated the sea and the night like a white shadow. At its side the steaming coastguard vessel "Micalvi" only awaited, in order to set sail, the loading of an expedition of gold prospectors who were going to Lenox and Picton Islands. The squeaking of the winches slackening the slings was mixed with the men's voices, among which were apparent several drunks who, wiser than I, moved from one life to another with an alcoholic lurching.

Three individuals directed the loading of machinery and supplies, and their brilliant leather clothing and the difficulty with which they arranged the gear revealed their inexperience as city men, hardly accustomed to that type of task. Their voices were high pitched, nervous and hurried, and from the thirty or so workers more than one curse slipped out under their breath upon seeing the uncertainty and hesitation of those bosses.

The sailors contemplated the noisy loading of the gold prospectors with a certain indifference, and more than one smiled upon remembering other expeditions that they had seen depart with as many hopes as this one, but much better organized, only to return later, decimated, poor, eaten up by hunger, mutiny and greed because of the possession of that metal.

At nine o'clock the ship blew its third regulatory whistle, put out the cable-laid ropes and moved slowly away from the pier while it put about its anchors and set a course for the southwest. The city was soon disappearing like a crown of jewels on the banks of the Strait.

There were on board, besides the rowdy gold hunters who never stopped arranging their equipment, settlers from the islands and woodcutters that the boat would be leaving in the most remote and solitary coves.

I leaned on a railing in one corner of the deck and began to whistle a melody that often brings to my mind pleasant memories, sensations, and colors, things like Bengal lights lit on Christmas nights in a distant infancy.

The boat moved on like a heavy lead monster, opening up a white wound in the sea and a fading halo in the night; the monotonous puffing and blowing of its machinery marked time with my song and so, united, it seemed that we were sinking together into those dark elements.

Around midnight, sleep's raven wing began to graze me. I had probably done nothing except wait for it on deck to avoid being awake in the unpleasant third class area. I didn't let it pass by, and I slid in between decks.

Third class is the same everywhere, on land as on the sea, and those of us who pertain to it are also the same. We all form a kind of borderline humanity; which is like the earth's crust, the exterior part jutting out, receiving the chafing of rough weather on the surface, the vapor of the stars, while the dark ball rolls and rolls in order to sustain itself in the night of abysses.

The "Micalvi's" third class confirmed the rule. Set up in the upper part of the prow's hold, it looked like a jail cell with its steel cots mounted one on top of the other; maybe this resemblance brought to mind the lesson that a prisoner once taught me: I put the straw mattress over my body like a blanket instead of using it like a mattress, and I lay down to sleep.

We found ourselves at dawn the next day in the channels that descend until they connect with the northwest arm of the Beagle Channel. The atmosphere was one of the clearest I have seen in my life. The hills we sailed between resembled herds of sea monsters cast upon the waters, with white backs smoothed by the wind's comb. The channel broke open and through the gap came the Pacific Ocean with its silly waters, which passed by rocking the ship from port to starboard, only to go and burst in a flowering of foam among the cliffs on the shore.

The gold prospectors sauntered through the castle, more tranquil and silent. Some rich settlers, with their wives and children, took turns at the bridge with the officer of the watch.

On the gangways, anonymous, dark people; I slipped in among them when the glare of light passed by me, and I went to lean on the stern near a group of four people. Among them a giant of a man stood out, with a broad head, whose eyes and lips could not be distinguished, for they were lost among a thicket of hair. According to what I found out later, he was one of the richest ranchers of the Beagle area, a Yugoslav who preferred the company of ordinary workers to that of the ship's officers.

The group remained in a position of conversation, but statically, in silence. After a long while, the huge Yugoslav raised an arm with the weight of a crane, pointed out the rocks that lay off in the distance, and said with an extremely rough voice, "I spent eight days on that rock one time!"

His voice was thunder, but he had a lisping accent and his pronunciation prolonged the s's and converted them into "ch's" like the unformed language of a very young child. All of which gave a more strange than comical impression.

"I almost died; I ate twenty raw beans a day!" he continued. "Up in there are Indians, but not a single one appeared!"

And he didn't say another thing. The group didn't make a single comment, stopped looking at the rocks and everyone returned to their static position.

Contrasting with this sobriety, a man of medium build, dark and thin, was shouting on the bridge, arguing with an officer.

"Puorco, madonna!" he shouted, with a mixture of Italian and Spanish. "A vosotro que interesare, pasaje, cobra chipe! Io me arregla solo, io no mas soportare tuto lo que viniere! Puorco, madonna!"

The officer maintained an unflappable calm, while the man who was speaking gesticulated as if he were going to attack him. This guy was a well-known seal hunter, Pascualini, of Neapolitan origin, famous in the region for his excursions and above all for having abducted Radowisky, the anarchist who "liquidated" Colonel Falcón in Buenos Aires, from the Ushuaia prison. He was protesting because they wouldn't agree to put him ashore right where we were traveling.

But he convinced the officer and the ship slowed down. With the engines in neutral, Pascualini lowered his boat that wasn't any more than four meters long, loaded in a sack of provisions and fastened one of the oars on the middle bench in the fashion of a mainmast. He raised as a sail a blanket tied to a spar made of a large broom handle, fixed the other oar as a rudder, sat down next to it and with a stentorian "adio" he shoved off and set his course, pushed by the southwest breeze.

"This guy is a bum of the seas!" said one of those on board. "He lives for a while among the Indians and then on any given day appears when a ship passes by, makes it stop like he just did and loads up his harvest of sea otter and seal skins."

Through three days of navigating, the "Micalvi" scattered its cargo in different areas. The gold prospectors stayed in Lenox and I was the last one to disembark, in Port Robalo, when the boat had almost completed its trip around Navarino Island.

Port Robalo is at the foot of a mountain range that almost drops straight into the sea; so the little valley that runs along the coast seems to be a haven for dwarfs in a land of cyclops. The Beagle, close to flowing into the Atlantic, forms a curious current there due to some pushing up of the rocks; the waters crisscross, forming a strange weft and they flee, forming dizzying swirls in the most intense moments of the tides.

Harberton was waiting for me there, a tall old man with a face that was dark and creased like oak bark. He wore a thick black cloth jacket, turned lichen-colored green by time; a similar hat, with raised brims, gave him the appearance of a Protestant pastor.

"Good morning!" he said to me in a harsh tone and in such a way as if we had always been together.

He led me to his house, which lay next to an oak grove and which was made with thick split tree trunks and roofed with zinc. Inside I encountered a young Indian woman and four children.

My work consisted of helping in the care of two thousand sheep, in the corralling of some cattle, in the yoking of a pair of oxen from time to time, in the tossing and retrieving of the fishing net when there was a necessity to provide the kitchen with fish, and in some other chores.

The work was very easy and I realized that my presence was almost too much, because Harberton did almost everything himself, almost leisurely.

On the other hand, I was quickly changing my opinion with respect to the place. There was plenty of spare time, and the work was done with the pleasure of a game. I milked cows, chopped wood in the forest, walked difficult areas in search of cattle and in the mornings when I gathered in the net I loved to see shiny snook jump into the bottom of the boat, like dozens of severed arms.

Everything went very well in that idyllic retreat, at first...

I say at first, because at the end of only two or three weeks I began to notice the strange influence that little by little carried me to desperation.

Harberton did not speak. After having given me instructions, shown me the roads and divided up the tasks, he remained completely silent.

His wife and children seemed to be accustomed to this silence; but for me, the presence of this silent man was little by little doing me harm.

He got up at dawn, put some meat or smoked fish and some bread and onions in his knapsack, and headed for the mountain from where he returned at nightfall.

On one occasion when a snowstorm let loose and he didn't return to the ranch all night long, I left the next morning to search the countryside for him, thinking that some misfortune could have happened to him. I found him on one of the highest peaks, protected by a natural cave formed in the rock; he was smoking his "octoroon" pipe and was contemplating the surrounding nature, his eyes staring off in the distance: the Beagle moved along down below, like a green path flowered with foam; it was the only thing different, everything else was completely white. The last spurs of the Andes that ended with Tierra del Fuego crossed like split moons, and Navarino Island itself resembled the beginning of another white, alien world.

The Indian woman didn't speak, either. After her domestic toiling she stayed in a corner, squatting, with a child among her skirts. The oldest of those was about eleven years old and was the son of Harberton's first wife, the other two from the second and the fourth one, from the third. The two former wives, also Yahgan Indians, had died fulfilling the destiny that pursues the women of that race when they become a white man's woman.

I took refuge in the children. I made them a big chalkboard and with a piece of dirt similar to chalk I taught them to read and write. I often taught them in front of some windmills that I made for them in the shape of airplanes, whose engaged propellers produced a sound similar to that of motors. I had them practice simple gymnastic exercises, jogging and games, until little by little I established with them a small social group, healthy and happy, which somewhat softened that rough monotony.

"Papa never talks!" the oldest boy told me one day.

"Yes, he does," I responded, "he talks to the trees, with the clouds and to the stones!"

The boy began to laugh and I couldn't help but do the same, although I would have willingly done the opposite.

"Why is this man like that?" I asked myself time and again with more and more insistence. It wasn't a curiosity to know what that individual was locking in, which perhaps was nothing more than stupidity or the exhaustion of just being old; nor was it self-love or a wounded sensibility but simply the desire to speak with a rational being. And the only one there was he and he denied me that precious gift!

One day I put an end to my obsession with this decision: "This man is not in his right mind," I told myself, "he is crazy with loneliness, with silence, with who knows what, and if I stay here I'm going to become as crazy as he is; so I am leaving with the first boat that departs!"

But not even a wretched Indian canoe arrived in Port Robalo. Only the coastguard vessel of the Chilean navy reached port as part of its duty every three or four months, and on this occasion five months had gone by without its stopping.

Luck, which gives something good to some and something bad to others, would have it that a schooner damaged in a storm passed by one afternoon to lie out the storm in the cove at Port Robalo. It was headed for Ushuaia and the Wulaia radio station found out that the vessel announced its passing by the island for the next Monday and it was already Friday.

I communicated to Harberton my decision to leave, and on Sunday night, by the light of a paraffin lamp, he presented me a correct settlement of my salary.

That night I said good-bye to the inhabitants and went to bed thinking that the next day I would happily abandon that land of destroyed mountains sunk in the sea, and above all the presence of that strange man, submerged in his silence like an iceberg that only shows a seventh of its great size, as rough and rocky as the nature surrounding it.

When dawn turned the cracks blue in the windows of my room, I tried to get up; but I found myself strongly lashed to the wood of the cot. In the depths of my sleep someone had secretly slipped in those cords that bound me like an Indian child on his carrycot.

I struggled as much as I could, I called and shouted with no result whatsoever. I remained there that way, alternating moments of bestial rage with resigned appeasement, of defeat; but my misfortune reached its climax when halfway through the morning I suddenly heard the shrill whistle of the vessel that announced its arrival to the port.

Only once in my life had I felt a similar desperation: I was sixteen when the treachery of an older brother had them lock me up in my room while I listened to the whistle of the ship that was going to weigh anchor. Ever since, when I hear those three regulatory whistles that the ship's siren sends out, I can't ever stop from trembling a little!

In a moment I heard some voices in the next room, steps and sounds of arguing and weeping. Suddenly a child's shout stood out among the confusion of noise, and the oldest boy, Dino, rushed into my room with a knife in his hand. He had realized my situation and was coming to help me, in spite of his mother's efforts to stop him.

"My hands first, Dino!" I shouted at him when I saw that in his haste he wanted to begin with the elastic cords that bound my feet.

In an instant I was free. I embraced my savior, grabbed my few belongings, and left, running; on passing I could see the frightened face of the Yahgan woman.

I ran down the slope to the beach like a madman, waving my arms so that the boat wouldn't leave me. Luckily, the lifeboat was just then being lowered from the davit.

In my haste I hadn't noticed that Harberton was on the beach waiting for it.

When he saw me arrive he approached me and with a tone in his voice and a look on his face that I will never forget, he said to me:

"Don't go! Stay! I'm going to die soon, and the children, and her, they're just a bunch of little animals, they won't know what to do! Someone will steal the place, become owner of this and will chase them away from here! Forgive me for what I have done, but I didn't want you to go! You can own all of this and take care of them like you have done until now! I didn't know what to say to you, I wanted to test you some more! For many years I have looked for a man like you! Don't go, I'll make you master of it all! Find one of my wife's cousins for a mate and stay!"

His voice was upset and I had the impression of hearing it for the first time. He was exhausted from speaking; his lips were trembling as in a prayer, and the look...ah! I will never be able to forget that pleading look...!

I began to hesitate, like so many times in my life. I looked at his face, rough like oak bark; I remembered his sordid silence, I looked at the stone by where some trees were leaning, curved by the wind, like begging hands. I looked at the steaming boat, at the whaling launch that was making its way to the beach and, just like every other time in which I have found myself undecided, I decided to go with where my heart was at that moment; this time, it was with the awaiting boat...

When I descended, on my return, to the fiscal pier at Punta Arenas, that little man in the gray overalls whose proposition had thrust me into such a strange trip came out of the cabin again.

I thought he was going to ask me the same question again: do you want to go to work on Navarino? when I saw him heading directly toward me; but no, with his rabbit-like face laughing, he said to me:

"You couldn't stand it any more?"

"I couldn't stand it any more!" I responded.

"Just like everybody else!" he replied. "No one let the cutter pass by more than once!" and he walked away, laughing senselessly.

"Yes," I told myself, looking at him, I don't really know if with scorn or rage, "the same as everyone else; but no one but me saw what the iceberg was hiding beneath the waters! No one glimpsed the tenderness of that submerged nature! One day I must return—perhaps—to Port Robalo! I'll be rich; I'll change the silence of the old master into joyful noise; I'll even enjoy the young widow; with the children, now youths, we'll rig out a thin cutter and we'll go around the islands harpooning seals Yahgan Indian style!

But I have not returned yet.

The Bottle of Caña

Two riders, like two black dots, begin to penetrate the solitude and the whiteness of the snow-covered plains. Their paths converge, and while they approach, their silhouettes begin to stand out with that slight uneasiness always produced by the encounter with another traveler on a solitary trail.

Little by little the horsemen draw nearer. One of them is a burly man dressed in a long black leather jacket, riding a solid chestnut horse, resistant to the hard roads of Tierra del Fuego. The other man, slightly built, is wrapped up in a coarse white cotton poncho, with a handkerchief at his neck, and riding a sorrel, pulling behind him a small shaggy chestnut which seemed to be lost under bundles of fox pelts.

"Good afternoon!"

"Good afternoon!" they greet each other as their horses join together.

The man in the leather jacket has a white face, pock-marked and unwashed, like some posts exposed to rough weather. The one with the poncho, a tender, rosy face whose red and humid eyes blinked as if they had been crying.

"How was the fox hunting?" asks the post-faced man, his voice trailing off as he quickly glances toward the pack horse carrying the furs.

"Just average," the hunter answers, looking candidly into the eyes of his companion who, always out of the corner of his eye, glances at him for an instant.

They continued on without speaking, side by side. The solitude of the pampa is such that the sky, grey and low, seems to have hugged the land so tightly that it has displaced every trace of life in it and has left alone—and more alive—that lethal silence, which now is pierced only by the crunching of the horses' hoofs on the snow.

After a short while the fox hunter coughs nervously. "Care for a swig?" he says, taking a bottle out of his woven wool saddlebag.

"Is it caña?"

"The best!" the young man replies, passing him the bottle.

He opens it and the liquid gurgles as he slowly drinks. The young man lifts it up upon his turn, with a certain satisfaction showing how much he likes the drink, and they continue on their way, again in silence.

"Not a bit of wind," the hunter suddenly says, after coughing nervously, attempting to strike up a conversation.

"Uh...huh...," the man in the jacket utters, as if he had been annoyed.

The hunter looks at him more with sadness than unpleasantness, and realizing that that man seems to be lost in some thought and doesn't want to be interrupted, he lets him be and just continues on, silently, by his side, trying to find a thought of his own in which to withdraw.

They travel together on the same road; but even more together than they, go the horses, who mark the rhythm of their strides, the chestnut glancing over every now and then at the sorrel who returns the glance, and even the pack horse trots along quickly to catch up to his companions when he falls behind.

Soon the hunter finds the entertainment with which his imagination has enjoyed itself for two years now. This time the sips of caña give the landscape more life than his mind usually does; he sees an island, emerald green, there at the tip of the Chiloé archipelago, and in the midst of it the white apron of Elvira, his fiancée, whose movement between the ocean and the woods, up and down, is like the wing of a seagull or the foam of a wave. How many times this dream made him forget the foxes themselves, while he galloped over the area where he set his traps! How many times, seized by a strange restlessness, did he mount his horses and ascend the hills and mountains, because the higher he went the closer he felt to that beloved place.

The caña arouses things of a much different nature in the imagination of the other man. A recollection, like a stubborn blowfly which cannot be frightened away, begins to haunt the mind of that man, and along with that recollection, an agonizing idea also begins to drive him, like a sudden frenzy, toward an abyss. He had promised himself never to drink again, as much for one reason as for another, but it is so cold, and the invitation was so unexpected that he fell into it again.

The tormenting recollection dates from more than five years ago. The very years in which he should have been in jail had the police discovered the author of the crime against Bevan the Austrian, the gold merchant who was coming from the Páramo and who was murdered on this very same road, right near the patch of black shrubs that they had just passed.

Strange thing! The anguish from the first wave of recollections was slowly giving way to a kind of imaginative amusement, like that of the hunter. It wasn't necessary—he thinks—to have much ability to commit the perfect crime in those solitary, remote places. The police, more because of procedure than zeal, searched for a while and then stopped investigating. A man vanishes? So many disappear! Some do not wish anyone to know when they depart, what roads they'll take, when or where they arrive. With others, something is known simply because springtime uncovers their bodies from under the ice!

The nervous cough of the fox hunter again interrupts the silence.

"Another drink?" he offers, taking out the bottle. The man in the leather jacket moves as if he realizes for the first time that someone is traveling at his side. The hunter hands him the bottle, as his eyes blink with their characteristic tic.

The other man opens the bottle, drinks, and this time returns it without even saying thanks. A shadow of uneasiness, sadness or confusion again crosses the face of the young man, who drinks upon his turn, leaving the bottle half-finished.

The strides of the horses continue crunching monotonously on the snow, as each man, riding side by side, continues with his own thoughts.

"With this last hunt I'll have the money necessary to leave Tierra del Fuego," the hunter thinks. "At the end of this season, I'll return to my island and marry Elvira." On arriving at this point in his habitual dream, he half-way closes his eyes, happy, absolutely happy, because behind that wall of happiness there was nothing else for him.

The other man had no wall of happiness; but there was a sick kind of pleasure, and like one who settles into the saddle to undertake a long journey, he settles into his imagination beginning with the now-distant moment in which he began the crime.

It is more or less in that same place where he came across Bevan; but the circumstances were different.

At the outpost in Cerro Redondo he found out that the gold purchaser was going to cross from the Páramo, on the Atlantic coast, to Río del Oro, on the Pacific side, where he would take the boat across to Punta Arenas.

In San Sebastián he found out the date of departure of the boat, and calculating the speed of travel of a good horse, he posted himself beforehand in the spot by which the buyer would have to pass.

It was the first time he was going to commit that kind of act and he found strange the certainty with which he made his decision, as if it merely dealt with something like cutting daisies in the country, and even more strange was the serenity with which he planned it all.

However, a slight discomfort, something frozen, troubled him at times for a few moments, but this he attributed somewhat to the fact that he did not know with whom he had to deal. A gold buyer couldn't be just any bird if he ventured out alone through that region. But at the same time something told him that that uneasiness, that "something frozen", came to him from deeper inside. Nonetheless, he didn't think he was a coward nor slow with his hands; he had already proven it in Policarpo, when because of some marked cards he had a shoot-out with several men, and definitely turned one of them around.

Of course this was not a question of a dispute. It was a little different killing a man in cold blood to take away whatever he carried, than to do the same thing playing "monte".

But what the hell was he going to do! The season that year in Tierra del Fuego had been very bad. It was slightly less than impossible to sneak contraband booze into a ranch. And the people didn't crowd around him when, deck of cards in hand, he invited them with a loud cordiality: "Let's play a little game, boys, just for fun." Besides, many of these folks were those who had already lost a year or more worth of sweat in the "little game", and it became more difficult all the time to pass through the places where more than one hot-headed victim had been stopped by the barrel of his Colt.

Tierra del Fuego was yielding no more to him, and the Bevan "business" was a good excuse to change residences and move to the other side of the Strait, to Patagonia.

"Bah!" he said to himself, the morning he stationed himself to wait for the gold buyer, to calm that frozen something which continued to surface now and then from somewhere inside of him. "If he had played 'monte' with me, I would have taken his last gram of gold; and in the end everything would have turned out the same, in a showdown in which only the liveliest would come out a winner."

When he stretched out along the edge of a gently rolling hill to watch for the arrival of the gold merchant, a flock of great bustards took off like a piece of the pampa coming loose and passed over his head, disintegrating in a triangular formation. He contemplated them, surprised, as if he saw something of himself leaving that land; it was a migratory flock which directed its flight in search of northern Patagonia. The same thing happened every year: in the middle of autumn all those birds abandoned Tierra del Fuego and only he and his horses remained stuck there. But now he, too, would fly away, like the bustards, in search of other skies, other lands, and who knows if not another life...

He never saw the pasture grass like he did that afternoon! The pampa seemed to be a sea of yellow gold, rippled by the western breeze. He had never before realized such a live presence of nature! Suddenly, in the middle of all that immensity, he really became aware of himself for the first time, as if he had suddenly found another being within him. This time, that inner cold surged forth more intensely and made him tremble. He was at the point of getting up, mounting his horse and fleeing that place at a full gallop; but he reached back, took out a flat canteen, unscrewed the aluminum cap and took a swig of the caña with which he was accustomed to chasing away the cold that came to him from within.

At mid-afternoon a black point which slowly became clearer, appeared on the far horizon. He immediately dragged himself down toward lower ground, untied the hobbles of the horse, mounted and took off pell-mell, like any traveler. Hiding himself behind the hill, he guided his mount in such a way that he could take the trail along which the other rider was coming, long before the latter would approach.

He continued on the trail with that stride which travelers take when they are in no real hurry to arrive. He turned around once to look, and by the way in which the rider had cut the distance he noticed that he was riding a good, big trotting horse and he was leading a pack horse, alternating riding them from time to time.

He took out the canteen again, took another slug of caña and felt more firm in the stirrups.

"If he passes me up with that trot," he thought, "It will be easier to nail him from behind. If he stops and we continue together on the road, it will be more difficult."

The horse was the first to perceive the trotting that was approaching; it cocked its ears, then moved them like two frightened birds. Then the man also felt the muffled beating of hoofs of the horses on the pampa; it was a dull pounding that came to reverberate strangely on his heart. The frozen wave surged forth again, and it made him tremble. It suddenly seemed as if the one being attacked was him, and without being able to contain himself he turned his head around to look. A huge man, on in years, was advancing with the rhythmic English trot, on a black horse soaked with sweat and foam; at his side trotted a dark brown sorrel, for relief. He noticed a harmonic corpulence between the man and his beasts, and for a moment he became frightened before the vigorous presence of the man who was pulling up.

Now on top of him, the horses stopped suddenly with a jerk of the reins, to his left. In spite of the fact that he had left room for him to pass on his right, the gold buyer prudently banked toward the other side.

He seemed to him to be more of a vagabond of the trails than a businessman dealing in gold. Basque beret, black kerchief at his neck, an ample leather smock, wide, loose-fitting pants and riding boots above whose short legs appeared course white wool socks. This outfit, old, shabby and wrinkled, harmonized with his long, tired, half-shaven face; however, in a quick glance he perceived a penetrating shine in his eyes and a sidelong glance revealed a hidden, controlled energy, which could vigorously mobilize, in an instant, like a spring, all of that enervated corpulence.

"Good afternoon!" he said, placing himself astride the other horse.

"'Afternoon," he answered him.

"Going to San Sebastián?"

"No, toward China Creek!"

He would never forget the accent with which he interwove this dialogue, since even the sound of his own voice seemed strange to him. He felt the man looking him up and down, trying to make eye contact; but he did not acquiesce, and so they continued in that way, silent, one beside the other, with the strides of their mounts muffled by the pampa grass.

Suddenly, with a certain wary slowness, he slid his hand toward his back pocket. He realized that the gold merchant perceived the movement out of the corner of his eye, and, in turn, with surprising rapidity and naturalness, he also put his left hand in the opening of his leather smock. The two movements were made almost in unison. But he took out the canteen of caña from his back pocket...and opening it up, he offered some to him.

"No, I don't drink, thanks," he answered him, taking out slowly, on his turn, a big red handkerchief with which he loudly blew his nose.

They remained awhile in suspense. The drink of caña made him recuperate the calmness lost in that instant of emotion; but no sooner had it been restored when the merchant, without taking his eyes off of him for a second, spurred on his horse and taking off with a rapid swerve to the left, shouted:

"See you!"

"See you," he answered him; but at the same time a violent blow of anguish took hold of his whole being and he saw the body of his victim, his clothing, his face, his very horses, all together, darkly, like the entrance of an abyss, like the pull of vertigo that desperately attracted him, and not being able to contain himself, almost without moving the hand which he held at his side, he took out the revolver that he carried between his belt and his stomach and fired almost at point-blank range, and he reached his victim right at the curve in the road.

With the force of the shot it took, the body of the gold merchant leaned to the left and fell heavily to the ground, while his horses took off, terrified, across the countryside.

He stopped his horse. He closed his eyes so that he wouldn't see his victim lying on the ground, and he sunk into a kind of stupor, from which he came back out with a profound sigh of relief, as if he had just crossed the threshold of an abyss or just ended the most exhausting journey of his life.

He opened his eyes again when his horse wanted to rear up at the sight of the cadaver, so he dismounted, calmer now.

The gold merchant's eyes had remained half-way rolled, as if they had been stopped at the beginning of their revolution.

The emotion exhausted him; but after such intense dizziness, he fell into a kind of laxness, in the middle of which, more sensible than ever, he was beginning to understand that "frozen something from within". He shivered, looked at the sky and it seemed to him that he saw in it an immense blue and white fissure, just like the one in Bevan's faded eyes.

From the sky he turned his glance to the stiff body, and without realizing what he was going to do, he came close, took hold of it, raised it up like a bundle, and as he was about to place it on his horse's saddle, the horse jumped and fled like a runaway across the plains, leaving him with the body in his arms.

Transfixed, he remained there with it on his shoulders; but it weighed so much, that in order to hold it up he made a huge effort with closed eyes; an effort that became painful; pain that dissolved into infantile distress, feeling immensely alone in the midst of a disheartening, hostile world. When he opened his eyes, the pampa grass had a brilliant color, was erect and red, like a sheet of fire that burned his eyes. He looked all around, disconsolate, and about one hundred meters away he saw a clump of black shrubs. He wanted to run to them to hide the body; he wanted to flee in the direction in which the horse had departed, but he couldn't, he merely took a few unsteady steps, and so as not to fall, he sat down on the grass. Trembling, he untapped the canteen and drank the remainder of the caña. Then, a bit revived, he got up, ever obsessed with the idea of hiding the body, and not finding a place, a new frenzy possessed him, another abyss, another dizziness and, taking his skinning knife from his boot sheath, he cut his victim into pieces as if he were a sheep.

In the peat bog located behind some black shrubs, he carried several clumps of grass and he began hiding pieces of the body which were wrapped up in clothing. When he saw that only the head remained on the peat, a thought that made him crazy with fright suddenly came to him: the gold! He had forgotten all about it!

He looked. On the grayish turf remained Bevan's head, looking with his dull eyes. He couldn't go back. There was nothing else, the entire peat bog began to tremble under his feet; the black shrubs, stirred by the wind, seemed to flee, terrified, as if they were actual beings; the pampa increased its fire, and the blue and white fissure broke up into pieces in the sky. He took the head in his hands to bury it; but he couldn't find a place. Everything fled, everything trembled; the cloudiness that he saw in the cadaverous eyes and in the curve of the sky began to cloud up also in his own. He blinked, and the cloudiness increased; a thousand little needle-like rays of light crossed his line of sight, they blocked the entire horizon, and then, like a blinded animal, he ran after the fleeing black shrubs, succeeded in throwing the head into the middle of them, and continued running until he fell on his face on the pampa, broken into pieces also, out of fear.

"What's the matter? You're trembling!" the young fox hunter interrupts, upon seeing his traveling companion shiver, while thick drops of sweat roll down his temples.

"Oh!" he exclaims, startled, and, as if calming down from a fright, a smile breaks onto his face for the first time, similar to that of impaled dead people, and it allows his depraved voice out: "The caña...the caña for the cold made me even colder!"

"If you want, there's a little left yet," the hunter says, taking the bottle out and handing it to him.

He takes the top off, drinks, and returns it.

"I'll kill this guy like a baby guanaco, with one whip blow," he thinks, shaking himself in the saddle, while the caña runs through his body with the same old malevolent wave.

"Did the cold go away?" the youth says, trying to strike up a conversation.

"Yes, now it did."

"This is my last hunt. I'll go north from here, to get married."

"Have you made some money?"

"Yeah, a fair amount."

"This guy will hand himself over, like a lamb," he thinks to himself, now warm to the bones because of the drink of caña.

"Five years ago I was traveling through this same place in order to go to the north and I lost all my money!"

"How?"

"I don't know. I was carrying pure gold."

"And you didn't find it?"

"I didn't look for it! I would have had to turn back, and I couldn't."

The hunter just stared at him, not understanding. "What a thing; they say that Tierra del Fuego has a curse! Something always happens to the one who wants to leave."

"I don't think anyone leaves here," he said, looking slyly at his victim's neck, and thinking he was like a baby guanaco who was right within his reach. "Bah!" he continued thinking, "This time I'll not fail. The one who leaves here will be me, not him. Only the first time costs you; afterwards, it's easier, and no longer will I get goose bumps."

Silence again weighs heavily between the men, and there is no noise save the monotonous crunch of the horses' hoofs on the snow.

"Now, now is the moment to kill this poor devil with a blow to the neck," he thinks, while the caña has abated and the forgotten frozen wave surges again from inside. But this time it is lighter, just as is the vertigo that begins to grab him more slowly and more serenely and the threshold of the abyss he must cross does not seem so great.

With a sideward glance he measures the distance. He turns the whip around, takes it by the leather strip, cunningly steadies the handle on his saddle. Ignorant of all this, the hunter seems only to think about the monotonous sound of the hoofs on the snow.

"I won't have to do anything with this one, the very snow will bury him," he says to himself, ready now to strike him.

He pulls lightly on the reins so that his horse lags behind a little and....

Just when he is going to strike, the hunter turns, smiling, his eyes blink, and in that blinking he sees identically, pathetically, Bevan's eyes, the deep fissure of the sky, the cloudy look of the severed head on the turf; the thousand scattered rays of light that like little needles again blur his vision, and, blinded, instead of striking his victim's neck with the whip handle, he hits the haunch of his horse, buries a spur in one flank and the animal jumps sideways, slipping on the snow. With another prick of the spur, the steed succeeds in getting up and stabilizing on his hind legs.

"Crazy horse! What's with him?" the hunter exclaims, surprised.

"This stubborn horse is bad and easily frightened!" he answers, returning to the trail.

Silence reigned once again, a lone, heavy, living silence, and again one hears the crunch of the hoofs on the snow; but little by little, a slight sound also begins to accompany that rhythm: the westerly wind begins to blow over the Fueguian steppes.

The hunter wraps up in his white course cotton poncho. The other man puts up the collar of his black leather jacket. In the distance, like a string fallen in the midst of all that immensity, a fence begins to appear. Afternoon is falling. The wind's whistle increases. The hunter shrugs his shoulders and from his mind he scares up Elvira's white apron, like the foam of a wave or the wing of a seagull carried off by the wind. The other man lifts up his weather-beaten face like an ox from whom the yoke has been taken off and he faces the gusts of wind. And that strong westerly wind, which every afternoon rises up to clean the face of Tierra del Fuego, also cleans this time that hard face, and it erases from that mind the last vestiges of alcohol and crime.

They have crossed the fence. The trails split again. The two men look at each other and say:

"Good-bye."

"Good-bye."

Two riders, like two black dots, begin to separate and to again penetrate the solitude and whiteness of the snowy plains.

Next to the fence lies an empty bottle of caña. Sometimes it is the only trace left of man's movement across that faraway region.